MAN
AT THE
DOOR

MAN AT THE DOOR

A MIKE O'SHEA NOVEL

DESMOND P. RYAN

LeVel
BEST BOOKS

First published by Level Best Books 2023

Author Photo Credit: Desmond P. Ryan

Originally published in 2019

Second edition

ISBN: 978-1-68512-546-2

Cover art by Level Best Designs

This book was professionally typeset on Reedsy.
Find out more at reedsy.com

To Pauline Gray. I owe you a pair of shoes.

Praise for Man at the Door

"Skillfully navigating his flawed and sometimes broken characters, Mr. Ryan leads the reader through wins and losses and choices that are as much analogous to real life as it is to police."—Henry Alexandroni, author of *Inizar: The Complete Trilogy*

"Ryan's flair for painting a vivid picture puts you right beside Detective Mike O'Shea and I found myself continually looking for parallels between Ryan's characters and the officers I have known over the years. A great read for crime fiction lovers."—Cal Miller, Crime reporter, retired *Toronto Star*, Member Crime Stoppers Board of Directors, honorary Toronto Police Service Detective

"Ryan has a strong voice and uses it to give the right details to provide a very compelling read—it's fast, gritty and with characters that'll stick with you after you've moved on to your next read."—H.C. Newton, *aka* The Irresponsible Reader book blogger

"Ryan's realism evoked many memories for me, and I've been out of the cops for 20 years now. But so much came rushing back, especially as I worked vice, and this is the litmus test for me when I'm looking for realism in crime writing about police work. If those memories come flooding back (some of them unwelcome, I have to say), then I know the author has done a very fine job. Take a bow, Mr. Ryan, you're off to a flying start as a crime author."—A.B. Patterson, former WA Detective Sergeant, Chief Investigator with the NSW Independent Commission Against Corruption, and author of the award-wining *Harry's World, Harry's Question and Harry's Grail*

"Ryan delivers what he promises—an authenticity derived from experience. He mixes the playful banter and acerbic humour cops need to keep their heads above water in a world full of heinous crimes with a compelling plot, which is woven into the crime that plays out in this book. It's crime fiction with a good ol' boys in blue camaraderie, authentic characters and an intriguing plot."—Cheryl M- M's Book Blog

Chapter One

hit! Detective Mike O'Shea looked at himself in the washroom mirror, careful not to pull on the stitches over his right eye as he dabbed at his face with a wet paper towel. Despite the crisp white shirt, conservative dark tie, and tried-and-true pinstripe suit, he still looked more like a third-rate boxer than the seasoned cop he was.

"Chick out there wants to know if you're finished preening yourself, whatever that means," a man dressed in baggy jeans and an oversize T-shirt commented as he walked past Mike to the row of urinals on the opposite wall.

Without answering, Mike straightened his tie, took another look at the contusions on his face, and walked into the courthouse hallway.

"All good?" Crown Attorney Bridget Calloway asked.

"Good as it's going to get."

"Are you sure you're up to this?"

Mike scratched the back of his head.

"Stop picking at it, Mike. The doctor said everything would get itchy before it healed. And it's only been a few weeks. Anyway, the judge has agreed to let you testify as long as he thinks you're okay. Scratching like a dog isn't going to help your cause."

"Hey, Mikey!" a man in uniform called out as Mike and Bridget walked to the courtroom. "Rock. Staaaaaaaarrrrrrr!!!"

1

Mike kept walking, a slight smile crossing his face.

"And remember, this is also your first day back after being beaten nearly to death," Bridget added.

"Yes, dear." Mike reached to open the heavy courtroom door for Bridget.

"Mike." Bridget stopped and faced him. "I'm not kidding. As the Crown attorney running this trial, I have some serious concerns about your short-term memory. If I know—and everyone who has read the papers in the last few weeks knows—that you're recovering from a serious concussion, don't think the defence counsel isn't going to know and use it to his client's advantage."

"Thanks, Counsel."

"I'm serious, Mike. I don't have the transcripts from your original testimony. Planned work slowdown by the transcribers. Some sort of union thing—"

"Go, union!"

"Which means that we're going to have to reintroduce a lot of your evidence-in-chief. Verbatim, more or less."

"No sweat."

"I hope not. Without those transcripts, any turn of phrase could completely change the context of what you originally said, and then we're screwed. So keep it simple, okay?"

"That's me. Simple."

"Agreed."

"Ouch!"

"And as your friend, I think you're pushing yourself too hard."

"As your *friend*?"

"Yes. As your friend."

"This manly look not doing it for you?" Mike asked with a grin.

"Not today, Mike." Bridget gave his arm a squeeze.

"I believe they are waiting inside for us." Mike gently guided Bridget into the courtroom, his hand on the small of her back.

* * *

The court clerk looked closely at Mike, curious to see the detective everyone was talking about. She swore him in and settled back into her seat in front of the judge. Mike was willing to bet that she, like the jurors, was growing weary of the grind of this messy trial and would be very glad when it was over.

"Good morning, Detective." Bridget looked up from the paperwork that she had laid out in front of her on the lectern and formally addressed Mike. She took a deep breath and adjusted the glasses she hoped would give her a more studious look. She glanced up at the judge who, she was sure, disliked her as much as she disliked him and then over to her right to the twelve good men and women corralled in the jury box.

Mike nodded at the young Crown attorney.

"Detective," Bridget began, turning to face the jury before looking back at Mike, trying to create the illusion that she and the jury were teammates and she was merely their spokesperson asking questions on their behalf. "Just to refresh the court, I understand that you have been a district investigator for the past ten of your twenty-seven years as a police officer. Is that correct?"

"Yes. That is correct."

"And for five years before that, a detective constable in the Juvenile Prostitution Task Force?"

"Yes."

"And today, we're here to talk about...?" Bridget sauntered over to the jury box before leaning casually against it, facing Mike from their vantage point.

Mike froze. *Shit. Concentrate. It's not that hard.* Fear was replacing focus as his mind began to wander. *Permanent brain damage. Focus. Answer the question.*

Mike's pause made Bridget's skip a breath. *Damn, I knew it was too soon,* she thought as she swiftly retreated to the safety of the lectern to consider what new approach she could take without, she hoped, tipping off the jury, the judge, or the defence.

"Let me rephrase, Detective O'Shea. You are in this court of law regarding—"

"A sexual assault causing bodily harm, Ms. Calloway," Mike said, just as

Bridget was beginning to consider the possibility that she'd have to request an indefinite adjournment pending Mike's full recovery. "And the accused male, Gregory Sanderson, is sitting right there, in the black suit with the red tie, behind the defence table. Beside the gentleman in the shiny blue suit." Mike pointed at the accused.

Bridget gave a tiny gasp of relief. Mike may or may not have winked at her. She was cautiously optimistic that her very capable prosecuting partner was back.

"Now, just to refresh our minds, Detective, you advised the court the last time you were on the stand that the accused before the courts," Bridget pointed at the defence table, her eyes not leaving Mike, "fathered his own daughter's child. Is that correct?"

"Objection." The defence attorney jumped up.

"Overruled. Continue, Ms. Calloway," the judge advised, not taking his eyes from the laptop screen in front of his face and continuing to tap fiercely on the keyboard.

"Your Honour," Sanderson's lawyer pushed on, "just to refresh your memory, the paternity of the child was never established. Furthermore—"

"Mr. Reiner, my memory is just fine. But just to refresh *your* memory, Madam Crown did, in fact, suggest that your client was the father of the victim's child. Now please sit down, Mr. Reiner. Carry on, Ms Calloway."

"But Your Honour—"

"*Sit down*, Mr. Reiner."

And so the morning plodded along. Fearing that she was losing the attention of the jury, Bridget found herself pulling more theatrical tricks out of her extensive repertoire than she would have liked. Sanderson's lawyer intentionally played to the tedium of the pacing in an attempt both to undermine the severity of the crime and to play up what he hoped the jury would see as the weakness of the Crown's case against his client.

Mike, meanwhile, tried his best to work with Bridget, staving off his own frustrations with this trial. It should have been a slam-dunk, but between his injuries causing an unanticipated delay in the proceedings and an angry judge, the case was turning into an even greater shitshow than these types of proceedings usually were. And then there was his nagging feeling that this fucker was somehow tied into the human trafficking ring and that bastard Malcolm, who had killed his partner, Sal, more than a decade ago, the bastard who was still at large for any number of bullshit reasons Homicide gave him.

More than anything, Mike wanted Sanderson convicted and rotting in a prison cell so that he could start to squeeze him for info on Sal's murderer. Fuck Homicide. They had dropped the ball. He'd let this bullshit drag on far too long. Time to get to the bottom of it. And Sanderson, Mike sensed, would be a good starting point. This slippery bastard was not going to get away. Neither would Malcolm.

Chapter Two

3:20 p.m., Thursday, October 4, 2018

"So?" Mike struggled to keep up with Bridget as she hustled through the courthouse corridors. "How'd we do?"

Bridget continued towards the Crown's office without responding, numerous dog-eared court documents bursting out of the worn brief she held tightly to her chest.

"What's wrong?" Mike's briefcase was swinging in step, the fluorescent lighting in the hallway adding a new layer of pain to his throbbing head.

"Did you wink at me in court, Detective?" Bridget demanded without looking at Mike or losing a step.

"Maybe. Is there a problem with that, Madam Prosecutor?" Mike smirked. "I saw you smiling back."

Bridget stopped abruptly. "Mike, we are in the middle of a really shitty trial. You have just had a significant injury. I can't—"

Mike came to an equally abrupt stop before proceeding to wink one eye and then the other. "Oh, I see. So the brain-damaged guy can't wink. Uh-huh."

"Mike, you know better." Bridget's voice lowered to a near-whisper as she scanned the hallway and suppressed a slight smile.

"Hey, Mike, give me a hand!" Detective Sergeant Amanda Black spun around the corner, an overflowing bankers box in her arms. "My Primary had a family emergency, the last copper to testify probably weighed less than me, and the Crown looked fifteen months' pregnant. Couldn't exactly ask any of them to carry this, could I?"

Mike struggled to grab the overflowing box that was being thrust into his arms, snapping his head back to avoid having his eye poked out by one of the oversize brown envelopes crammed into it.

"God, I miss those days of perfect skin," Amanda commented, looking Bridget over admiringly before turning her attention back to Mike. "At my age, it's all smoke and mirrors. Speaking of which, I hear Reiner is the defence on your child abuse case. Fucker. If anyone can turn a gourmet meal into a dog's breakfast, it's him. I assume there are more victims? They never stop until we stop them, do they?"

"No, I suppose they don't." Mike fumbled to control his briefcase in one hand while wrestling with the box.

"Oh shit. You just got back to work, didn't you? Here, give." Amanda grabbed the box of files back from Mike. At barely five foot two and weighing no more than a hundred and two pounds soaking wet, she was known among her officers as 'the pit bull in stilettos' and not an individual to be questioned, especially by lower-ranking cops. "How the hell are you?"

"Good. It's my head that's injured, not my back." Mike tugged the box back from her.

Amanda relinquished the bankers box, then adjusted her elegantly tailored skirt. "Tell me you haven't returned to work?"

"Light duties. Straight days. Half-days, actually. Following up on missing persons occurrences and any sudden deaths where the city has to get involved to find next-of-kin or whatever. You know, just something to keep me busy."

"That's good, Mike, really good," Amanda nodded, taking stock of the nicks in Mike's face. "Listen, I'm sorry I never got around to see you. It's just—"

"Don't worry about it, Amanda. Ron came by every day, and Bridget here popped in a few times."

Amanda shot a glance at Bridget. "Really? Well played. She's young. She's smart. She's beautiful. You're, well—"

"How about I let you two catch up. I've got a ton of work to do. Mike, get some sleep. You're back on the stand first thing tomorrow morning." Bridget nodded at the two cops, then made her way around the corner Amanda had just come from.

"Well played," Amanda repeated before continuing down the hallway at a pace that rivalled Bridget's, once again causing Mike to trot to keep up.

"Oh no," Mike shrugged the thought off. "It's not like that. She just needs me to be on my game to testify against that piece of shit I have for an accused. Fucked his daughter. And yeah, likely more victims. You still in contact with the guys from the old morality squad?"

"He sounds lovely, and most of the old squad guys are retired. Why do you ask?"

"Just a hunch."

"I'm not going to ask. You know we have Mark Johnstone in custody and the prelim is coming up fast, right? We're charging him with the murder of Sergei Kuzminov, obviously, and attempted murder on you. Are you up to doing a victim impact statement for me, or is it too soon?"

"How about we hold off? Still don't know the long-term effects."

"Fair enough. No rush. I just like to have my ducks in a row. I'll get it from you some other time."

Amanda's mind was already on other things. She'd have to call the woefully inexperienced Crown assigned to one of her homicide cases to discuss strategy this evening. Before that, she'd have to get to her older daughter's city-wide track and field meet. Hopefully, she wouldn't get called out to a homicide in the meantime; there was another team lined up before her on the blackboard in the office. It would be nice to spend a full night at home for a change. She knew her husband would certainly appreciate it, if only to have help with the girls.

Chapter Three

6:10 a.m., Friday, October 5, 2018

Having arrived at his desk a few minutes too late for his liking, Mike instinctively grabbed the ringing telephone. "Detective O'Shea. How may I help you?" *And who the fuck calls at 6:10 a.m.?*

Ron Roberts, already busy with the paperwork of an early-morning arrest, nodded a silent welcome across the desk to his partner. Mike looked at Ron and noticed dark bags under his partner's eyes.

"Hello, Detective. I am hoping you can. My name is Glen Brebeuf. I reported my friend missing yesterday and am wondering what's happening with that investigation."

"Well, Mr. Brebeuf," Mike began, setting his coffee down, "since you just reported her missing, I don't suspect too much."

"Oh."

The single syllable landed with a thud in Mike's ear. Having worked for years with the families of young girls caught up in the sex trade, he was quite familiar with the sentiment behind the utterance.

"What's your friend's name, Mr. Brebeuf?" Mike struggled to shed his coat while balancing the phone receiver between his ear and his raised shoulder.

"Sibby...uh, Elizabeth MacDonald. I reported her missing yesterday afternoon. The officer who took the report said someone would be getting back to me within a day or so to let me know what was happening."

"Okay, Mr. Brebeuf. Let me just get myself settled in here and I'll find that report." Mike rummaged through a pile of papers on his desk as he pulled off the other sleeve of his suit jacket and dropped the garment onto the back of his chair. *Paperless society, my ass.* "Reported yesterday, eh? Elizabeth MacDonald. Shouldn't be too hard to find. Oh, wait. Here's something. Says here that she's seventy-two?"

"That's right," replied Brebeuf eagerly, "although to see her, you wouldn't think she was a day over fifty."

"Is that right?" Mike replied absently as he sat down, scanning the paragraph that passed itself off as a report.

"Yes. She is…was…incredibly active. Very forward-thinking. And a very beautiful—"

"I'm sorry, Mr. Brebeuf," Mike interrupted, turning the single page over several times, hoping that something more would appear with each turn.

With his desk so close to Mike's, Ron could not help but overhear his partner's end of the conversation. His experiences over the past thirty or so years gave him a good idea of the kind of caller on the other end of that line. *Better you than me, partner.*

"Glen. Just call me Glen."

"Okay then, Glen. So how is it that you know this missing woman?" Mike's curiosity pricked up. Women very seldom went missing. They either left miserable relationships or were killed within them. Either way, they didn't go missing.

"Well," Brebeuf's voice faltered, "as I mentioned to the officer yesterday, it's kind of complicated—"

"Life is complicated, Glen," Mike interrupted, looking across the desk at Ron, who nodded in silent agreement.

You were either banging her or she owed you money, Mike figured. *Considering her age, she probably owed you money. Or you were banging her daughter. Or her son. Whatever.*

"Yes, I suppose it is. But the real reason I'm calling is because I don't think she's missing. I told the officer that yesterday, but I don't know if he understood what I was saying."

"Neither do I, Glen. What *are* you saying?" *'Report submitted as per Sergeant*

10

45532' Mike read at the bottom of the page. Cop-speak for *'I think this is a crock of shit but I'm putting in a report to cover my ass.'*

"I think something bad has happened to her."

"What do you mean?"

"I think someone has hurt her."

"And why do you think that, Glen?"

"Because I'm her best friend, and she wouldn't have gone on a holiday without telling me, because I'm the only person she's ever had drop by to water her plants when she was away."

"Well, that's certainly something." *Too damn early for this shit.* "Why don't you give me a couple of minutes to look over the report and I'll give you a call back?"

"I'm just on my way in to work. I'll be driving right by the station in about ten minutes. Why don't I just stop in and see you, Detective…?"

"O'Shea. Mike O'Shea. Sure. I'll look forward to it."

Mike hung up the phone.

"I thought you were still on light duties," Ron commented.

"I am. Can't you tell? Got a guy coming in in a few to talk to me about a missing woman he reported yesterday." Mike shook his head in disbelief, waving the single piece of paper he had to work with at Ron. "And this is all I've got to go on."

"Want me to deal with it?"

"No. I'm just gonna talk to him a bit. See what he knows. Why he's so worried. I'm good." Mike turned his attention to the monitor in front of him, hoping as he logged into his computer that there had been a more comprehensive report submitted electronically.

"Suit yourself. Oh, and before I forget, there was a box. Had your name on it. Left here after the son of your Robby Williams—"

Mike's neck cracked as he snapped his head up to look at Ron. "When?"

"A couple of days after you got assaulted. It was just behind the front desk. I didn't think it was a good idea to leave it here, so I took it home."

"You took it home?"

"Yes, I did. There's a lot of…well, information that might be of interest to

11

you in it, and I didn't want—"

"Did you look at any of it?"

"Not much, but yes, I did."

"And?"

"I think it's of more interest to you than me. I'll bring it in tomorrow, and we can put it in your truck straight away."

"The stuff's that good?"

"No, not good at all."

Mike looked closely at Ron for some sort of a reaction, but there was nothing. He took off his suit jacket and draped it over the back of his chair before turning his attention to the missing person report that had popped up on his monitor. It mirrored the document he held in his hand.

Elizabeth MacDonald, 72 years of age. Reported missing yesterday by Glen Brebeuf, 41 years of age. Complainant attended the station to report that he stopped by at the now-missing woman's house this date at approximately 12:00 p.m. for lunch, as he had been doing every Thursday for the past several years.

Focus, Mikey. Nooner, eh? Even old broads need loving, I guess.

When he knocked on the door, an unknown male answered and advised that Miss MacDonald was not home.

Miss, eh? Interesting.

The unknown male further advised that he had been asked by Miss MacDonald to water her plants while she was on holidays. The complainant reports that his friend would never do this, and he has been watering her plants for years.

Apparently.

As a result, the complainant thinks his friend is missing. The reporting officer requested a car attend the scene. Further information indicates that the attending officer attended the address, knocked on the door, and there was no response.

Because she's either on holidays or missing, bonehead.

Sergeant 45532 advised. Report submitted as per Sergeant 45532. No further action to be taken at this time.

Mike looked away from the monitor and turned over the paper that he was still holding in his hand, hoping to find more details on the back. Nothing. Nada. Incredulous, he punched the occurrence number into the records database.

Still nothing.

That's it? No supplementary report from the attending officer? No further direction? She's seventy-two years old. This should have gone to a Level Three Full Search immediately, regardless of how flaky the complainant may or may not have been. And they didn't at least get into her house? Or canvas the neighbours? Very odd. And what about the complainant, this Brebeuf character? No indication of whether or not they checked him out. And what's with 'the man at the door'?

"Everything alright?" Ron asked as his partner grunted and mumbled across the desk from him.

"Just ducky," Mike snorted. "You know, it doesn't take much to do things right, does it?"

Ron smiled. "Uh-oh. You're starting to sound like me."

"Oh, Christ! Say it ain't so! Seriously, though. Old doll reported missing yesterday, fuck-all done about it, and now the guy who reported her wants her found. What the hell am I supposed to do?"

"Want me to handle it?" Ron offered again.

"Since when did you become the compassionate one?" Mike fumbled in his pants pocket for his bottle of prescription painkillers.

"Competence and compassion are not the same thing, Mike."

"Did you just say that I'm the incompetent one?"

"I said nothing of the sort. In any event, why don't you go grab another coffee or something and I'll take a look at this."

"How soon can you get that box to me?"

"Not before tomorrow. Marie has the car today. Appointment with some specialist out in the middle of nowhere."

"And you didn't go with her?"

"How could I?" Ron asked, waving his hands around at the stacks of paper he had created on his desk.

"She's really—"

Before Mike could finish his sentence, the phone on his desk rang again. It was the officer sitting at the front desk advising that there was someone waiting to speak to him.

Mike slammed the phone down harder than he had meant to as he leaned over to pull the tiny pill bottle out of his pants pocket. He held it up to his face and squinted. "What the hell does it say? Take every four... is it...? Who types this small? Oh, fuck it!" Shoving the bottle back into his pocket, Mike snatched the jacket from the back of his chair as he headed for the doorway. "Shit. See you in a bit."

"I'm here if you change your mind. Remember, you're on light duties. Nothing too involved. Or strenuous. Or complicated. Or..."

Mike left Ron's voice behind him as he threw his jacket on, straightened his tie, grabbed a steno pad, and made his way out the door.

Chapter Four

T he reception area for the 6 District station was an embarrassment. The chipped asbestos-tile floor always looked dirty, no surprise since the cleaning staff dwindling every year due to the city's operational budget cuts seldom had time to wash it properly. As a result, the Sunday morning weekly waxing locked in the previous week's worth of misery. Over the course of fifty years, Mike figured, there was likely at least a quarter of an inch of grime pasted onto the tiles. The corpse-grey walls did nothing to reflect any light that managed to make its way through the permanently filthy windows, even on the brightest of days.

There were no seats for bereaved family members waiting to collect the belongings of their loved ones or for the children who were court-ordered to be passed between toxic ex-spouses at a police station. Instead, there was a well-worn bench covering the radiator that ran the length of the windows. It was not unusual for people to prefer to stand.

"Mr. Brebeuf?" Mike looked at the boyishly thin man standing across the counter from him.

"Yes. Call me Glen. Detective O'Shea?"

"Please come around."

Brebeuf was an ordinary-looking man, but Mike sensed that there was something not quite right about him. He led the complainant through the glass double doors and down the stairs to the musty basement and into the dated interview room. Even though he had no intention of doing a true interview, this drab room was sadly the only place in the obsolete police facility where they could speak privately. And even if this guy was a complete flake and the report bogus, Mike figured the least he could do was appear interested.

"This woman must mean an awful lot to you if you're willing to come in to the station on your way to work, Glen," Mike said as the two men settled into the cold metal chairs across the table from each other rather than the more comfortable living-room setup behind the chairs that was intended for 'soft interviews' such as this one.

"Yes, she does."

Mike dropped his steno pad on the table and pulled the cap off his pen. "So what do you know, Glen?" He looked at Brebeuf and mentally heard his mother's voice describing the man.

"Sibby Mac is not missing, Detective. She's dead."

Mike set the pen down. "Hold that thought. I'm going to turn the camera on behind you and get this conversation on video, just to make sure I don't miss anything." Mike fumbled for a couple of minutes before finally getting the outdated equipment fired up.

Neither man spoke until Mike sat down again, looked at his watch, and noted the time on the pad in front of him.

"I did not kill her, Detective. I don't know who did, or who would even want her dead, but I know she's dead."

"Mr. Brebeuf, I am now going to caution you." Mike was not prepared to rule out the possibility that he was speaking to a murderer. This would not be the first time in his career that someone came in under the pretense of making an idle inquiry, only to drop a full confession in his lap. Light duties or not, it was now showtime. "While you have not been formally charged, I am of the opinion that you know something about the disappearance of Elizabeth MacDonald. While you may or may not be criminally involved, it is my duty to inform you that you have the right to retain and instruct counsel before we continue. Do you understand?"

"Yes."

"Fair enough. Okay, Mr. Brebeuf—"

"Glen."

"Glen. What do you know about the disappearance of Elizabeth MacDonald?"

"Not much. That's why I'm here. I do know that Sibby—"

"Sibby?"

"Sibby Mac. Everyone called her Sibby Mac."

"Why?"

"Because that's how she introduced herself, Detective."

Bit of a wanker, that one, Michael.

"You speak of your friend in the past tense. Why is that, Glen?"

"Because I think something horrible has happened to her," Brebeuf mumbled.

"I'm sorry. I didn't hear you. Can you repeat that, please?"

"Because I think something horrible has happened to her. I knew her for twenty years. She and I were best friends. I knew everything about her, Detective."

"Everything?"

"Yes, everything. I knew of every man she has fucked—"

"Whoa whoa whoa!" Mike glanced at his watch again as he made a stop-right-there gesture with his left hand, then scribbled the time down with his right. "Why don't you begin by telling me how you know Eliza— Sibby?"

"I met Sibby twenty years ago when I was a summer student working for the government. She worked there, too."

"As a summer student?"

"No, she was an executive."

"So how did you meet?"

"At a mentoring session. Most execs bail on those functions, but Sibby was an incredibly dedicated person who loved to help develop talent."

"Talent?" Mike raised one eyebrow.

"Talent," Brebeuf repeated. "Whether it was mentoring subordinates in the ministry or working with community groups or just helping out her neighbours. She was a very giving woman."

"Okay. So there you were, twenty years ago. She would have been...?"

"Fifty-two, Detective. I was twenty-one."

"Oh." Mike sat back a bit.

"Yes. I was mid-way through my undergrad degree in foreign affairs. Like I said, we met at this mentoring function, and she really took an interest in me."

"I bet she did," Mike muttered.

"It was purely professional, Detective, I assure you. I worked in her department for the next three years until I completed my master's. And then we got to know each other outside of work."

"Got to know each other how, Glen?" Mike straightened his back in the old metal chair and leaned forward slightly.

"We became lovers, Detective. That's what you're asking, aren't you?"

"I'm not asking anything, Glen. I am just trying to figure out the story."

"We were lovers, on and off, for several years, but..." Brebeuf paused, almost wistfully.

"But what, Glen?"

"But she didn't want to get married. So I married someone else. I was thirty-two and she was sixty-three."

Mike did the math in his head as Brebeuf carried on talking.

"She wasn't the marrying type. Too old for children. She thought I should be a father and needed to find someone to do that with. Six months later, I got married."

"So let me get this straight." Mike shook his head in moderate disbelief. "You had this affair going with our missing woman for seven or eight years—"

"An *intimate relationship* with her. Yes. On and off," Brebeuf corrected.

"On and off, and then she dumps you—"

"She wouldn't marry me," Brebeuf corrected again.

"And you meet and marry someone else to give you a kid because this woman thought you should be a father?"

Brebeuf looked blankly across the table at Mike.

"How's your marriage going?" Mike finally asked.

"I'm not here to discuss my marriage, Detective." The sharpness of

Brebeuf's voice poked at Mike's ear. "Look, I wasn't the only guy she was involved with."

"Okay, then." Mike took a breath to regroup. There was a thin line between allowing a subject to talk and allowing them to take control of the interview. Time to rein it in, but not too abruptly.

"Sibby was her own woman. Never married. Never wanted to. She enjoyed life."

"So she was a swinger?"

"No, not at all. But she was not ashamed of her sensuality. Not like most other women."

Mike thought he saw Brebeuf's lip curl. Nerves or a snarl or...?

"She also wasn't vulgar about it," Brebeuf continued.

"What does that mean, Glen?"

"She had rules," the man said simply. "She did not sleep with married men, for starts."

"So that let you out," Mike rubbed his hand over his cheek and discovered some unexpected stubble his razor had missed this morning.

"Yes. And she made it perfectly clear that she was not interested in any long-term relationship."

"Except for you. Why?"

"Because we were friends, Detective. There's a difference between friends and that other business."

"What *other business*, Glen?"

"You know what I'm talking about," Brebeuf muttered, looking down at the table in front of him.

"Okay, then." Mike's brow furrowed. "So you get married, have a kid, and now you're going to her house for...what? Lunch?"

"Every Thursday, unless she or I—"

"Or your wife?"

"My wife has no idea—"

"That you've picked up with this older woman after all these years?"

"That I go to an old friend's house for lunch once a week to discuss current events before returning to the office. No, she does not."

"Wow!" Mike could not stop himself from shaking his head in disbelief.

"Would your wife believe you, Detective?"

"*I* barely believe you, Glen." The words hung in the air.

Mike looked down at his watch. *Time to wrap this interview up.* "Do you think your friend is on a holiday somewhere?"

"No, I do not."

"Do you think she is missing, Glen?"

"Certainly missing. Likely dead."

Mike took a deep breath as he looked at the man sitting across from him. Experience told him that he had everything he was going to get from this interview.

"Okay, then. We will find her, one way or another. Are you available for us to talk to you again?"

"If that's what's required, yes. I'll do whatever you need to find Sibby Mac."

"Fair enough. Thanks for coming in. I think the first step is to have a good look in her house."

"I have a key." Brebeuf fumbled in his left front pants pocket.

"Great. Won't have to kick any doors in. May I have it?"

"I'd rather come with you."

"I can appreciate you wanting to help, but it won't be me going. Whoever is going will likely be heading out just as soon as you and I finish up here. Weren't you on your way to work? I can call you when they're done, and you can pick the key up on your way home, if that's your concern."

"I don't mind missing a couple of hours of work. It's the least I can do for Sibby."

"Suit yourself."

* * *

As he was leading Brebeuf back to the front desk, Mike noticed Sergeant Karl Hageneur coming up the stairs behind them. "You busy?" he asked the uniformed foot patrol sergeant as they reached the reception area.

"Just going to grab some breakfast. What's up?" Karl was a solid man, true to his German heritage. He and Mike had come on together, and the one thing that had always stood out in Mike's mind was the size of Karl's hands. In fact, all of Karl's features were huge. At six foot four and built like a brick shithouse, he was the guy you wanted beside you in a fight. Or executing a search warrant where those involved were likely to get silly. He was rumoured to have been a pretty good football player in his day, and his size alone secured his position as a defenceman on the District hockey team. While he wasn't exactly handsome, there was something about him that made him very popular with the ladies. No one had ever met them, but Karl apparently had a wife and a couple of kids. He was that guy whose personal life was private, but whose reputation as a copper's cop was almost legendary.

"Got a Check Address for you and maybe a couple of your guys if you're interested," Mike offered, gesturing for Brebeuf to take a seat on the bench.

"Sure. What is it?"

"Missing woman. Seventy-two years old. Reported yesterday. No Level Three done—"

"Holy crap! Heads might roll for that one!"

"Hopefully not. Anyway, the complainant is sitting over there. Friend of the old girl's. He has a key to let you in." Both cops looked over at the man perched somewhat gingerly on the cover over the radiator.

"Damn. And here I was looking forward to an early-morning door break." Karl, a smile practically consuming his face, exuberantly thumped Mike on the back with his enormous hand.

Mike cringed, his body still sensitive after his recent encounter with Mark Johnstone and his metal pipe. "I don't imagine there's too many doors you couldn't break down, Karl, but this one is easy. Anyway, I'll get you a copy of the occurrence. Not much to it. Buddy over there—Glen Brebeuf is his name, by the way—dropped by the old girl's yesterday for lunch and someone else met him at the door."

"Uh-oh. I see. It's like that, eh?" Karl shook his head knowingly.

"Your bet is as good as mine on this one. Anyway, the guy tells him that our girl has gone on vacation, but Brebeuf isn't buying it. Reports her missing and is here this morning to see what we've done.

"Which is?"

"Nothing."

"Right."

"Good luck."

Chapter Five

The house was a semi located in one of the nicer areas of the city, where homeowners took great pride in their tiny walkways and petite gardens. The wrought-iron fences that separated these gardens from the sidewalks were more ornate than functional. If outward appearances meant anything, a death among these folks by any means other than old age seemed unimaginable.

As they approached what looked like a tiny dollhouse that was the home of one Elizabeth MacDonald, Sergeant Karl Hageneur and his four officers could not have looked more out of place. Despite their best efforts to park as far off to the side as possible, their three marked police cars jammed up the one-way street that would have been considered a laneway in any other part of the city. The officers' crisp uniforms were in sharp contrast to the casual wear of the early-morning dog-walkers and the trendy suits of residents hustling to the streetcar that would take them to work at the downtown office towers. Most people who would normally have walked by stopped for a few moments to offer a theory or two to each other to explain this early-morning police presence. Perhaps fearful of the truth, no one approached the officers for clarification.

Had he not been with the sergeant and his men, Brebeuf, with his cuffed pants and shiny tasseled loafers, would have blended in with the hip transit riders.

"How about you let me open the door and you just wait out here?" The softness in Karl's voice made his direction seem more like a suggestion and mirrored the gentle grasp he had on Brebeuf's hand as he began peeling fingers off the house key. Brebeuf looked up at the gentle giant and silently submitted.

Karl carefully opened the front door, calling out to Elizabeth MacDonald as he entered. This wouldn't be the first time a cop had walked in on something that ought to have been left behind closed doors. At the same time, he was aware that this house could, in fact, be an actual crime scene. As a result, he and his men had to balance the necessity of a thorough search of the house with the need to preserve what could be potential evidence or, more to the point, not destroy anything.

Flanked by his four officers, Karl entered the house. Small kitchen at the front on one side of the door, living room the size of a suburban den on the other, dining room running the width of the house at the back with glass doors leading out into the tiny backyard. An open set of stairs piled with books divided the front and back of the house. Even though the white walls were covered with artwork that looked original and shelves lined with knickknacks, the rooms did not look cluttered. Everything seemed to be in its place. Karl stifled a sigh of appreciation, recalling the box-store sell-offs and what could only be described as the child-friendly mash-up style of his own house.

It was the kitchen took caught Karl's attention. Solid brass pots and pans hung artistically from the ceiling suggesting that great care had been taken to ensure both aesthetic and practical applications were possible. An impressive set of knives stood by the gas stove in a block for easy access. A row of well-worn cookbooks lined a very high single shelf that spanned the entire circumference of the kitchen. The cupboards, although dated in their facing, contained the most beautiful set of dishes Karl had ever seen. Place settings for twelve, Karl noted. *Interesting for a woman who lived alone.*

As his officers fanned out—a couple springing up the stairs while the other two hunched down to get into the low-ceilinged basement—Karl noticed the island in the kitchen. Every house had a place where anything that did not have a home seemed to reside. In this tiny house, it was here.

Karl reached into the back pocket of his uniformed pants to pull out his memo book when, to his surprise, his hand rubbed up against Brebeuf. "Sir," Karl said, "you're going to have to wait outside."

"You think something's happened to her, don't you?"

"I don't know, sir, but you're going to have to wait outside."

"Sibby loved to cook, you know. In fact, she loved to entertain. Any excuse for a dinner party. Or any party at all, for that matter."

"Real party girl, was she?" Karl commented, stepping back out of the kitchen with Brebeuf in tow.

"Not the way you mean it, no. She was a very generous woman. She was good to her friends. She enjoyed them. She enjoyed herself. She took pleasure in pleasure for its own sake."

"Fair enough." Karl nodded as he continued to subtly manoeuvre Brebeuf back out of the house.

"She had that gift of making you think you were the only person on the planet when she spoke to you, you know what I mean?"

"Sounds like you got it bad, buddy." Karl squinted in the morning sun as he and Brebeuf stepped outside the house.

"No." Brebeuf shook his head slowly. "No, it wasn't that at all. She was like that with everyone. She has this amazing gift—"

"I'm sure she did. Does." Karl corrected himself before taking Brebeuf's arm, surprised at its muscularity. "Why don't you go wait over there in that police car? I'll get one of my men to sit with you until we're done."

"No, I'm fine here," Brebeuf said with a touch of defiance.

"Or you can go on home, and we'll give you a call later with an update." Karl smiled in that negotiation-finished manner he had honed over the years.

Brebeuf reconsidered. "No, I'll wait with the officer."

After calling over one of his officers and dispensing with Brebeuf, Karl made his way towards the small group of people who had begun to gather next door to the house. Glancing back over his shoulder and nodding towards the open door of the house behind him, Karl called out, "Anyone know anything about the whereabouts of Elizabeth MacDonald?"

The three or four neighbours standing with their dogs looked at each other blankly, shaking their heads.

"Well," Karl sighed, "if anyone hears anything…"

"Oh, you mean Sibby? Sibby Mac? Is that whose house you've been at?" a woman who had just joined the dog walkers chimed in.

"Oh God, no. Something has happened to Sibby Mac? It cannot be!" a middle-aged man shouted.

"Sibby Mac? Who would hurt Sibby Mac? What the hell is wrong with this world?" another man muttered.

"Not Sibby Mac. Not *our* Sibby Mac. Hang on. I'm going to call Richard right away. He won't believe this," a man dragging a weary dog on its leash said as he fumbled for his cell phone.

Within what felt like a few seconds to Karl, this group of curious onlookers became an increasingly large flock of frightened neighbours. Four or five became seven or eight became twelve or thirteen.

"Excuse me, Sergeant," one of them said, pushing through the crowd with his bicycle. "My name is Bruce. I write a weekly neighbourhood blog. Can you tell me what's going on here?"

Karl stared at the older man incredulously. Maybe it was the man's oversize helmet, or maybe it was his undersized bike shorts. Whatever it was, Karl didn't quite know, in the moment, how to respond.

"It's just a little thing I do," the neighbour continued, smiling modestly. "Mostly giving people updates about what local shops and restaurants are opening or closing and what have you, but everyone knows Sibby Mac, and I'm sure we all want to know what's happened."

Karl decided to ignore the man and motioned towards his men. "Can you guys get the names, addresses, and phone numbers of everyone here, please," Karl directed, turning his back to the crowd to address the officers. "I'm thinking someone may want to speak to them later. Are we finished with the house?"

"Yep," the most senior officer responded.

"But…." Constable Preston McAfee, who was doing a six-month training spot in the foot patrol, shook his head as Karl stared beyond them at the house. While he was not known to be the sharpest tool in the shed or likely to move beyond a uniformed position, Preston had a reputation for being diligent in his duties. Karl gave him a slight nod of acknowledgment before nodding to his men to get to work.

While his officers dispersed into the crowd, jotting down names and phone numbers as they went, Karl went back to the house to have another look around.

Re-entering, he tried to keep along the informal path his officers had already made to avoid additional contamination of the scene.

At least they haven't broken anything this time.

He reassessed the house as methodically as he could, conscious of his own size, particularly when he was practically brushing up against the tiny porcelain figurines on the shelves. Living room: check. Dining room: check. Kitchen: check.

Up the stairs, mindful of the books that were loaded on each step, to the second floor. One door to his immediate left, two doors to the right. Bedroom running the width of the house at the front, bathroom and bedroom at the back.

White carpet in both bedrooms and the tiny hallway. Fluffy white carpet. Boot prints. Lots of boot prints. *So much for minimizing scene contamination.*

Karl returned to the main floor. Nothing out of the ordinary. McAfee must have been mistaken.

* * *

"Your head is looking better," Ron Roberts commented, looking across his desk at Mike.

"Pardon?" Mike stopped pecking away at his keyboard to look over the monitor at his partner. Ron looked tired as he stood at his desk, sliding the final piece of paper in the Crown brief that would accompany the accused to today's bail court. While his white shirt was as crisp as always, his cufflinks glistening, and his tie clipped efficiently between the third and fourth button from the top, Ron's shoulders sagged as if they were carrying the weight of the world on them.

"Your head. Looking better. Just noticed now. I'm a busy man these days, you know. My partner went off and got himself beaten to near-death, and I'm stuck holding down the fort." A faint smile came to Ron's face, then just as quickly faded

"Yes, I see that," Mike retorted, looking back down at the notes he had made after speaking to Glen Brebeuf.

"And you were right back then. Marie isn't doing very well. Her doctor thinks—"

"I'm sorry."

Ron's eyes returned to his paperwork as he double-checked his brief. "What has the boss got you doing today? You actually look busy."

"How do you feel about going for a drive? Just for a coffee?"

"Mike," Ron said with a sigh, setting the brief back down on his, "you know you're on light duties…"

"Yes, I do." Mike locked eyes with Ron, stifling a smirk.

"And it would be against regulations for you to leave the station during those designated light-duty hours…" A slight hint of playfulness tinged Ron's voice.

"Very against regulations. Likely against some procedure, too."

"But I suppose I have some subpoenas to deliver and I am under the impression that going out to enjoy a simple cup of coffee is not in violation of the terms of light duties as defined in Rules & Regs."

"Or procedures. Yes, that is exactly, if not verbatim, my understanding of the terms as well."

Mike shoved the original Missing Persons report into a folder and grabbed the steno pad next to his keyboard before springing up from his chair and slipping his suit jacket on.

"I see I'm delivering those subpoenas now." Ron tapped the Crown brief on his desk to make sure that the papers inside were uniformly settled. He had to admit that he was glad to have his partner back or, at the very least, something more than the papers in his hand to distract him from his own concerns.

Looking over to Mike standing in the doorway, he added, "You might want to grab your coat. A bit chilly out this morning if we're going to be poking around a crime scene."

Chapter Six

8:42 a.m., Friday, October 5, 2018

Given his light-duties status, Mike knew he should have immediately passed the investigation off to Ron Roberts and continued on with the benign paperwork assigned to him for the duration. As his partner passed him his coffee and pulled away from the drive-through window, however, Mike could hear his mother's words ringing in his ear: *It's easier to ask for forgiveness than to ask for permission.*

"Jesus, Ron," Mike yelped, spilling coffee on himself. "Whatever's happened has already happened. No need to go lights and sirens!"

"I'm not going lights and sirens." Ron countered as he deftly swerved through the narrow alleys that passed for streets and avenues in this neighbourhood.

"I'm sure you would if this car had them."

"I just don't like to dilly-dally. When I was in traffic—"

"You're not in traffic anymore."

"I know."

Ron brought the car to an abrupt stop.

"Jesus, Ron!" Mike cried, looking for something to mop up the hot liquid that had spilled onto both his coat and suit jacket, mercifully missing his paisley tie and white shirt beneath it.

"There's napkins in the glove box if you need them. Where's Hageneur?"

"Can you wait a minute?" Mike pleaded as he fumbled to wipe himself off.

"What?" Ron plopped himself back down in the driver's seat.

"Can you just slow the fuck down for once? Let me have a sip of my coffee. I gotta find my pen. I thought I brought a steno pad with me." Mike fumbled to return the wet napkins to the glove box while taking a sip of the still too-hot coffee and patting his jacket down to feel for a pen.

"You left it on your desk. Brain still a little scrambled, I see. Never mind. I've got a spare one here. Where's the Crime Fighting Kit I made for you?" he added, referring to the folder full of pens, pencils, rubber gloves, police tape, and the other necessities of life for an investigator that he had prepared for Mike on their first shift working together.

Mike was rubbing his forehead, which had begun to pound. He looked down at his watch. Almost nine. *Took the pills at six. Due for more in about an hour. Likely be done by then. Wait until I get home. How bad can it get?*

"Here." Ron passed Mike a steno pad that he pulled out from his own Crime Fighting Kit lying on the back seat. "Maybe you should let me take the notes, eh?"

"You're the chauffeur on this one, partner," Mike half-joked.

"I'm just trying to help."

"I'm sure you are."

Ron bustled towards the tiny MacDonald house, while Mike followed a step or two behind, trying to take in the big picture. He rubbed the back of his head a bit self-consciously as he saw the meticulously cut-above-the-collar uniform-style hair on the back of Ron's neck. The curling strands of his own hair making their way past the collar on his jacket were a bit on the scraggly side, especially for a divisional D. The sparkle of the morning sun reflected in the shine on Ron's shoes was lost on Mike's; the only thing shining on Mike was the glossy coffee spill on his jacket.

Ron stopped to wait for Mike to catch up with him while noticing Preston McAfee smiling like a fool at some woman he hoped was not from the media. "We should be taking the notes, not the uniforms."

"*Our* job is to pull this all together into a neat little package for the Crown." Mike took in the gawkers and bystanders crowding around the uniformed officers as he looked for the sergeant. "Let the uniforms do their jobs."

"I know who is required to do what," Ron sniffed before beginning to walk again.

"I'm sure you do."

"It was never like this in Traffic."

Unlike the solitary world of traffic investigation that Ron came from, Mike was accustomed to working in a team. As a result, he was comfortable having uniformed officers do the preliminary work of gathering the names of the people who would become a part of his case, if there was a case.

"I don't see Forensics."

Mike stopped in his tracks. "Are you doing this one, or am I?"

"I think you are out of your league on this one—at least for now."

Mike stepped away from him. *Fuck you.*

"You're on light duties, Mike. Reviewing occurrences is what you've been assigned to do. Interviewing people is not. This going for a coffee is one thing, and I was okay with us dropping by the scene. After all, we are investigators. Getting into the thick of it, however, is out of the question. Now I can cover us until we get to the scene, but that's as far as you can go. I'll say that I decided to drop by and accept whatever consequences come with that, but that's it. Right?"

Mike didn't hear a word Ron said. He was surveying the area around what his gut was telling him would, in fact, be a homicide investigation. *His* homicide investigation. So far, except for the body and the murderer, all the players were present: the officers, the witnesses, and the gawkers.

And Elizabeth MacDonald? The brief background check he had done indicated that she was a retired senior executive in the Ministry of Finance who was instrumental in drafting a number of significant reforms. A patron of the arts who organized fundraisers to bring obscure art exhibits to the AGO. A certified Cordon Bleu chef who volunteered at St. Mary's preparing food for the homeless. A beautiful woman who, according to the various photos readily available on the Internet, never seemed to have a lack of equally beautiful men available to her. *Smart. Connected. Creative. Social conscience. Beautiful. And now...?*

He noticed that Ron had begun walking around her house, checking to see if the front windows were locked and how easy it would be to get into the backyard and unnoticed into the house through an unlocked back door.

For his part, he stood looking at the front of the house. Time had shown Mike that his first exposure to a scene gave him his best opportunity to understand the what, where, when, why, and sometimes, who, of any crime. At a crime scene, first impressions matter.

Ron paced up and down the walk, counting the seven steps up to the front door, counting the pieces of carefully spaced flagstone. Mike looked at the walk himself. Clean, not cluttered, and highly functional. No chipped cement or weeds growing up through dirt left unattended. Even though it was only about ten feet long, this walk gave the impression of an invitation to the house.

Ron pointed to the roof. "You don't see that very often, except around here."

"What?" Mike was brought back to this world.

"Slate roof. Expensive. Durable, mind you, but… Marie and I thought about doing our roof in slate, but the quote was far too high. This woman must have had money."

"I guess."

Mike looked up to the large window on the second floor. No lace or shutters there. Heavy drapes. As a career shift-worker, he recognized the functionality of them. Must be the main bedroom. *Either she was a late sleeper who needed dark during the early daylight hours, or she didn't want anyone to see the lights on up there during the night.*

"But at the end of the day, it's still a semi," Ron continued, motioning to the doorway to the left of Sibby Mac's house. "Likely no fire-barrier in the attics of these places. Paper thin, these walls. Might as well be sitting in your neighbour's living room having your conversation, for all the good these walls do. Could work to our advantage. They would have heard something if she put up a fight."

"Maybe she left willingly on a holiday." Mike's head was beginning to pound.

"Really? Is that what you think? I don't believe you. I don't believe *you*

33

believe you." Ron winked at Mike, then glanced towards the crowd clogging the nearby sidewalk. "Judging by the look of that group of people over there, I'd bet every one of them knows everyone else's business."

"So I guess we're in on this investigation together?"

Ron just shrugged off the question. He pushed past Mike and pointed up to a slight chip missing from the second step down from the little porch. "Look at this."

"Hmm. Must have happened when she had something delivered." Mike rubbed the back of his neck, hoping to ease his throbbing head.

"Or when something was taken out." Ron bent down for a closer look, resting a knee on the step below the one in question. "Looks fairly new. Wonder where that missing piece is?"

"Forensics will find it."

"I'll make a note for them." Ron scribbled something on his steno pad. "Just to make sure they don't miss it."

"I doubt they will."

Mike walked up the seven steps past Ron to the wooden porch, careful not to disturb the chipped step.

Seven steps to Heaven. Mike found himself humming softly. *Miles Davis, 1963.* He looked at the house next door—also seven steps. He stopped humming. "Brass door handle. Don't see that very often."

Ron pushed past his partner to take a closer look, his head inches from the handle. And Mike's groin. "Looks like it's been well-used. Shinier than my shoes. She either had a lot of service people in or was very social." He stepped back, almost bumping into Mike. "I'll never understand why someone, particularly in this neighbourhood, wouldn't have a metal door. Much safer."

Mike shoved Ron away, the three-by-six porch definitely not big enough for the two of them. "Maybe because they're ugly?"

"This fancy lace curtain isn't going to keep anyone from smashing the glass and just turning the door handle to get in," Ron said, turning the handle himself.

Mike stepped inside the open door, Ron following. They could hear air blowing.

"Forced air heating," Ron commented. "Didn't notice an air conditioning unit out front."

"Could be in the backyard, Ron."

"These houses don't have backyards. Don't know how anyone could live in a place like this. So on top of each other. Might as well live in a condo."

"Dunno."

"Your house is like this though, isn't it? I still don't know why you sold your other place. You'll never find a lot that size anywhere near the city again. That long driveway, that—"

"Detective Roberts?" a voice called from the street. "Station's been trying to get hold of you on the radio. Call from home. Your wife..."

Both men froze. All colour in Ron's face drained immediately. "I have to go." Ron's body was shaking as he fumbled in his pants pocket for the car keys. "Homicide will be here soon. One of the uniforms can take you back to the station. I have to go."

And with that, Mike was alone. He took a deep breath before stepping back into the house. From the front door, he could see straight through a large, uncurtained window into the backyard.

A garden. A tiny, perfect garden. Mike smiled as he saw a bird splashing itself in the ceramic bath in the corner of the yard, surrounded by a riot of vines and plants with colours and textured leaves that looked as if they belonged in a glossy gardening magazine. So different from the cement parking pad at the back of his own house. Mike noticed the air conditioner discreetly tucked away behind some bushes right beside the house. *I'll have to let Ron know.*

He looked at the dining room at the back of the house. Interesting. Dining room table laid out formally with a setting for six and chairs in place. No papers, no books, no lost socks waiting for their mates. *Why? Was she preparing for a dinner party or was she always prepared? And would it be three couples or five people and her? Who were the people who populated your life, Sibby Mac?*

Between the dining room and the living room, Mike saw the open staircase

35

leading to the second floor, books piled on every step. Surprising. *An uncluttered staircase is an uncluttered life, me son,* Mary-Margaret's voice rang in his ear.

Mike had assumed that as a senior employee with the Ministry of Finance, Sibby Mac would be a bean counter. The decor of her home definitely suggested that she had an eye for detail. And yet these stacks of books sitting on the stairs...?

Not wanting to disturb what his senses told him was a crime scene, at least not any more than it had already been disturbed, Mike remained at the front door as he peered around the wall to his left into the kitchen. The heart of any house, but of this house in particular. Bright and warm, functional and clean. The little bit of sunlight that the tiny window allowed in reflected off the shiny brass pots and pans dangling from the ceiling. Around the room above the pots and pans was a single shelf lined with cookbooks. *No mac and cheese for this gal.*

Something shiny by the stove caught Mike's eye. A metal book holder. *For novels while you cooked, or for cookbooks?*

Then he took in the overflowing island in the middle of the room. *Bingo! The Bermuda Triangle, where everything ends up. An investigator's gold mine.* The bits and pieces of a person's life that don't fit nicely anywhere else end up here. Like the empty wine bottle. Box of paperclips. Elastic bands. Scraps of paper: lists, maybe? Pens. Pencils. Heavy-duty garbage bags. Gardening shears. Bag of potting soil. Laptop. Reading glasses. Bottle of nail polish. Emery board. Five, six, seven, eight books. Couple of decks of playing cards. Lighter.

Wait for the photos from Forensics before taking this apart. Except for the laptop; after Forensics has printed it all, get the geek squad on it. Gonna be lots to see there, particularly if she found her men online.

As Mike studied the kitchen one last time before turning to leave the house, something caught his eye. Blood. Not much, but enough. A drop by the stove, a larger splash under the fridge. And over there, against the cupboard near the floor. Is that a clump of...what? Scalp?

Mike smelled car exhaust, like in an underground parking lot. He felt something warm splattering on his face and then a weight against his body. His heart began to pound. He wiped his brow with his forearm. He looked at his sleeve. Nothing.

Michael, there was nothing ye could have done differently. Ye are not to blame, my son. Neither Sal nor Janice nor God Himself blames ye. Let it go, lad.

Mike gave himself a shake. The smell was gone. The weight was gone. He took another look at his sleeve to confirm that there was no blood on it. It took a few more moments and several deep breaths before he was fully convinced that he wasn't in the underground now. That he wasn't holding Sal's dead body in his arms. That all of that happened almost fourteen years ago, and that he was okay. Back at work. At a crime scene. A different crime scene. *Shit.*

Mike took a closer look at the floor. He saw the almost imperceptible pinkish-red streaks of wiped blood. He saw a bloodied piece of paper towel against the cupboard. He saw what the uniforms had missed.

He turned on his heel, retracing his previous steps as best he could as he walked out of the house, closing the door carefully behind himself.

"Well?" Karl sauntered up to Mike.

"Sibby Mac is not missing. She's been murdered. I'm giving Homicide a ring."

Chapter Seven

9:52 a.m., Friday, October 5, 2018

"Detective O'Shea, I presume?" Amanda Black's voice could be heard even before the distinctive tapping of her stiletto heels reached Mike and Karl.

Mike smiled broadly as he turned to face her. "Are you the only investigator they have at Homicide now, Detective Sergeant Black?"

"Stay in your lane, Detective. I ask the questions here. And aren't *you* supposed to be thumbing through occurrences in some back office?"

"Well, yes, but I was just out for coffee—"

"Cut the bullshit, Mike. I'm not getting any younger. Just ask my colourist. What have you got?"

Mike retold the story.

"No Level Three yesterday? She's seventy-two, for God's sake. Three years younger than my mother. Least they could have done to cover their asses. Automatic Level Three for seventy and over. Says right in Procedures."

"I know, but—" Mike endeavoured to continue.

"Bones was right," Amanda mused, thinking back to her first partner in Homicide. "'*Something will go horrifically wrong in the first few hours of every investigation you get.*' He promised me this would happen, Mike. Promised! Fucker. Okay, can't change the past. Moving on. House thoroughly checked? Nice suit, by the way. Not dressing yourself anymore?"

"House has been searched," Karl stated. "No body located.

"So we have a missing person?"

"Mi— Detective O'Shea seems to think otherwise."

"Did your officers check under the beds, Sergeant? Or make sure there are no murderers hiding in the cupboards? Wouldn't be the first time the uniforms have missed those vital bits of information. Like yourself, Sergeant, apparently missing that vital bit in Rules & Regs that clearly states that all male officers shall be clean-shaved for duty." Amanda looked up from the leather portfolio she was opening to shoot a disapproving glance at Karl. "Given that you are a role model for your officers, Sergeant, may I suggest that you sort that out sooner rather than later. I've got a little pink razor I use for my legs when I'm at the gym if you'd like?"

"No, thank you, Detective Sergeant. It's a...medical...thing," Karl stammered.

"I'm sure it is. Missing presumed murdered? Should be blood or guts somewhere. That's Homicide Speak for clues, Sergeant. Remember that." Amanda turned her attention to Mike. "Well?"

Mike recounted what he had seen, Amanda nodding approvingly at each detail Mike provided.

"A couple of drops usually won't get me out of bed, but I trust your intuition, Mike. God knows why. And I was just around the corner. True story. And there *was* a homicide at 3 a.m. this morning so this *would* be my body regardless. Anyway. Where's my complainant? Any next-of-kin need notifying? And who the hell are all these people?" Amanda jerked back as she looked at the crowd milling about on the street, feigning surprise as if she had just noticed them.

"No idea about next-of-kin. Complainant is sitting in that scout car. These are the neighbours." Mike rubbed his forehead, squinting in the sunlight. *Fuck, my head is killing me. Maybe it's her.*

"Friendlies. Good. Otherwise, they would make one hell of a lynch mob." Amanda turned her full attention to the onlookers. "Not our usual crowd, I see. Apparently affluent or, at least, educated. Well-spoken. Snappy dressers. Good thing you don't dress yourself anymore, Crumply-Pants. Wouldn't have worked out too well with this crowd. Anyway. Who is the spokesperson for the mob? Bobble-head with the bike? Please tell me it's not the bobble-head with the bike. And tell me he's not wearing a onesie, speaking of DIY fashion disasters. You know, I just interviewed a witness yesterday who looked kind of like Mr. Bobble-head over there. Avid cyclist, so he said. Also should not have been wearing a onesie. Lovely man, but very, *very* different. Irony of it is that he's likely to be my star witness. Hope to God he has other clothes when it comes time for court. Okay. Well, who is it that I'm talking to over here?"

Stepping away from Karl, Mike led Amanda to the group of the dozen or so neighbours who had now gathered. He rubbed his right eye with his fingers. *I need to go home. This is not getting any better.*

"Good morning, ladies and gentlemen," Amanda began her performance. "My name is Detective Sergeant Amanda Black from the Toronto Police Service Homicide Squad."

A wave of *ooohs* and *ahhhhs* went through the crowd. *Fucking posers,* Mike thought, looking over at Amanda as he stood back. *We do all the work, and fucking Homicide gets all the glory. And she just eats it up.*

Amanda *was* eating it up, so much so that she waited for the murmur to subside, not unlike a seasoned stage actor waiting for her audience to simmer down before beginning her signature monologue. Over the years, Amanda had learned how to use this mystique to her advantage in all her homicide investigations.

"I have been called out in regard to your neighbour, Elizabeth MacDonald—"

"Sibby Mac," a voice from within the flock corrected.

"Pardon?"

"Sibby Mac. We all know her as Sibby Mac. No one will know who you mean if you call her anything else," a thin, grey-haired, grey-skinned, grey-clothed woman with a scrawny old grey dog continued with increasing assurance, making her way to the front of the crowd.

"Sorry. Sibby Mac," Amanda acknowledged the woman with a slight smile and then raised her head again to address the assembly. "I am here in regards to your neighbour Sibby Mac. At this point, it would appear that something untoward may have happened to her."

Again, a murmur of *ooohs* and *ahhhhs* went through the crowd.

"I want to stress the word '*may*' to you. Obviously, my investigation is just in its infancy, and I am anticipating that you will assist me...us..." Amanda turned back to Mike, who nodded his acknowledgment, "in any way you can."

"Would you like us to get you a coffee, Detective Sergeant?" an older man with a cane asked. "Or perhaps a cup of tea?"

Amanda's jaw dropped.

"Coffee or tea? Or maybe some hot chocolate? I suspect that you and your officers are going to be here for a while. I used to do the crime beat for the CBC years ago, you know. I am quite familiar with how you people operate." The man looking knowingly around at his neighbours, who all seemed to agree that he was, in fact, an authority on such matters. "A cup of...*joe*? Perhaps a little croissant as well, although Joel may already be sold out. He bakes them fresh, but you have to get there early..." The man's voice trailed off as he glanced sadly down at his watch before returning an expectant gaze on Amanda.

"That's lovely," Amanda replied, regaining her composure. "Perhaps later. Right now, what I need is for each of you to speak to one of my uniformed officers to provide us with as much background information about Eliza—Sibby Mac as you can."

"Doug and I are just around the corner, dear," advised a brightly dressed woman apparently in her mid-eighties. "If you need the loo or just want to pop in for a break, feel free. We usually have the door locked, but with all of you people here, I don't see the need. We have a couple of shih tzus. Yappy little things. Doug says he can't stand them, but he truly loves them. They won't hurt you; they only bark. And shed. So says Doug. Feel free to come and go as you please."

"That's very kind of you, but..." Amanda did her best to keep a straight face. *Do these people not realize that there could be a murderer amongst them?*

"Everyone around here just loves Sibby Mac to bits. She is an absolute angel. I don't know what you know about this neighbourhood, dear, but we all look out for one another," the woman continued, smiling knowingly at her neighbours as they turned and looked en masse beyond their own street towards the starkly contrasting dilapidated rooming houses just beyond them. "We all know each other's comings and goings. Not that we're being nosy, of course. But we care about each other. And I'm sure that all of us will be more than happy to tell you anything you want to know about our little guild. Anyway, my name is Matty. Matilda McKinley, as I am professionally known, but everyone around here just calls me Matty. I'll be sure to let Doug know to expect you."

"Great. Lovely, in fact. Perhaps you could tell my officers over there," Amanda motioned to the three or four people who had already approached the uniformed men, "what you know about Sibby. And please keep your doors locked. All of you. My officers and I will be sure to knock if we stop by."

The crowd nodded collectively in agreement as they made their way in an orderly fashion over to the officers.

Amanda walked back to Mike. "What strange and unusual planet did I just land on?" she whispered to him, both of them watching Karl oversee his officers scrambling to keep up with the dictation. "When was the last time you saw people lined up to give statements who weren't trying to bargain their own charges away? Fascinating."

Mike's cell phone rang. "Hello?" he fumbled to answer the call, not bothering to acknowledge Amanda's comments.

"Thank God you picked up! I thought you were dead! In all the years, you've never done this to me before." Mike could hear a combination of annoyance and fear in Bridget Calloway's voice on the other end of the line.

"Oh shit!" Mike looked up at the sun before formally noting that it was well past 10 a.m., when he was supposed to be in court.

"Tell me you're in the hospital, Mike. Then tell me you're okay."

"Oh shit!" Mike repeated.

"I am really worried about you. Where are you?"

"At a scene."

"Mike, you're on light duties. What the hell are you doing on the road?

Didn't you hear the neurologist say that these next few weeks are critical for your recovery?"

"I forgot," Mike lied.

"Yeah. Great. And you thought it was a good idea for you to testify. Come on, Mike. We've been through too much for this." Bridget paused long enough to sigh. "Anyway, today is your lucky day. Sanderson is a no-show and the judge just issued a discretionary warrant for his arrest."

"Discretionary?"

"Yeah, because his counsel said he was sick, just as the judge was going to issue the bench warrant. So consider this your one and only hall pass, Mike. Listen, I've got a pile of other matters to catch up on, but we'll chat later, maybe over dinner?"

Mike was trying to think of something to say, besides how much his head hurt. And his eyes. And his neck. And...

"Or not," Bridget continued, awkwardly filling the silence. "I am really worried about you. You have never even been late for court before. This isn't you. Please get someone else to take over whatever it is you're doing and go home, okay?"

Mike stared at the phone in his hand as he drew it away from his ear. He hung up without saying goodbye.

"All good?" Amanda asked.

"Yeah, fine."

"Good. You have a couple of boys, don't you?"

"One is mine. Other one is my wife's...ex-wife's, I guess...her son. They, uh..."

"Oh. Right. Yes, I heard. Sorry." Amanda stopped talking for a moment to actually take stock of Mike. Despite the nice suit, she would have to say that he was looking rough.

Mike shuffled uncomfortably.

"Someone looking after your son now?" Amanda looked down at her watch, glad that she had not received a call from home before Tony could get her younger daughter off to school. *Good thing the other one is out of the house early or he'd really have his hands full.*

"He's old enough to look after himself."

"Spoken like a true father, Mike. Now," Amanda's investigator hat was back on, "I hope those knuckle-draggers haven't totally contaminated my scene. Who is my complainant?"

"Guy by the name of Glen Brebeuf. He's over there," Mike motioned to the police car behind them.

"Get him in for an interview as soon as you and I are done here. I want you to do a full-on, rights-to-counsel cautioned statement with him. Pure version first. Don't interrupt him. If he wants to talk, let him go. Just you in the room with him. Have an audio recorder going as well. Has he been talking to anyone since you got here?"

"I don't know. I don't suppose so. Uniform's been with him the whole time" Mike's eyes were watering, and his head felt as if it was about to explode at any moment.

"If he didn't kill her, he's going to help me find out who did. And I'm thinking that he'll talk to you more than he'll talk to me."

"Really?" Mike cocked his head in disbelief, not that he doubted his interviewing abilities, but that Amanda would defer to him.

"Yes. He's a boy. You're a man. I'm a woman. Boys like him want to be buddies with men like you, and women like me scare boys like him. Talk to him, Mike. Sooner than later."

Before Mike could consider whether or not Amanda had flattered him, she was off heading towards Karl's uniformed men and the crowd of potential witnesses, the staccato sound of her heels tapping in Mike's ears.

Chapter Eight

12:27 p.m., Friday, October 5, 2018

"**W**henever you're ready, Mr. Brebeuf," Mike began, glancing at his watch before looking across the table at his complainant. *Shit. Supposed to be done a couple of hours ago. Overtime on light duties? Oh well. Headache subsided. Maybe just the light bothering my eyes. Or fucking Ron. Or her.* Mike shrugged slightly, thinking of the whirling dervish that was Amanda Black.

"Glen," the man sitting across from Mike in the dingy interview room once again corrected. He sat up straight, adjusting his tie and pulling down the suit jacket that had begun bunching up around his shoulders. Mike thought he looked like someone preparing himself more for a television interview than for a police questioning that had the potential to go quite badly for him.

"Glen, yes." Mike looked back at the camera to make sure the red RECORD light was on. *Be glad to get into the new station. Everything automated, so they say.* "You've already been cautioned and have indicated that you understand the possible consequences of lying or telling anything other than the truth in this interview, and for the camera, you have already provided positive identification. Now, what can you tell me about Elizabeth MacDonald?"

Brebeuf took a deep breath as he settled back in the old office chair, staring directly at the camera just to the right of Mike's head. "I met Sibby Mac— Elizabeth MacDonald—twenty years ago."

Mike groaned to himself. *This is going to be a long interview.*

"I was twenty-one and she was fifty-two," Brebeuf went on, reiterating much of what he had stated in the interview Mike had done with him earlier that day.

Unlike the previous interview, however, Mike was now studying everything about Brebeuf. This man, as unremarkable as he may have initially appeared, was no longer just a complainant on a Missing Persons report. With very little doubt in the mind of either man that Elizabeth MacDonald was dead, Glen Brebeuf was now a person of interest, if not the actual murderer, in this matter.

"I remember the first time I saw her..."

Mike's senses were fixed unapologetically on the man sitting across from him, watching and listening for flinches or twitches. The first few statements in any interview were usually just the baseline for the interview. The important words that would incriminate or exonerate the interviewee would come later.

Hands and voice are steady. No beads of sweat. Yet. Fucking headache is coming back. Clearly not Ron. Maybe fluorescent lights in here.

"When I first saw her at that Ministry of Finance mentoring session, I thought she was *nothing*...."

There was a pause just long enough for Brebeuf to catch himself. And for Mike to raise an eyebrow.

"Not nothing like that. Just nothing like...not an executive, you know?" Brebeuf presented a plausible clarification.

"Hmmm." Mike did not buy it. *Objectifying the subject. Easier to kill.*

"She introduced herself to me as *Sibby Mac*. I had read the little program they gave us when we came in and there was no Sibby Mac listed anywhere..."

Organizes thoughts in a detailed manner. Crime scene washed cleaned. Almost.

"...which is also why I figured she wasn't anyone...well, important. It wasn't until the formal part of the morning when she was introduced as Elizabeth MacDonald that I realized who she was."

Brebeuf stopped speaking. Mike was beginning to consider the possibility that he could be interviewing a killer. Her killer. "Anything else?"

"To say that I was starstruck is a bit much. More like bewitched..."

Bewitched?

"...I'd say. I mean, here was this powerful woman who just seemed to carry the room. I don't know. I'd never seen anything like that before. Or since..." Brebeuf's voice trailed off.

Amanda was right: You're a boy. Women scare you. The old girl was a woman. Who scared you. Enough to kill her how many years later? Because your life...what was it...'didn't quite turn out....'? Shitty motive, but men have killed for less.

"I ended up working there for the following three summers, and then I moved on." Mike saw Brebeuf's jaw tighten slightly, his eyes drop before quickly looking back at the camera. "As one ought to."

You've been told you need to. Recently? By whom? Mrs. B.?

"I kind of thought about her after that, but not in any real sort of way, you know. I was busy doing my own thing, dating lots back then, and I can honestly say I don't recall every woman I slept with. I'm sure you know how that goes, Detective."

Brebeuf stopped and winked, leaning slightly forward as he did so. Mike stared deadpan, then leaned slightly back. *You're lying.*

"But yeah, I guess you could say I kind of had a bit of a crush type thing on Sibby. After I graduated with my Masters, before Sibby helped me get into the MOH—"

"MOH?"

"Oh, sorry. Shop talk for Ministry of Health. Thought you'd know that. Anyway, before then, I was working for a small company a couple of blocks away from the Finance offices—"

"Ministry of Finance?" Mike clarified, glancing subtly back at the video camera.

"Yes. The Ministry of Finance. Like I was saying, though," Brebeuf repeated slowly, the flash of annoyance swelling in his voice subsiding almost as quickly as it had begun, "I worked for this company a few blocks away. It wasn't every day, but I'd have to say that I did sometimes wonder if Sibby still worked in that building." Brebeuf paused and dropped his shoulders, cocking his head slightly to the right, a slight smile crossing his lips as he stared into the camera over Mike's head.

47

Trying too hard.

"One afternoon, when I was grabbing a coffee at this little shop around the corner, I looked up and there she was. I mean. *There. She. Was.*" Brebeuf's head straightened, his face becoming animated as he leaned in very close to Mike, emphasizing each word before putting his elbows on the table and resting his chin in his hand.

Mike did not move.

"I don't know if you've ever had this happen to you, Detective, but it's like you see a woman and everything around you drops away. I know. Crazy, eh?" Brebeuf's body exploded dramatically back in his chair, his arms flailing before dropping to the exposed metal armrests on the chair. "Especially coming from a guy like me. I'm not exactly what you'd call the most passionate man on the planet."

Little man. Been rejected one too many times. Sees what he believes to be the object of his desires and...?

"But that's what happened. I mean, she walked into that coffee shop, and it was all I could do to hold on to my coffee. I was, what...?"

Lonely? Desperate? Broken? Mike looked directly at Brebeuf, who smiled back at him.

"...twenty-four then. And she would have been fifty-five, but she looked a-*mazing*. Nothing like the girls I'd been dating."

Because she wasn't a girl. She was a woman. And she scared you.

"She comes over to me, puts her hand on my shoulder, and says," Brebeuf's voice rose in an airy sigh, "'Glen. How nice to see you. I was hoping I would meet you again, and here you are. Are you well?' And she says it just like that."

Did she? Or is that what you wanted to hear her say?

"I know. Who says that, right? But she did. And I will never forget that moment. It was like when lovers meet at some random airport somewhere."

Giddy. Just like a kid. Good. Mike leaned as far back as his chair would allow him, closing his eyes as he rotated his neck to relieve the increasing tightness in his upper back before refocusing on Brebeuf. *Confession time. No prompting. Keep it loose.*

"Before I knew it, we were having dinner together, and then we were in her bed, and, well…" Brebeuf smiled softly, his eyes dropping to the table, as if he was momentarily lost to another place and time.

You're full of shit. She was older than my mother, even then. Never happened. Mike actively worked at not contorting his face in disgust, choosing to sport his well-cultivated look of indifference instead.

"I ended up staying the night," Brebeuf continued, seemingly oblivious to Mike's reaction to his words, "which, at that age, I *never* did, and she made me breakfast. Who does that, Detective? I mean, really. Have you ever had a woman make you breakfast after the first time with her?"

There was an uncomfortable pause as Mike blinked a couple of times.

"Sibby Mac always made me breakfast. Every time I stayed over."

You never did have sex with her, did you?

"So there we were. Lovers."

"And you were okay with that?" Mike's headache was back. He looked down at his watch. *Pill time.*

"Yep," Brebeuf proclaimed. "Very okay, as a matter of fact. We both were, even though she knew that I was likely sleeping with whoever else would sleep with me…"

Interesting choice of words. Sloppy. Like the crime scene cleanup.

"Back then, I had an okay job, making okay money, and," Brebeuf lowered his voice, "I was getting laid as often as I wanted."

Mike looked down at his watch again. *Let him talk. We're almost done.*

"Life was good for the next seven or eight years. Over time, I got to know that I wasn't the only man in her life, but that was okay."

"So why is she missing?" *Time for this interview to be done.*

"Dead, Detective. I think she's dead," Brebeuf corrected without emotion.

"Okay. Let's go with that. If Elizabeth MacDonald is dead, why are you the only one reporting it?"

"Maybe because I'm the only one who cared about her."

"So the other guys…?"

"Fucked her," Brebeuf spat out. "But I *loved* her. They didn't."

Both men sat back in their chairs and stared at each other, each locked in his own thoughts for several moments.

"How do you know?" Mike finally pressed.

"Because she told me," Brebeuf nodded. "But she didn't love them, either. They just liked *fucking*." Brebeuf spat the word again.

"Who were these other guys," Mike's face was tightening, "that she slept—"

"*Fuck*ed," Brebeuf corrected.

"Where did she meet them?"

"Online."

"Kinda dangerous, isn't it?"

"You'd think. But she wouldn't *fuck* friends," Brebeuf explained, continuing to spit out the word 'fuck' as if it was the most scrumptious candy imaginable covered with soap, "or a friend's husband. And she never *fucked* anyone who was married. Or picked guys up in bars to *fuck* or anything like that."

"You seem kind of hung up on this fucking thing, Glen. Want to tell me about that?"

"I hate it. I hate what it means. The only woman I've ever *fucked* was my wife. Sibby *fucked* a lot of men."

"But you never...fucked...?"

"No. We didn't." Brebeuf crossed his arms, pulling them tightly into his chest.

Mike consciously relaxed his body to contrast Brebeuf's increasing tightness, aware of the camera and how the DVD it contained might be considered if it was shown to a jury at a murder trial. "You...?"

"Made love," Brebeuf declared, his lower jaw jutting slightly forward.

"But you never...fucked...did you?" Mike tilted his head to one side, as if hearing Brebeuf's truth would make more sense if he just let the words fall into his head.

"We mostly cuddled." Brebeuf was now blinking repeatedly, his body seeming to crumple into a heap held up only by his clothes.

"Some problems with the plumbing, Glen?" Mike finally softly suggested.

"What do you mean, Detective?" Brebeuf's back straightened as if he'd just received an electric shock.

"We've both been around the block a few times I'd say, Glen. When a guy

50

says fucking, he's having sex. When a guy says cuddling, he's not. You never did have intercourse with Elizabeth MacDonald, did you?"

"No." Brebeuf shot a quick, wounded glance at Mike, then looked down at the edge of the table that separated the two men. "I, uh, couldn't...you know...get it up. She never made me feel bad about it. We'd just lie really close together instead. Spooning."

"Sounds like a...nice...woman." Mike's eyes sought out Brebeuf's, hoping now that the younger man had shared his secret, he'd confess to something bigger.

"Yeah, not like some of them, eh, Detective?" A flash of anger crossed Brebeuf's face as he jerked the knot of his tie tightly up to his throat. He continued to stare at the table.

"Not like some of them," Mike repeated. *Strangled, perhaps?*

"And maybe that's why I kind of fell in love with her?" Brebeuf asked, finally looking up.

There was a pause, both men momentarily lost in their own thoughts.

No, Mike reconsidered. *You didn't kill her. You needed her too much for her to be dead.*

"When I told her... When she noticed," Brebeuf corrected, "she was very kind. She offered to break it off. The cuddling, I mean...and she was really encouraging about my meeting someone who would more...fit the bill...for me."

"Sorry?"

"You know, someone who would have my children, eat dinner with me every night, go to some cottage we would no doubt own, and all of that jazz." Brebeuf recited his list with the passion of a burned-out car salesman quoting all of the features on some old beater in the back lot. Then he looked down at the table before taking a deep breath and looking directly at Mike.

Mike held his gaze.

"Six months later, I was married. I have a daughter now, one of those suburban monster dream homes with two cars in the garage, and..." Brebeuf half-smiled at Mike, his eyebrows rising and falling quickly. "A hypo-allergenic dog. Because every kid needs a dog, so I've been told, and I'm allergic to animal dander."

"And how's that working out for you, Glen?"

"My wife is a wonderful woman, Detective. And an excellent mother, but I'm not in love with her. She's no Sibby Mac, in *or* out of bed."

"Not a cuddler?" Mike pushed his chair away from the table.

"Separate bedrooms. Which is fine by me."

"But you do have a child?"

"Like I said, my wife is the only woman I've ever *fucked*. And that was a long time ago."

Mike thought he saw Brebeuf almost shudder. "Got it."

"I went back to Sibby after I got married. She turned me down. Said I couldn't sleep over anymore. I felt so alone. I…um…actually cried, Detective. I was…am…*that* in love with her."

"And now?"

"I don't sleep over anymore." Brebeuf chuckled bitterly. "Sibby said that we could still be friends, so I go over to her place for lunch once a week. And we talk about real issues, something other than how strapped we are for cash all the time. You know how it is when the wife is a stay-at-home, Detective. All they do is spend the money you work your ass off for."

"Mmm."

"Sibby and I are really close. Much closer than the wife and me. Sibby confides in me. Asks my opinions about real-life decisions she's making."

"Mortgage payments aren't real life, Glen?"

"I couldn't care less," Brebeuf snorted. "With Sibby, we talk about books and ideas and—"

"She ever talk about anyone who she thought might want to hurt her?"

"Never. And we were best friends, I guess."

"What do you mean, 'I guess'?"

"I've never had a best friend before," Brebeuf whispered.

"I can see that."

"Which is why," Brebeuf resumed, his voice filling out again, "I know that Sibby would have never gone on a holiday without telling me. She had no reason to. Even if it was a last-minute thing, she would have let me know, one way or another." He quietly leaned back and gently placed his hands in his lap.

"So," Mike said, recalling that Brebeuf had a key to Sibby Mac's house, "she let you keep the key?"

"No. I got the key when we became friends. No one who *fucked* her had access to her home."

"But you couldn't."

"No, I couldn't. Not her or anyone else, really."

There was an uncomfortable pause.

Brebeuf broke the silence with a flurry of confidence. "And am I willing to get on the stand and say all of this to a judge and jury? Yes, I am. I love Sibby Mac. We have the best intimate relationship that I've ever had. I know that she is not on vacation, and I highly doubt that any of the men she *fucks*, past or present, are the murderer. There would be no reason. She was kind. She was good. She was fair. She gave every one of us what we wanted—"

"Except you?"

"No." Brebeuf paused for a moment. "I got what I wanted, Detective. If this had been back in the day, I might have said differently, because back then, I wanted to *fuck* women. I really did, but—

"What about men?"

"Absolutely not."

Touched a nerve there?

"I've made my bed with the wife. I'm content to lie in it. The only regret I have is that I didn't marry Sibby."

"She didn't want to marry *you*," Mike reminded Brebeuf.

"And I didn't want to marry my wife," Brebeuf blurted out, swiping at his eye.

"But you did. And you have a daughter. And a dog."

"And my best friend is gone." Taking a deep breath, Brebeuf pulled himself together. "I have to get back to work now, Detective. If you need me, please don't call me at home."

"One last thing. The man at the door: Have you ever seen him before?"

"No. Never."

53

"And the time is…" Mike looked down at his watch, squinting as he tried to focus on the numbers, his head pounding, "2:38 p.m. Thank you for your assistance, Mr. Brebeuf."

Chapter Nine

2:41 p.m., Friday, October 5, 2018

J anelle Austin was closer to forty than thirty and, on days like this, she
felt it. Chasing down leads that would ensure her pieces would appear
in the first four minutes of the 6, 10, and 11 p.m. news was getting to
be a grind that her weary body was starting to rebel against. And yet here
she was—increasingly heavy, yet still flawless, make-up covering the years
of hard drinking with cops, prosecutors, and defence lawyers all in the name
of Today's Top Story—standing at the front desk of 6 District, waiting to
speak to the lead investigator or anyone else who would give her the money
shot.

Noticing Mike O'Shea opening the glass door between the operational
side of the station and the public foyer to usher a man into the civilian world,
she cued her cameraman. "Excuse me, Detective Sergeant. What can you
tell me about Elizabeth MacDonald?"

"That's 'Detective,' Janelle. You know better than that." Mike recalled how
she had referred to him as a coward just after Sal's murder almost fifteen
years ago. "And you know that I have nothing to say to you at this time, or
likely ever. Now if you'll excuse me, please."

"Wait a minute," Brebeuf jumped in. "I know something about her."

"And you are?"

"Glen Brebeuf. She was my best friend. I'm the one who reported her
missing."

"Great. Can you spell your name for me and tell me what you know about Elizabeth MacDonald?" Janelle looked over at Mike, one eyebrow raised, before returning her attention to her new subject matter expert.

"Glen, I don't think—" Mike began.

"She was murdered," Brebeuf blurted out. "Detective O'Shea and I were just discussing the suspect."

As Mike gave a heavy sigh and looked down at the ground, Janelle's eyes lit up. The Money Shot!

"Is that so, Detective Sergeant?" she asked, trying to suppress her excitement.

With the camera rolling and a keen understanding that saying 'no comment' was the same as 'police cover-up' to the television station Janelle Austin worked for, Mike knew that he had no choice but to continue with the interview.

"We do have several leads into the disappearance of Elizabeth MacDonald and have not ruled out the possibility of foul play, but," he advised, straightening his tie, "pending further investigation, we will not be releasing any details."

Janelle ignored him and focused on Brebeuf. "As her best friend, Mr. Brebeuf, you would certainly be aware that Elizabeth MacDonald, or Sibby Mac, as she was known to friends and lovers alike, was renowned for her sexual exploits."

"She wasn't like that—" Brebeuf began.

"Of course," Janelle continued implacably, "you knew that she had quite an active online profile looking for partners interested in bondage and S&M activity, didn't you? She was clearly a serious player in the world of sex games. Isn't that correct?"

"Not at all. She was—"

Mike interrupted. "We don't believe Ms. MacDonald's disappearance has anything to do with her Internet activities."

"So it was someone she knew?" Janelle asked.

"At this point—"

"Sibb69," the shrewd reporter said, jumping back to her original line of questioning, fully aware that sex, not logic, sold sound bites. "Does that mean anything to you, Mr. Brebeuf?"

"She wasn't—"

"Or TyMeUp?"

"Yes, but—"

"Did *you* know her by any of those names, Mr. Brebeuf?"

"I am aware of those names, yes, but what I'm saying is—"

"That this is a case where one of those names—one of her doorways into the world of bondage and domination and sadism and masochism—got her into trouble?"

Brebeuf looked stricken.

"I think we're done here, Janelle," Mike stated in an attempt to rescue Brebeuf from saying something that might jeopardize Mike's investigation.

"I'm sorry, Detective, but you didn't seem to know much about this," Janelle sniffed, smiling warmly at her mark. "Mr. Brebeuf, would you say your friend's sexual activities likely played a part in what you are sure is her murder? Did this 'sex play,' as people from within that community refer to it, get out of hand often, or would you say that what happened to her was likely an accident?"

"I don't know—"

"Or would you say, as a member of that community yourself, I'm assuming, that this is something that usually remains unspoken?"

"Glen, walk away," Mike instructed. "Go out that door. Get into your car. Go."

"Sibby Mac was not a part of any online BDSM community," Brebeuf sputtered.

"I have here," Janelle countered, "several correspondences between Sibby69 and numerous individuals. Are you telling me that Sibby69 is not Elizabeth— Sibby—MacDonald?"

"I don't know if she was."

"So there were other ways of connecting?"

"I'm sorry?"

"You say you didn't know her as Sibby69, but you were one of her sexual partners. How, then, did you connect? Was it through private clubs or so-called key parties or—?"

"I met her years ago at work," Brebeuf huffed. "When we were both at the Ministry of—"

"So you're telling me that there's a BDSM meet-up through our governmental offices?"

"No. Not at all."

Mike interrupted. "Janelle, I think you're barking up the wrong tree here"

"Were *you* aware of her online profile, Detective?"

Mike's head began to pound.

"And," Janelle continued, her head tilted slightly as she pulled the microphone back for herself, "were you aware of how many people Sibby69 corresponded with in relation to sexual activities?" She shoved the microphone back into Mike's face; however, she continued without giving Mike a chance to respond. "I'm not saying that she's connected with them all. No one could be, but it seems that there are more than enough suspects within that pool to draw from if you're looking to find out what happened to Elizabeth MacDonald."

All Mike could think of was the work it would take to eliminate each and every one of these so-called suspects. And that he was likely to be the guy who would be assigned to do it.

Janelle turned back to Brebeuf, intentionally softening her voice to achieve the appearance of sympathy that she had honed so well over the years. "Thank you so much for your time, Mr. Brebeuf. I am terribly sorry about your friend and hope that whatever happened to her and that whoever is responsible for it will be uncovered sooner rather than later. Thank you so much."

All business again, she waved off her cameraman. "Okay. We're done here. Let's go."

Mike ushered a bewildered Glen Brebeuf down the front steps of the station. "I think you might want to have a quick chat with your wife on the way home before this airs at 6 tonight, Glen." *And I need to figure out how to explain this sound bite to Amanda Black before 6:04 p.m.*

58

Chapter Ten

4:10 p.m., Friday, October 5, 2018

As Mike let himself into the house, Max hurled himself down the stairs, his long legs easily managing two steps at a time. "Granny's here!"

Mike shrugged off both the comment and his trench coat. "Okay."

"No, Dad. She's *here*," the gangly teenager said, stopping abruptly in front of his father as he pushed his thick hair off of his forehead with one hand and pointed over his shoulder with the other.

"Ah, Michael!" Mary-Margaret O'Shea called out as she floated down the stairs from the second-floor back bedroom where she had taken up residence. "I've got a kettle on just this moment. Take yer shoes off and sitcheedoon." As she made her way to the kitchen in her knitted wool slippers and compression socks, she gave her son a peck on the cheek.

"Why are you here?"

Mary-Margaret stopped mid-step and turned to look back at her son. "Because I'm yer mother and I love ye. But since havin' that cuppa will not wait for the likes of yer impatience, I'll have a seat meself and we'll have a wee chat." She gave Max a wink as she set herself down on one of the two wing chairs at the front of the house. "Surprised she left these. Must not have fit in the movin' truck. I've come to stay for a bit."

Mike stood stunned and motionless in the entranceway of his home. "I see."

"Now, Michael, not a word." Mary-Margaret threw up her hands. "Ye have had quite an upset, what with the assault and all, and knowin' ye as only a mother can, I know ye won't be eatin' well. That lass of yers…" She looked at Max and warned, "This is not to be repeated, Max," and then continued, "…has left ye high and dry. I've just barely left me job at the Church, and me son needs me. If this isn't God takin' care of us all, I don't know what is."

Mike continued standing there, dumbfounded.

"Max, take yer Da's coat. He's lookin' a little unwell." Mary-Margaret settled into her chair.

Mike passed his son the coat he had forgotten he was still holding. "Mom,"

"Sitcheedoon," Mary-Margaret commanded. "After more than thirty years as the right, left, and every other hand of whatever Father happened to be runnin' the Church at any given time, I know when a poor soul has been overwhelmed by life. We've had more than a few parishioners come in broken, and after a chat and a strong cuppa, left all the better for it. Now, since ye are pushin' things, here's where I see us goin'."

Feeling weak in the knees, Mike let himself collapse into the nearest chair. Max flipped his father's coat over the banister and sat down on the second step, knees up at his chest and eyes widening, ready to hear a good story.

"I'm stayin' here until ye get back on yer feet, Michael," Mary-Margaret stated firmly, standing up to face her son. "We'll be doin' the Sunday dinners here, so I'll need Max," her raised eyebrows met with Max's eager nod, "to come with me to pick up some of me pots and pans. I don't know if *she* took them all or if ye just never had any, but I have no idea how ye people ate in this house, Michael. Not a good pot to be found in any event. I don't want ye boys to think that I'm here at yer beck and call, though. I've got me own life and don't expect to be givin' it up now."

Mike opened his mouth but was unable to get any words out.

"I know what ye are thinkin', Michael: 'There she is, long-time widowed, just now retired, nothin' to do but meddle in me life.' Not at all. I've got me yoga three times a week, me book clubs, me volunteer work at the Church. That new girl they have is all about the technology; couldn't organize a funeral to save her life. *And* I walk Sally-next-door's dog every Tuesday and

Thursday. That's her long days at work, poor thing. A stewardess at her age. Who would have thought it? Which reminds me, ye will have to find yer own way home from school on those days, Max."

"No problem, Granny." Max grinned.

"I usually go for a massage after the dog walk on Thursdays; it's a tiny wee thing but it pulls so on me shoulder. After slingin' ye and yer brother and sisters around on me own all of those years, Michael, it's a wonder I don't have permanent damage. In any event, I'll have breakfasts ready and a dinner either on the table or in the oven if I'm not home. I don't watch the tellie so there's no conflict there. I like me evenings quiet, though, because that's when I do me readin' from me book clubs. Oh, and I'll need another suitcase of clothes while I'm here. Just because I'm nursin' an invalid doesn't mean I have to look like a ragamuffin. Ye will help yer Granny with the suitcase, won't ye, Max?"

Max nodded emphatically. Mike, meanwhile, shook his head slowly under the onslaught of his mother's words.

"Well then," Mary-Margaret settled back into her chair, "where's that cuppa, Michael? I don't suppose sittin' around feelin' sorry for yerself day in and day out will help anything. Ye have got to keep goin', son. That's exactly the advice that I got after yer father passed—God rest his soul—although having yer wife walk out on ye is, I'll be the first to admit, a bit different. Likely harder. Knowin' she's out there, gettin' on with life while ye are mopin' about the house here. Ye canna let yerself get down like that, Michael. The last thing our wee Max needs is for ye to take to yer bed. No, I never did that, and neither will ye. We're strong people, we O'Sheas. But let's have that cuppa. And while ye are at it, can ye bring us all a cookie? Not the biscuits, mind. The cookies with the chocolate on top. The ones I brought."

Mike got up to answer the shrill call of the boiling kettle. *At least I'm at work for four hours a day. Hopefully, I'll be up to six and then eight and then back to the shift,* he calculated as he stood in the kitchen warming the teapot. But then he caught himself. *You're a terrible son, Michael. Her heart is in the right place. It'll only be a couple of weeks at best. And it'll be good for Max.*

Chapter Eleven

4:30 a.m., Monday, October 8, 2018

Four-thirty a.m. came early. They had told him that he could come in at whatever time worked for him while he was on light duties as long as it was during dayshift hours. But for as long as Mike could remember, dayshift started at six, so he was determined to keep to that start time.

He heaved himself out of bed and was wandering towards the bathroom when…

"Jesus, Mary, and Joseph, Michael!" Mary-Margaret jumped back, her hand to her chest, partially to ensure that the top of her nightgown was sufficiently closed, and partially to grasp dramatically at her heart.

Coming face-to-face with his mother as she was walking out of the bathroom, Mike exclaimed, "Mom, what are you doing up at this hour?"

"I could ask ye the same. It's the middle of the night, son. Go back to bed!"

"I'm up for work."

"Oh! Then let me get me housecoat on. I've not got yer breakfast ready."

"I don't eat breakfast, Mom. Just a coffee for the road."

"That's no way to start a day, Michael. No wonder ye are not healin'! Give me a moment."

There was no point arguing or discussing or even speaking. Mike knew this. He walked into the bathroom and turned the shower on. The initial drops of water from the shower felt more like needles on his face. Even though the worst of the bruising had almost faded, his head was still tender to the touch.

As he made his way down the stairs, straightening his tie and adjusting the cuffs of his shirt inside of his suit jacket, Mike heard his mother in the kitchen.

"Ye didn't tell me ye got up so early, Michael. I just assumed that ye would be lyin' in until at least six. I've hardly had time to get the oats softened."

"It's okay, Mom. I don't eat breakfast."

"And therein lies the root to likely most of yer problems, son. From this day forward, no one leaves this house without breakfast. At least, not while I'm here."

Mike tried to reach around his mother to get to the coffee machine.

"Out!" Mary-Margaret pointed to the dining room on the other side of the wall that divided the kitchen from the rest of the main floor. "Sitcheedoon and I'll have yer rolled oats ready in a flash."

"Mom, I don't want—" Mike clicked on the coffee maker, noticing the rain hitting the window on the back door just beside the stove.

"It's not all about ye now, Michael. Ye have a son that needs ye. Now that ye are on yer own, ye can't be takin' foolish chances with yer life. Bad enough ye are a policeman."

"I'm a detective, Mom. It's different." Mike pulled a plastic travel mug shaped like a semi-clad woman down from the cupboard above the coffee machine.

"And is it, now?" Mary-Margaret looked askance at the half-naked woman leering suggestively at them before returning her attention to the pot of water on the gas stove.

"It was a gift. A gag gift."

"I see." Her right eyebrow still raised, Mary-Margaret continued, "Nonetheless, who is it that almost got his head bashed in sittin' in a car looking for a killer? Oh, wait. It would be Mister Big Shot Detective Michael O'Shea, wouldn't it, now? Or were ye too busy looking at girlies? Not a policeman, me arse. And what kind of a mug is that to be cartin' about, what with an impressionable young man in the house? I'm beginnin' to

MAN AT THE DOOR

think it's little wonder Carmen left ye after all. Well, there'll be none of *that* going forward. A fine example ye are settin', Michael! And look at me, gettin' meself all worked up so early in the day."

"Mom, I'm going to work now." Mike leaned over and kissed his mother on the forehead before turning and leaving the room, his knuckles tightly holding the offending mug, which was now full of coffee. "Enjoy your oats. And good luck getting Max to eat them."

"Oh, I picked up some pastries for Max. What little boy doesn't love pastries in the mornin'? But hear me now, Michael. Yer rolled oats will be waitin' for ye on the table when ye get home. And I'll be up with them tomorrow mornin' for ye. And I don't want to be seein' that filth again while I'm in this house."

"Why is it that Max gets pastry in the morning and we never did?"

"They didn't have pastries then."

"But—"

"Michael, it's five o'clock in the mornin'." A twinkle lit up Mary-Margaret's pale blue eyes as she made her way towards her son, taking his head in both of her hands, forcing him to bend his head towards her so she could hold his face. "Are ye goin' to argue with yer old ma at five o'clock in the mornin' or are ye goin' to go off and do yer...ah, yes...detective work?"

"Fair enough, Mom. And thank you. Enjoy your dog walking."

"It's yoga today, Michael. And ye call yerself a detective, do ye? Perhaps ye would do better as a policeman." Mary-Margaret released her son's face, but not before she had planted a mother's kiss on his lips. "Off with ye then. And for the love of God, be safe, me son. There's not a day gone by since ye signed up when I haven't worried about ye. Now go before I change me mind and make ye wait for the rollies. And do up yer overcoat: It's bucketin' down. And leave that mug at work!"

* * *

"Detective Mike O'Shea. How may I help you?" *Who the fuck calls at 6:00 a.m.?*

64

"Mike? Amanda Black calling. Glad you're in."

"Where else would I be?" Mike ran his hand through his rain-soaked hair as he looked around the empty office. The midnight Ds had already left without waiting to be relieved. Cells must be empty. He saw a note tossed on his desk with four words scribbled on it.

Roberts off. Wife sick.

Ron Roberts never took a sick day. Not even after his wife's surgery a couple of months ago. He told Mike they had found something on her ovary. Just a lump. Mike's heart sank. *Maybe it wasn't just a lump.*

"True. Listen, a couple of things about that interview you did with Glen Brebeuf on Friday."

Mike sighed. He knew it was a shit interview. It wasn't an interview at all, really. It was a couple of hours of some guy blabbing on about his unrequited love for some missing old doll. Mike had not asked any of the hard questions. He should never have done the interview in the state he was in. He should have passed it on to Ron. *Shit.* He knew better.

"I need you to get him to go over the things we saw on the kitchen counter. Get him to tell you where everything came from. Sooner rather than later. Forensics has finished with the scene, and the photos should be available soon."

"Why don't I just take him back to the house?"

"This is likely a homicide investigation now, Mike. Think endgame. Trial. While my gut tells me that Brebeuf is not our murderer, if my investigation leads me otherwise—"

"Then what better way to demonstrate that we ran a full, frank, and fair investigation?"

There was an uncharacteristic silence at Amanda's end of the phone.

Mike continued, "I mean he's put himself at the scene on or near the day of, and he's stated that he'd been at the house many times before that. His prints are already all over the house, and Forensics will have already pulled them. If he has nothing to do with the murder, this is just a much easier way for him to ID the stuff. If he *is* involved, he might fumble at the scene and say or do something to strengthen our case against him."

"Let me think…." Amanda paused. "Okay. I don't like it, but I'll agree to it. Just make sure you document very carefully everything he says or does. How soon can you get him in?"

"Likely by eight. I can give him a call now and have him drop by on his way to work. Apparently, he drives right by the station every day."

"You're still on light duties, aren't you? Maybe I should have Ron go instead."

"He's not in. I'm all you've got."

Amanda paused again. "Shit. Okay, just be careful. Our victim was quite the philanthropist."

Mike chuckled. "Is that what you call it?"

"Grow up, Mike. And focus. She had a large social set. That means you need to find an address book. We need to eliminate everyone in that book."

"Sure. I'll take a look."

"And hurry up and get better, will you? Our admin clerk is having a helluva time trying to enter your overtime hours into the system while you're on light duties."

Chapter Twelve

8:17 a.m., Monday, October 8, 2018

"I hate rain," Mike muttered, sweeping the water from his trench coat with the back of his hand as he got into the driver's side of the unmarked police car.

"You're not a gardener, are you, Detective?" Glen Brebeuf offered, leaning his attaché case neatly against his shin before adjusting his seat and fastening his seat belt.

"No, not at all. You?" Mike turned the key in the ignition, simultaneously clicking the windshield wipers on high.

"No. Sibby gardened, though." Brebeuf peeled off his glasses, wiping the raindrops from the lenses with his tie.

"Of course, she did."

"She had many interests." Brebeuf inspected the glasses as he held them closer to the windshield, catching any bit of light that the grey morning could offer.

"I bet."

"Yes. And she was quite the collector. There's a thirty-year-old Jag sitting in the garage in the back. Probably doesn't even have ten thousand K on it. That would be the car to buy if you could ever get your hands on it."

Mike glanced over at his passenger before throwing the car in gear and driving away from the police station. "You like cars, Glen?"

"Not enough to kill for one, if that's what you're asking."

"No, that's not what I'm asking. I'm asking if you like cars."

"Yeah, I do."

"What are you driving?"

"A big honkin' SUV, Detective." Brebeuf spat the words. "A *metallic blue* Chevy Tahoe that always smells like urine and wet dog."

"Why is that, Glen?"

"Because that's the colour they had in stock on the day my wife woke up and decided that I ought to trade in my Mustang for the biggest SUV she could find. And I have a kid who pees herself every time she's in the car for more than twenty minutes. And a dog that gets wet." Brebeuf stared straight ahead.

The wipers swept hopelessly back and forth across the windshield in an attempt to keep it clear.

"You don't seem very happy, Glen."

"No, I'm not. I'm going over to my best friend's house to help the police find out what happened to her. You seem to think that she's just on a holiday somewhere, but I think she's dead. Not a very happy-making situation, is it, Detective."

"I guess not."

Stopped now at a red light, Mike absently watched pedestrians trying to protect themselves from the heavy sheets of rain with their umbrellas while dodging puddles. "You said the other day that you had two cars in your garage. What's the other one?"

"I dunno. I never drive it. My wife drives it."

"And you don't know what it is?"

Mike looked at Brebeuf before turning his attention back to the road in front of him. No video camera now. No cautioned statement. Just a couple of guys talking about cars. And maybe a murder.

"I said I never drive it," Brebeuf repeated, looking away from Mike, his voice so low that it was almost swallowed up by the sound of the rain pounding on the car.

"But you said you were a car guy. A car guy would know what kind of a car he has."

68

"You're right. I *am* a car guy. And I would know what kind of a car *I* drive, and I do. *I* drive an SUV. My wife drives the car."

Mike glanced over at Brebeuf again. The interior of the vehicle suddenly felt much smaller. And colder. "You don't like your wife very much, do you, Glen?" Mike wished he could have watched how Brebeuf was reacting to his questions, but he had to focus on the road, the rain seeming to get even heavier as they made their way to Sibby Mac's house.

"I told you on Friday, Detective. I love my wife. She's an excellent mother."

"But you don't like her very much, do you?"

Neither man spoke as Mike drove cautiously on, the wipers barely able to move fast enough to keep the windshield clear.

"I hope for your sake that this rain lets up soon," Brebeuf finally said.

"Why is that, Glen?" *This is the part where I send someone over to check your home address for your wife's body, isn't it, Glen? When did you do it? Friday when you got home after dropping your daughter off at the grandparents for a weekend sleepover? Or did you wait until this morning, while she was sleeping in her little bed? Or did you do them both, Glen?*

"I thought you said you hated rain."

"I do, Glen," Mike said, ending the round as they pulled onto Sibby Mac's street. "Doesn't mean I don't see the merit in it, though."

"Kind of like how I see the merit in my wife, I guess."

"I guess."

Mike pulled the car in tight to the curb right in front of Sibby Mac's house, then pressed his left arm against his body to feel the butt of the Glock in the holster strapped just underneath his armpit. *Always good to travel with a friend.*

* * *

The two men walked quickly from the car to the front door. Mike fumbled for a few moments with the house key he had taken from his pocket.

"Here, let me. The door can be ornery. There's a trick to it."

Standing back, Mike watched Brebeuf effortlessly unlock the door and push it open.

"You've done this before."

"I told you I always watered her plants when she went on vacation, Detective," Brebeuf sniffed.

Even though Mike had been to thousands of crime scenes during his career, none were more unnerving to him than homicide scenes, particularly after the body had been removed and the air had had time to settle. Maybe it was the influence of his mother's version of Irish Catholicism, so deeply steeped in spirituality and otherworldliness, or maybe it was just his own imagination, but Mike always felt as though the deceased was watching him trample through their last worldly address. *Shake it off.*

Mike directed Brebeuf to the kitchen and pointed to the cluttered island. "I'd like you to take a look at this." He noticed the chalked circles that were Forensics' calling cards around various patches of red on the floor and wall and hoped that Brebeuf would not. "What do you see?"

Brebeuf pointed to the roll of plastic wrap that lay within the quagmire of random things. "This isn't hers."

"What isn't hers?"

"This. Plastic wrap. Hated it. Doesn't belong here." The words practically exploded out of Brebeuf's mouth.

"I'll make a note of that. Tell me what else you see."

"The cards, the scrabble pieces... She cheated, you know."

"Okay." Mike looked around the room to see if there was anything else to bring to Brebeuf's attention.

"And she was terrible at it. I think it was the only thing she *was* terrible at. Everything else..." Brebeuf's voice seemed to change very subtly, and Mike noticed the man's shoulders starting to shake.

Shit. He's crying.

"I'm sorry, Detective," Brebeuf sniffled. "I thought I would be okay with this, but I guess I'm not. Can I have a picture of all of this and just write down what it is and where she got it from? I'm really not up to this now." Turning abruptly, he walked out of the kitchen.

"Yeah, sure." Mike followed behind as Brebeuf locked up the house. As the two men walked down the steps, Brebeuf stopped abruptly at the bottom one.

"She'd be so annoyed if she saw this."

"What's that?"

"This." Brebeuf pointed up at a gouge in the wood of the second step from the top. "I knew he would damage the stairs with that trunk."

"Who?" Mike's hand froze on the car keys he had been hunting for in his coat pocket.

"The man at the door. Said Sibby had asked him to get rid of that trunk of books she had in her guest room while she was away."

Mike looked sharply at Brebeuf.

"She *loved* books but hadn't even opened the trunk since we packed it up...ten, maybe?... years ago. It weighs a ton. Kinda surprised that she would get rid of them. Anyway, I told him I'd help carry it to his car so he wouldn't gouge the stairs, but he insisted that he could manage on his own. I stood right there on the porch and watched him drag the damned thing out of the house. Saw him bounce the trunk down the stairs and knew he'd need help to get it into his SUV, so I grabbed the back and we both hoisted it up. I didn't notice that he'd chipped the stair, though."

"So you helped lift this trunk into some SUV and you never said anything about it in our interview?"

"You didn't ask."

Mike snatched the house key from Brebeuf. "Let's take another look in the house." He mounted the stairs and opened the front door with none of the fumbling of the first time. Brebeuf bounded up the stairs after him.

The two men had barely stepped through the doorway before Mike grabbed Brebeuf by the scruff of the neck and pointed to the books on the stairway to the second floor just beyond the dining room. "Is that where she normally kept her collection of books?"

"No," Brebeuf said, the colour in his face visibly washing away. "Those stairs were always clear. Those books are...from the trunk."

"So if the books are here and Sibby Mac is gone, what do you think was in that trunk?"

"Oh God!" Brebeuf slumped against the door frame.

"Let's get in the car, Glen."

Mike led the distraught man back down the front steps and pushed him gently into the front seat of the unmarked police car. They drove back to the station in silence.

Chapter Thirteen

9:35 a.m., Monday, October 8, 2018

"That was quick." Amanda beckoned Mike into the office she had commandeered for the duration of her investigation, a coup that she was rather proud of given the limited space in the tiny 6 District building. The light from the computer monitor bounced off her face as she returned to scanning and sorting loose papers that she pulled from various boxes around her and then filed in boxes behind her.

Mike leaned against the doorway, the water from his trench coat quickly pooling below him. "Our guy got a bit weepy there and wanted to leave."

"So you let him?" Without wasting a breath, Amanda waved the front page of the day's newspaper she had brought in with her. "Look at this: 'Missing Miss a Mistress?' How the fuck do they get away with this? This just screams lawsuit to me. And you know, it almost reads worse when a woman writes this kind of crap. Unbelievable. Anyway, you let Brebeuf walk away?"

"Yep. Can't make him go through the house. Whoever killed her took her out in her own steamer trunk. And our boy may be in on it, intentionally or otherwise."

Amanda stopped rummaging through the papers. She looked over the monitor at Mike, giving him her full attention. "Talk to me."

"Glenny says he helped the man who answered the door carry out a particularly heavy trunk when he came calling for lunch the other day at the old girl's house. Thought it contained books until he saw the books that were supposed to be in the trunk on the stairs leading up to or down from our...what do they refer to her again as?...'Missing Miss's?... bedroom." Mike's words sat heavily in the air between them for a moment.

"What?" Amanda's voice rose almost as quickly as she did.

"Yeah. *Forgot* to mention it in the interview," Mike continued, undoing the buttons of his coat. "He began crying about some plastic wrap that didn't belong in the kitchen and wanted to leave. We'd just got out of the house when he pointed to a gouge in the wood of one of the stairs and said it likely happened when this guy was dragging a trunk down the steps. Being the upstanding kinda guy our Glen is, he offered to help. Both of them put it in an SUV parked in front of the house."

"Tell me we have him saying all of this on camera?"

"Nope. But I've got it in my notes." Mike pulled a worn steno pad out from the inside pocket of his coat.

"Not enough. I want this guy taped up."

"Too late. He's gone."

"Mike..." Amanda began, settling back down into her chair.

Mike stepped into the office and around the desk to see the screen on her computer. "You have Forensics' photos there? Pull up the exteriors of the house."

Amanda impatiently clicked through several prompts until she had the desired images in front of her.

Mike pointed at the screen. "There! If you look closely, you'll see that gouge in the second stair from the top. Apparently, the trunk bouncing out of the house caused it. As well as hating plastic wrap, according to our boy, Miss I Get Around wasn't terribly happy about gouged stairs, either."

Amanda clicked on a photo of a carpet. "That would explain this then,"

"That worn piece on the carpet. How big is it?" Mike asked, his eyes focusing on the image.

"Three by four and a half feet."

"Where is it?"

"Bedroom at the back of the house."

"That's the guest room. And that would be where the trunk full of books was before it was emptied. Look at the depth of the imprint on the carpet."

The two investigators studied the image on the screen, nodding in silence.

"Find a pic of the stairs," Mike directed.

Amanda clicked through a series of photos until she found one showing books piled high on the stairs.

"And there's the books from the trunk," Mike pointed out. "I'd put money on our girl having gone out in that trunk."

Amanda studied the screen intently.

"An uncluttered staircase is an uncluttered life," Mike said.

"What?"

"One of my mother's expressions. She claims it's an old Irish saying, but I think she just makes this shit up." Mike focused back on the picture on the screen. "Anyway point being the rest of the house is immaculate, except for the books on the stairs. Because she didn't put them there. Whoever did likely cleared out the trunk to put her body in it to get it out of the house."

"Hold that thought. I'm calling Forensics to make sure they dust every one of those books for prints. God, I wish Amy was on this one. Hopefully, Klunder... Well, they're all good. That's why they're there."

She turned to her phone. "Detective Sergeant Black. Who's doing the MacDonald scene for me?" *Good work!* she mouthed to Mike.

Mike looked down at his watch before making some notes in the steno pad.

"Brebeuf's prints will be on the books, regardless. He put the books in the box to begin with," Mike whispered to Amanda as she updated Klunder.

"My D here says there'll be prints matching our victim and our complainant, regardless. Call me if you find anyone else's." Dismissing Klunder with the push of a button, she said to Mike, "We used the luminol. Place lit up like a beacon."

"Wonder if hers is the only blood we'll find?" Mike mused, wondering if Sibby Mac would have had time to put up a fight.

"We'll find out soon enough. This is your neck of the woods, Mike. I need you to go to any stores in the district that sell plastic wrap and grab their security tapes for last Thursday and a week or two before that. We'll pull the stills of every person buying it and see if we can ID anyone. Maybe do some photo lineups with the neighbours to see if they recognize any of the customers as our man at the door. While you're doing that, I'll have whoever the walking wounded around here is—"

"That would be me."

"Oh, right. Okay, well then, I'll see who we can get to run all of the SUVs registered in Toronto to begin with and then move outwards from there. Brebeuf didn't happen to say what kind of SUV it was, did he?"

"No, but one of them is going to be his. He drives a Tahoe."

"Of course, he does. Ugh. This guy is everywhere, isn't he? Let's keep an eye on him. Anyway, grab a coffee, and I'll see you back here for my morning briefing. You didn't happen to get the colour of it, did you?"

"Shit. No, sorry," Mike said, embarrassed by the rookie mistake. "You know I'm only working until ten, right? Half-days?"

Amanda glanced at the clock above the door. "Come on, Mike!"

"Near-death beating, remember?" Mike halfheartedly offered. "Or so I've been told."

Amanda recalled Mike slumped over in the seat beside her, life slipping away from him, as she frantically tore through the city to get him to the hospital. "How could I forget? Probably the worst night of my life. Even worse than my first honeymoon. How are you doing, by the way? Bruising has gone down, I see. Still a bit of yellow, though. Did you get any update on long-term effects yet? Not like anyone's going to notice with you, but still..."

"Dunno. Too soon to tell."

"Leave Plastic Wrap Man then. I'll voluntell someone else to do it later. Dunno if I have time to grab a shitty coffee from the machine or if I should just send someone out to get me one." Amanda stood up and walked towards the door. She took a quick peek up and down the hallway before returning her attention to Mike. "Make sure you put in a quick supp for today before you go, okay?"

"Sure. I'm assuming next-of-kin has been notified?" Mike glanced at the newspaper headline.

"Last night. Big family." Amanda looked down at her watch and then at the clock on the wall. "No time for even a shitty coffee. Never thought I'd hear those words come out of my mouth. Anyway, three brothers and four sisters, partners, kids, dogs, cats, all living in and around Glasgow. Nigel, lovely man, retired surgeon, one of the brothers, is my point person. You know," Amanda paused, "regardless of who the deceased are or how they came to our attention, I find dealing with their families, for the most part, to be a very enriching experience."

Enriching. Mike briefly considered the families he had dealt with over the years while he was in the Juvenile Prostitution Task Force. Some were crushed to learn that their daughters or sisters were having their bodies listed for rent on the back pages of trade magazines, while others couldn't care less. Most of the ones who cared were still angry with him for being the bearer of bad news, although the occasional letter or card at Christmas still found its way to him.

"Is he flying over or…?"

"No, not yet. No need to. I'm going to be giving them a daily update. If this investigation is like my other ones, it'll be about 3 a.m. before I finish my day. With the time difference, that'll be about 8 a.m. their time. I can give Nigel a call first thing in the morning, his time, and he can have all day to tell the rest of the clan."

"And you're back at it again within a few hours. Impressive."

"That's Homicide. Every time I want to hit the snooze button on my alarm, I remind myself that what I do is an honour: I get to investigate the death of a human being."

"I get it," Mike admitted with a smile. Even though the stakes were a little different, he had felt that same sense of honour at various moments throughout his career.

"Do you know that some higher-ups at the Ministry of Finance have already offered to give us a whack of money for," Amanda made air quotes, "'equipment and other operational needs' to wrap this up quicker? As if throwing more money at me will make me work harder." She snorted. "Every one of my cases matters to me. Those assholes just want to keep their little club clean. They don't want her personal life splashed all over the papers. Well, a bit late now."

She glanced at her watch and then looked over at the newspaper on the desk again. "This crap looks like something that would come out of Janelle Austin's mouth. Surprised she hasn't been by for her pound of flesh yet. Did I set the meeting for 10:30? Where is everybody?"

"They're probably on their way and I already spoke to her."

"What? You spoke to the media about *my* investigation? And you didn't tell me about it?"

"She was still considered missing then. *My* investigation," Mike countered.

"I'll give you that. But from now on, nothing leaves this room without my stamp of approval on it going forward, right? Right?"

"Whatever you say, boss."

"Now, get me that supp and get the hell home. I need you well rested tomorrow morning so you can go through her Internet records and ID everyone. Maybe we'll get lucky and one of them will drive an SUV. And be missing a roll of plastic wrap."

Chapter Fourteen

7:37 p.m., Monday, October 8, 2018

"Ach, Michael, that nap clearly did nothing for ye. Ye are lookin' like a bat woken from his belfry on a Sunday mornin'. I'm just this moment steepin' a pot of tea. Sitcheedoon and I'll make a cuppa for the both of us."

"I bet I know just how that bat feels," Mike groaned, staggering down the stairs. He managed to make it to the chair by the front door as Mary-Margaret stepped back into the kitchen. As much as he hated to admit it, having his mother around right now was likely a good thing.

"Well, ye're supposed to be on these 'light duties'—whatever that is," she called out, "and here we're not seeing ye in until after five in the evening, barely able to drag yerself up the stairs. I'm surprised ye woke up at all before mornin'. No, what ye are doin' here doesn't sound too light to me, me son."

"I know," Mike sighed, massaging the top of his head with one hand while steadying himself in the chair with the other. "I got caught up in a homicide."

"Homicide? Well, that's something'!" Mary-Margaret poked her head around the door frame. "Hold that thought while I get a tray and some biscuits."

Mike rubbed his forehead. Not quite pounding, but close enough. What was it the neurologist had said?

His mother set the tray of tea and biscuits down on the coffee table in front of their two chairs and took a biscuit for herself before settling in. "Is everything alright, luv?"

"Yeah, fine. It's just work," Mike sighed, leaning in to pour a splash of milk in his cup while the tea steeped in the pot.

"It's more than work, Michael. Ye canna fool yer mother."

"Ron, my partner—odd kinda guy, but solid—came to see me every day when I was off after that assault. Got me thinking. His wife had some growth thing going on down there," Mike gestured awkwardly at his pelvis, still embarrassed to talk about women's anatomy in front of his mother, regardless of how clinical the terminology might be. "He didn't say, but I'm thinking it might be cancer."

"Oh, Jesus, Joseph, and Mary," Mary-Margaret leaned back and sighed, bringing her hands up to her heart. "Any children?"

"No." Mike poured the tea into his cup, watching it turn from a milky-grey to a dark reddish-brown. He set the spout over her cup, but she shook her head and held up her hand to indicate that the tea wasn't steeped enough for her liking.

"Just the two of them, then. What a shame. And it's so much harder for a man without a wife than a woman without a husband. The world can be such a hard place, can't it?"

She paused for a moment as she contemplated the unfairness of life, then changed the topic, her mood picking up. "So tell me about yer homicide."

"Old broad," Mike exhaled the word, and then seeing the disapproving frown on his mother's face, restarted. "Older woman. Seventy-two. Reported missing, presumed dead."

"Name?" Mary-Margaret poured and dressed her tea, then settled herself back in her chair, a second biscuit in hand, ready to hear the story.

"Elizabeth MacDonald. Known to all as Sibby Mac."

"Sibby Mac. Good name. Catholic name. Married? Family?"

"None."

"Shame."

"Retired government executive. Never married—"

Mary-Margaret clicked her tongue in sympathy. "Poor wee soul."

"Hardly. Had many…uh, suitors."

"Ah, well then," Mary-Margaret paused for a moment to take a gulp of tea and a bite of biscuit while she considered. After a moment or two, she concluded, "Good for her!"

"What?"

"Well, good for her, I say. A woman has a right to enjoy her body, don't ye know, Michael? There's a lot of chatter in the Church about women's bodies as vessels of humanity, which is all well and fine, but we're more than that. And she with no husband. She's not hurtin' anyone now, is she?"

Mike took a sip of his tea. "Did you have many suitors, Mom?"

"Whatever do ye mean, Michael?" Mary-Margaret guardedly asked as she leaned over to pick up a couple more biscuits from the tray.

Mike glanced over at her. "You know. After Dad...?"

"There was no one after yer father. He was the love of me life," Mary-Margaret began, sitting back with that rigid posture reserved only for dowagers and dancers. "He was—"

"I know, but did you ever—"

"What, Michael? Have *sex* with another man?" Mary-Margaret huffed, her chest heaving with indignation, "As if I'm going to be having that discussion with the likes of *ye*, me son!"

Mike involuntarily shuddered. "Fair enough. Sorry."

The two sat in uncomfortable silence for several minutes.

Mary-Margaret spoke at last. "So tell me about this Sibby Mac. Spunky name, that. Sibby. Sibby Mac. I like it. Yes, tell me more about our wee Sibby Mac."

"She's not ours, and I don't know if she was wee at all. But she was retired and quite...uh, active."

"So ye have said, Michael. What else do we know about her?"

"Not much." Suddenly feeling very tired, Mike slurped his tea.

"So why do we think she's dead and not just missin'?"

"At this point, we don't. There's some circumstantial—"

"Well, I'm not a big-city detective like me son here, but I would think that would be a question that needs answerin', wouldn't ye, Michael?"

"Yes. Yes, it would be."

"So what do we know of her? Government retiree, lives alone by choice. And?"

"Not much yet. Lots of books in her place." Mike's mind wandered back to the books on the stairs and the trunk, and the realization that Glen Brebeuf possibly—no, probably—actually helped to carry out his lady friend's body.

"Likely belongs to a book club or two, then," Mary-Margaret concluded.

"Not everyone who reads books belongs to a club, Mom."

"No, ye're right. But she met a lot of men. They usually don't sell men with the books, Michael. Ye have to go out and find them. I've met a few gentlemen through my book clubs—"

"Have you now, Mrs. O'Shea?"

"Gentlemen, Michael. Who are there to discuss the books. I'm the widow in me marriage, not the one who's dead. If ye are wantin' to meet people, ye have to belong to things. Clubs. Might be somethin' for ye to keep in mind now. Anyway, carry on about our Sibby."

"I think she met...uh, gentlemen...through the Internet, Mom."

"Oh. Well then, that's somethin' different, then, isn't it? Good on her. This will surely be an interestin' case and I look forward to hearin' all about it." Mary-Margaret refreshed her cup of tea, "In the meantime, ye had better get yerself off to bed. Ye are startin' to look like a bag of hammers, to be perfectly honest. All this talk of books reminds me that I'm a couple of books behind in me readin' and here I'm losing time flappin' me gums on about yer case. And I'm in at the Church all afternoon tomorrow for Arthur McCann's funeral."

"Didn't you retire from that?"

"Ach," Mary-Margaret cleared her throat with moderate disdain before taking a sip of tea. "That new girl. I'm sure she'll be fine once she finds her feet, but she hasn't worked herself in yet."

"Giving away what they would have paid you for, Mom?"

"Don't speak of the Church that way, Michael. They were very good to us when yer father passed."

"They paid you a pittance, Mom. How is that being 'very good to us'?"

"Michael, I wish ye would stop being so angry with God and His Church.

It's not His fault that yer Da died. It was an accident. And thank that very same God for the Union steppin' up like they did and gettin' us that pension money. Otherwise, we'd all five of us been out on the street the very next day. And as for the Church, they didn't have a job to give me, truth be told. It was Father David who found something and made application for me to work there. And they paid me far more than they should have."

Knowing he was treading on dangerously thin ice, Mike continued on in spite of himself. "Mom, you worked day and night for them." *In for a penny, in for a pound.*

"No, Michael. I worked day and night for *me*. Imagine a young girl of thirty, four children, newly widowed with not a whiff of family here and no job or prospects. The Union took good care of us, yes, but if not for Father David and the Church, I would surely have died of loneliness. Ye wee ones and yer Da were me world, Michael. We came here when I was sixteen and he eighteen, with nothing but our dreams. I was just a child of seventeen when ye came along—"

"I know, Mom. I've heard this part about a million times," Mike's voice was gruffer than he had intended.

"And now ye'll hear it a million and one. As I was sayin'—"

"Granny, can you pick me up from my friend's place tomorrow after school?" Max hollered down the stairs before leaping from the fourth step down into the living room. "Oh, hi, Dad. When did you get home?"

"Yer Da's been home since about dinner time. Took straight to his bed, poor lamb. Workin' too hard as usual, I'd say. And yes, I can pick ye up anywhere ye wish. What time are we looking at, then?"

"I dunno. I'll call you?"

"I'll surely be sittin' by the phone." Mary-Margaret took the last biscuit from the tray. Mike grinned at the hint of sarcasm in his mother's voice, not entirely sure that Max picked up on it. "Leave the address for me, and I'll see ye at your chum's place at 5:30. After that, I'll need ye to come grocery shopping with me, darlin'. I don't know how ye people survive in this house."

"We manage," Mike said dryly.

"Barely, I'd say. Now before ye start scaring the boy by droolin' down yer gob, get yerself off to bed, Michael. I still think it's far too early for ye to be back at work at all. And that's all I'm going to say about that. For now. And Max, go into the kitchen and fix yerself a wee snack before ye head back up. And on yer way, bring out a few more of those biscuits for yer Gran, will ye? Someone seems to have eaten all of the ones I brought out." Her eyes twinkled as they adoringly following Max out of the room.

Mike could actually feel some spittle rolling down the left side of his face. Having his mother stay with them for a while was definitely a good idea.

Chapter Fifteen

7:54 a.m., Tuesday, October 9, 2018

"There are two things in life you should never be late for," Amanda began, pulling down the visor to check her face in the mirror. "A media scrum and a hair appointment. Both of them can change everything. That and shoes. Game-changers, Mike. Absolute game-changers."

"I'll keep that in mind." Mike shook his head, absently glancing down at his own shining shoes while he ran his hand through his hair, fearful that a clump of it might come out this time. After checking to make sure there was still more hair on his head than on his hand, Mike scanned the street behind police headquarters for a parking spot, congratulating himself on finding one between a couple of the media trucks that had just been set up.

"I really appreciate the ride. Today, of all days, had to be the day my car had to go in for a minor," Amanda commented, referring to the maintenance schedule all police-owned cars were on. "Good thing I've got that new kid with me to take it in. Otherwise, I'd be screwed. You'd think with all the technology out there, they'd be able to build a car that can go more than three months without needing an oil change."

"You'd think," Mike commented to the suddenly vacated seat beside him. Before he could manoeuvre into the parking spot, Amanda had popped open the door and was racing through the back entrance of the once-impressive building, past the pack of reporters that would populate her 8 a.m. press conference. Mike rubbed his head again, aware of a bump that didn't seem to want to go away, and made his way back to the 6 District station. *No telling where the scrum will lead,* Amanda had told him. *No sense wasting time waiting for me. I'll call you if I need a ride.*

* * *

He had intended to return to the station, but the car seemed to find itself back on the tiny street where Sibby Mac had lived and, quite likely, had been murdered. Mike pulled over a few houses west of the home that was now a crime scene and rolled down his window. The birds were singing the way they sang when he was a boy, before he knew anything about pain or sorrow.

"Excuse me," a tiny voice spoke, far too close for Mike's liking. "You're the detective looking for Sibby's murderer, aren't you?"

Mike snapped back to the present. "Huh?"

"Can I bring you a coffee or a cup of tea?" It was the thin, grey-haired, grey-skinned, grey-clothed woman with the scrawny old grey dog whom Mike had noticed in the crowd of neighbours the day before. She was smiling cautiously.

"No, thank you. I'm fine."

"Very sad thing this murder, isn't it?" the woman persisted. "She was a lovely woman. Very warm. A good neighbour. Kind. I don't like what the papers are saying about her. If I'd known they were going to go down that road, I would never have spoken to them yesterday." The woman's voice trailed off as the dog collapsed beside Mike's car and lay there panting.

She continued. "Sibby did a lot for the community, not just the arts. She started up the soup kitchen at St. Mary's, you know. They serve over a hundred meals a day there now. Didn't see *that* in the paper, did you?" Mike suspected that the woman would have huffed, had she had it in her to do so, but instead, she just let out a little sigh. The dog rolled over onto its side with an equal degree of resignation. "All that woman wanted to ask about was Sibby's *sex* life. As if *I'd* know anything about *that.*"

"Seems to be a big deal," Mike offered.

"To whom? Me? The neighbours? Listen, Detective, nobody in this neighbourhood gives a pig's foot about what anyone does behind closed doors. We've all got our secrets. It's just too bad that Sibby's private life has to overshadow everything else she's done."

"Were you close?"

"We're all close here, Detective. Most of us have lived here for years, since the time when they couldn't *give* these houses away. That's how we could afford ours, my husband and me. It was the same for most of us who've been here any length of time, really. Places were unlivable when we bought in. All a pile of dumpy old rooming houses. When I think back, I can't imagine what we must have been thinking when we bought," the woman almost smiled, "but now even the smallest of the small is worth over a million."

Despite being well aware of the value of the houses in this neighbourhood, Mike found himself looking around and giving a low whistle.

"I just wish Norm was here to see it," the woman sighed.

"You said you spoke to someone yesterday?"

"Mistake. I should have known better. Janelle Austin. Used to be a good reporter back in the day, but I think," the woman's voice lowered as she made a drinking motion with her hand, "she drinks. Anyway, I won't keep you. Just wanted to let you know that Sibby was not some 'Mistress of the Dark' like the newspapers are saying. Have a very good day, officer."

* * *

"Where the hell have you been?" Amanda caught Mike as he was walking by the office she had commandeered.

"Waiting for you."

"I called you about ten times. You didn't pick up. Do I really want to know where you were?"

"I was…" Mike began, looking down at the phone he pulled from his trench coat pocket. *Shit. Seven missed calls. Must have had it on silent.* "Talking to one of the neighbours. Did you know that our deceased started up that soup kitchen at St. Mary's?"

"Yep. Not nearly as sensational as being a dominatrix, is it?"

"What?"

"That's the latest. I've put in a call to shut this smear campaign down. Hopefully, the editors will start reining in their writers, but I doubt it."

Amanda stepped back into her office, grabbed half a dozen eight-by-tens from her desk, and shoved them at Mike. "Here. Take a look. Our boys pulled some picture from the security tapes of the only guy buying plastic wrap during our time frame. Good thing it's not a hot-ticket item. Do you recognize him?"

"Should I?"

"James Sobatics. Used to be a federal member of Parliament. Stepped down about four years ago, for, he claimed, 'personal reasons'. Code for 'the missus has had enough of my screwing around and will feed me my balls for breakfast if I don't stop.' Still likely has his hand in both games, but more behind the scenes now. Is Ron in?"

"Dunno."

"Great. Well then, once again, you're my man. I need you to do a little background on Sobatics. Let's see what he's all about, with special attention to the last year or so." Taking the photos back from Mike, Amanda set them down on her desk, then turned to lean against it, arms folded, facing Mike. "When are you back on full duties?"

"Why? Need me?"

"Need a warm body is more like it." Amanda looked over her shoulder at the cell phone vibrating on the desk behind her. "Shit. I should take this but I'm going to let it go to voicemail. So yes, I need you."

"Been a long time since I've heard that."

"Seriously, Mike." Amanda moved behind the desk, fumbling for a pen as she went. "You know your job. You're thorough. You're dependable. Christ, you sound like the new vacuum cleaner I just bought for my cleaning lady."

"Well, that's something, I guess."

"Not like I'm pushing you or anything, but," Amanda held up her hand as she listened to the message on her phone, jotting a name down on the corner of a scrap of paper on the desk before continuing, "get your ass back on full strength. My partner has hip dysplasia or some macho bullshit football injury that's got him laid up for a few weeks, and they're not giving me anyone else." Amanda dropped into the chair behind her desk. "You're a damn good cop. We work well together. And you're dressing better. Is your mother dressing you now, or are you dating Bridget Calloway?"

"Neither." Mike chuckled. "Listen, I'm tickled pink that you love me as much as a vacuum cleaner, but I've got my own investigations on the go."

"Like what, Mike? A few Fail to Complies that Ron has thrown your way to keep you out of trouble?" As she spoke, she was tapping in a number on her cell phone.

"No, a pile of interviews with girls who have been diddled by some fucker that they just issued a bench warrant for." Mike could feel his head beginning to pound at the thought of Gregory Sanderson.

"I'm sorry, Mike, but you don't have a choice. I'm taking you for the next four weeks. I've already cleared it with your new boss."

"We have a new boss?"

"Paul Landon. Just arrived," Amanda replied, listening to her phone ringing on the other end as she continued talking to Mike. "Hell of a nice guy. Came from Corporate. Pencil pusher. Admin type. Not a knuckle-dragger. Knows his place. Spoke to him yesterday afternoon. He's okayed the deal."

"What about Ron?"

"Yes. Hello," Amanda waved Mike off as she turned her chair to face the corner of the room. "This is Mrs. Black, Kristie Black's mother. To whom am I speaking, please?"

Chapter Sixteen

9:45 a.m., Tuesday, October 9, 2018

"James Sobatics. Fifty-seven years old. Married to Katherine Sobatics for thirty-one years. Both lawyers by trade. Four kids together: James—goes by Jimmy, twenty-nine; Chloe, twenty-seven; Ashley, twenty-five; and Russell, nineteen."

"Afterthought?" Amanda smiled.

"Even lawyers make mistakes. Anyway, called to the bar from Osgoode at twenty-five, as was the missus. He worked for the firm he'd articled with for the next three years, moved to a different firm, left presumably because he didn't make partner after five years, entered politics, and went to the Hill at thirty-five as an assistant. She stayed in Toronto with the firm she was at. He got elected in their riding here at forty, handled a few portfolios including Finance as an interim minister very briefly, then came back to Toronto at fifty-three at Mrs. Sobatics's beckoning, as you had surmised earlier. Still in tight with the Feds, and now we have video footage of him buying plastic wrap around the corner from our homicide scene."

"You know, you might actually be better than my vacuum cleaner. Good work."

"Thanks. After almost thirty years on the job, you get to know a lot of people. And people talk, someone once told me."

"It was a Google search, wasn't it?" Amanda said with a smirk.

"Anyway, I'm gone for the day. Off to see my doctor." Amanda's whole body sagged in disappointment. "Don't worry. I expect to be back tomorrow for a full day."

Amanda's elegantly plucked eyebrows jumped.

"Are you swooning, Detective Sergeant Black?"

"No, I'm just trying to decide whether I should choke you for leaving or hug you for coming back." Amanda gathered up the file that Mike had dropped in front of her. "Don't let this get around, but I might be warming up to you, Crumply-Pants."

* * *

"Can I see you up in my office for a moment, Detective O'Shea?" an unfamiliar voice called from the doorway of the D office.

"Yes, sir." Recognizing the insignia on the uniform, Mike immediately stood up and grabbed his suit jacket from the back of his chair.

"No jacket required," the thin bespectacled man said. "Follow me."

Mike flung the jacket back on the chair and followed the new unit commander down the hall and up the stairs to his office.

"Close the door, will you?" The man gestured at the round conference table across from the door.

Last time I was in here was the night Robby Williams did a header off his balcony. Haven't heard anything more about that investigation, Mike thought as he stood by the table, reminding himself of the ongoing internal investigation that might or might not implicate him in his old boss's suicide.

"My name is Paul Landon. I understand that you're one of my best investigators, Mike."

Mike shook the outstretched hand.

"Please. Sit."

Mike sat awkwardly in the same chair he'd sat in the night of Robby's death. The unit commander sat in the same chair that Shannon Somerville, the lawyer the union sent for him, had occupied.

Mike's eyes darted around the room. No matter who occupied them, unit commanders' offices all seemed to look the same. Until now. Something was very different this time. There were no plaques to remind the occupant of where he had come from, or pictures with smiling faces of those he would have climbed over to get to where he was now. There were no Rockwellesque prints that seemed to pass as art for these men. Instead, there was a photo of this man with a woman who looked about his age and three adult children. There were framed quotes that Mike recognized as being from Dickens, Chaucer, and Plato. There was an ugly, obviously hand-made, ceramic objet d'art on the floor in the far corner of the office.

"I understand that you're on light duties, Mike."

"Actually, sir—"

"Paul. Call me Paul. When we're out there, you can bow and genuflect profusely, but in here, I'm Paul. That okay with you, Mike?"

"Sure, Paul. I'm actually just on my way to a doctor's appointment."

"Then I won't keep you. I've got two things I need you to know. Three. Well, four. First, I'm the new unit commander here. I've heard a lot of good things about you. Second, Detective Sergeant Black has asked to borrow you for a few weeks. I hold her in very high esteem, and if you have no objections, I've agreed. Third, is there any truth to the rumour that your partner may be pulling the plug?"

"Ron? Retiring? Doubtful. I mean, he's got more than enough time, but I don't think he's got anything else to do, you know?"

"Good to know. Staffing issue either way because fourth, I have a sort of favour to ask of you."

"Okay."

"Now, I know it may seem like a bit much for me to ask anything of you, given that you don't know me at all, but like I said, I've heard good things about you, both as an investigator and as a man. I've got a bit of a situation… Well, no, it's not. I've got… Well, I need a strong personality to help me with something that's landed in my lap. It's new to this organization, and I think you're the one who can walk through this with me."

"I'll bite."

"I can't say too much about it now out of respect for the individual involved, but I need to have you on deck. Again, I can appreciate that this is a lot to ask of you, but I suspect you're the right person for this challenge."

"Well, sir—"

"Paul," the unit commander corrected with a broad grin.

"I'll do what I can, Paul, but I really have no idea what you're asking of me."

"Nor do I, but I suspect you'll rise to the occasion. I know you've got places to go. I just wanted to introduce myself and let you know as best I can what will be coming down the pipe. I don't like surprises, and I work on the assumption that others don't, either. Fair?"

"Fair, yes. Thank you, Paul."

"Oh, and before you go, can you just sign this?" Landon stretched out his long legs to pull his wheeled chair uncomfortably close to Mike's. "It's the report from the Special Investigations Unit with regards to Robinson Williams's death. You've been cleared of any wrongdoing. I understand that he was your boss a while back. I'm so sorry for your loss."

Mike scribbled his signature without looking at the report and then stood up, stunned. *No one else has ever said they were sorry.*

"And one last thing, Mike. I was at Detective Constable Salvatore's funeral. I have never been so proud to be a police officer as I was that day. I will never forget your compassion as you handed Mrs. Salvatore her son's forage cap. You did us all proud."

"Thank you, Paul. Thank you on all counts."

Chapter Seventeen

1:45 p.m., Tuesday, October 9, 2018

Mike had heard somewhere—couldn't recall where or when—that Dr. William Buxton, who headed up the department at St. Mike's, was one of the top neurologists in the country. He had to take his informant's word for it. Except for a couple of minutes here and there, Mike had only ever dealt with the resident, Dr. Wu. She seemed nice enough: young, energetic, optimistic.

"How are you feeling, Mike?" she asked as she breezed into the examination room, sizing Mike up before sitting down in the plastic chair across from him. She pulled the ends of her open lab coat out from under her as she settled in. "They say one size fits all, but I think they mean no sizes fit anyone. So how are you?"

"Great." Mike sat up straighter.

Dr. Wu pulled a folder out from the large binder she had been carrying. She opened it and flipped through some loose pages, refreshing her mind with the details of Mike's condition while looking for any notes that might have been added.

"Any changes since the last time we spoke?"

"I'm back at work."

"But only for a couple of hours a day, right? And they don't have you doing anything strenuous?" She looked questioningly at Mike. "No major physical exertion like heavy lifting, lots of stairs, anything that could be considered physically demanding?"

"No, but I don't see what that has to do with my head."

"It's just about getting rest." Dr. Wu made some notes in his file. "And driving. I didn't see any restrictions, so I'm assuming that you are driving. But not for long periods of time, I hope."

"A couple of blocks to work and back."

"No problems with your vision then. Okay. And your overall health? I see the contusions on your face are healing nicely. This one over here might leave a scar, but it looks—"

"Hot?" Mike grinned at her.

"I was going to say 'like it will fade', but whatever. And your thought processes. How is your recall? Any headaches?"

"Recall isn't too bad. Headaches are. Shouldn't they be getting better by now?"

"Headaches? Hard to say. May I?"

Before he had a chance to respond, she stood up, snapped on the latex glove she had pulled out from her ill-fitting lab coat and was gently touching the purplish line over Mike's left eyebrow. "Might be some residual swelling settling down, or it might be something else." She peeled the glove off and tossed it into the waste bin on the other side of the desk. "Are you getting lots of rest, Mike?"

"Oh, yes." Mike hoped she wouldn't see through his lie.

"Then it must be the swelling settling, although it's been a while. How about your ability to find and place appropriate words. How is that going for you?"

"Not bad."

"Ability to follow a conversation?"

"Depends whether or not I'm interested in what you're saying."

"Fair enough. How about we run some tests?"

Dr. Wu took the large binder from the desk and flipped through its pages until she found a series of words and phrases she had Mike read to her. She then had him describe a series of pictures. From there, she led him through several word-association and memory tests before setting the binder back.

She sat down at the desk again and made more notes in his file.

"How'd I do?"

"Not bad. Not as well as I would have expected almost two months after the assault, but you seemed to get a bit tired near the end. Anything else going on that I should know about?"

"My wife left me."

"Oh. I'm so sorry."

"It's okay. Not the first wife to go."

"Still. The end of a significant relationship can—"

"Save it, Doc. I've got my mother, who has moved in with me until further notice, for all of the soft and cuddly advice I need."

"Oh, I see. And how is *that* going?"

"Fine."

"Okay. Well, I'm noticing that your speech is a bit slurred now, Mike. Is that normal?"

"Not until after I've had a few pints, no."

"I'm sorry?"

"I was joking."

"I see." It was obvious to Mike that she did not. "You mentioned before that you're a reader. I noticed that you were having some difficulty when you were reading out loud. Is that normal?"

"No."

"How would you say your overall ability to concentrate is?"

"Sorry?"

"Let me rephrase—"

"I was joking. Again." Mike sighed. "I think my concentration is pretty much as good as it has ever been, though."

"How would you measure that?"

"I was back giving evidence on the stand and I seemed to do okay."

"Oh, I see. That doesn't sound like modified work duties to me."

"Well, I had to convince a few people..."

"So you think you'd be doing better if you were back at work and taking on more responsibilities?"

"Definitely."

"Are you able to avoid stressful situations and high-impact physical exertion in the capacity you're in? You said you're a detective."

"Absolutely. I mean, really, all I do is type at a computer. Not like those guys on TV."

"Do you want to go back to full duties, Mike?"

"Yes, I do."

"I'm going to have to consult with Dr. Buxton on this one because I'm really torn. For our purposes, your test results show that you're functional, but that's a pretty low threshold and I have no baseline on you to work with. I have some serious reservations of my own based on my knowledge of you, but again, I'm working within a very limited scope. Hang on a minute, will you? I'll see if I can have him come in and talk to you."

Dr. Wu disappeared and within a few minutes, an older man whom Mike vaguely recalled seeing once before appeared, followed closely by Dr. Wu.

"Mr. O'Shea, I'm Dr. Buxton. We've met before, shortly after you were admitted last time. Dr. Wu tells me you want to return to work. Is that so?"

Mike had to think for a moment. The room suddenly seemed quite crowded, and Dr. Buxton's businesslike delivery was in stark contrast to Dr. Wu's warm tone.

"Yes," he stated, much louder and clearer than he had intended.

Dr. Wu handed the file to Dr. Buxton, who glanced at it and frowned. "I can see from your chart that given the length of time that has elapsed since your injury, it is most likely that whatever swelling your brain experienced has gone down."

"Okay."

"Not really. What that means, Mr. O'Shea, is that wherever you're at today is likely to be where you'll stay." He looked at Mike. Mike looked over at Dr. Wu. Dr. Wu's glance darted back and forth between the senior doctor and their patient.

Dr. Buxton continued. "The brain is a funny thing, Mr. O'Shea. A lot of research has been done and a lot of books have been written about it. More recently, we like to talk about how the brain can rewire and rebuild itself.

Makes for excellent reading based upon some interesting studies, but at the end of the day, each brain is unique, and each recovery is different."

Shit. That doesn't sound very good.

"Age and overall health at the time of the injury play a significant role in that recovery. I see that you are in good health, but you're also no spring chicken, as they say."

Mike glanced over at Dr. Wu, who was now focused exclusively on Dr. Buxton.

"Now don't get me wrong," he continued. "I've had much older patients who have made near-complete recoveries after brain injuries of a catastrophic nature. I wouldn't classify your injury as catastrophic, but it *is* quite significant. Which is to say, I've seen worse do better."

Mike looked down at his feet, his heart sinking. Dr. Wu pursed her lips, looking apologetically at Mike.

"All things being considered, however," Dr. Buxton concluded, "I will recommend that you return to your regular work."

"Excuse me, Dr. Buxton, but I was suggesting that Mr. O'Shea might want to take some more time—"

Dr. Buxton interrupted. "What do you do for work, Mr. O'Shea?"

"I'm a cop. A detective."

"Very good. Yes, I can see that. Must be a very fulfilling occupation for someone like you."

"Which is why—" Dr. Wu politely continued.

"Dr. Wu, Mr. O'Shea is clearly a working man. Someone who derives great satisfaction out of putting in… What was it one of your former chiefs was fond of saying? 'An honest day's work for an honest day's dollar'? Am I correct in assuming that you are that type of man, Mr. O'Shea?"

"Yes."

"As such, Dr. Wu, a person like this needs to get back to work." Dr. Buxton turned his attention to Mike, "I will recommend that you return to your detective work then, but I advise you to book a follow-up appointment with me for a year from now."

"A year?"

"Yes. If whatever impairments you have now are still present at that time, then they are what we consider to be permanent impairments. Which is why, Dr. Wu," the veteran neurologist stated to his resident, "I would suggest that Mr. O'Shea return to work now. Not much is likely to change. This may be, as they say, as good as it gets, and Mr. O'Shea will have to either work with what he has or find other work more suited to his impairment."

Shit! That doesn't sound good.

"Now, Mr. O'Shea, I would advise against false hope, while at the same time encourage you to continue to get plenty of rest and avoid physically demanding situations. Be sure to return to my office before the one-year mark if anything changes for the worse. If the changes are dramatic or immediate, come through Emerg."

Before Mike could say anything, Dr. Buxton was turning to leave the room. Dr. Wu cleared her throat.

"Oh, right." Dr. Buxton looked at Dr. Wu before smiling uncomfortably at Mike. "Do you have any questions of me, Mr. O'Shea?"

"What do you mean," Mike gathered some air in his lungs before he continued, "by 'permanent'?"

"Permanent," Dr. Buxton snapped at Mike. "You know what that means, I'm sure. Forever. As in never going away. Anything else?" He seemed to be annoyed at having been delayed by such a pedestrian query.

"No, that's it. Thanks."

"See you in a year then. What's going on with the patient in the next room, Dr. Wu?" Mike heard him saying as the two doctors swept out of the examination room.

Mike sat for a moment alone, considering the information he had just received, choosing to focus on being allowed to get back to full duties more than on the possibility of being forever impaired. Then he straightened up and walked out of the room, head held high, if only out of habit.

Chapter Eighteen

6:03 a.m., Wednesday, October 10, 2018

"Well, partner," Ron grimaced at Mike, not looking up from the piles of paperwork sprawled across his desk, "ready for another half-day at the office?"

"Nope, I'm back full time," Mike replied, turning on his computer and placing his full mug of coffee from home on the desk before heading to the ancient coat rack in the corner of the office.

"Already That's awfully quick."

"Yep. Saw my doctor yesterday. Told him I was fine. He signed off on me."

"But you're not."

"Close enough. Anyhow, the wheel keeps on turning and I've got shit to do." Mike hooked his coat on the rack and gingerly set himself down in the chair at his desk across from Ron's, the monitor of his computer screen glowing at him. "Amanda Black's pulled me in on her Sibby Mac thing, and I've got that sex assault trial running as soon as they find Fucknuts—"

"Oh, sorry. Forgot to tell you. Guy from 7 District called. They found him."

Mike's head shot up. *Game on!* He stopped short. *Holy shit, that hurt! Stiff. Pain. Pills. Where?* He leaned his body over to the left as he fumbled in his right pants pocket to find the bottle of painkillers.

"Traffic stop, of course. Warrant wasn't on the system yet, but I put out an internal alert when Calloway called looking for you the other day to say that he'd skipped."

"Nice." Mike gave a tiny approving nod at Ron, straightening up as he placed the pill bottle on the desk in front of him.

"So your man will be up in court this morning for the bench warrant. I told the D who called that I thought the Crown likely still had the jury on call and would probably be able to recall them by tomorrow." Ron shoved a piece of baby-blue notepaper at Mike. "Here's Calloway's direct line at the court. I looked it up for you, although you probably have it, don't you? In any event, I told the other D that the two of you would sort it out."

Mike rose slightly, reaching across the desks to Ron's outstretched arm, retrieving the number he in fact already had. "Hmm. This might change things a bit for the Sibby Mac detail."

"Oh, and about that, the boss came in this morning. I told him what was going on with you. What I *thought* was going on with you. I'm going to be covering if you have to leave."

"It's not even 6:15 yet," Mike grumbled, frowning as he looked down at his watch.

Ron shrugged, a half-smile crossing his face. "It's not every day we have a high-profile homicide in our district."

"High profile?"

"You haven't been out front yet, have you? There are at least half a dozen people—well-dressed people—waiting to speak to Amanda Black with information. Reporters were buzzing around yesterday afternoon, too."

"Have we got the room set up?" Mike fumbled in his desk drawer for some blank DVDs for interviews. "Has anyone called Amanda?"

"Relax, Mike. These are neighbours just wanting to be 'helpful.' I already spoke to them. They all have valid ID in their leather wallets and designer purses. All quite content to speak to Detective Sergeant Black *whenever she is ready*." Ron spoke the last four words in a sing-song voice, struggling not to break out into a grin.

Mike settled himself back down in his chair, shaking his head. *Shit, gotta stop doing that*, he thought as a wave of pain washed over him.

"The boss was a little concerned when he walked by them on his way in this morning, which is why he came back here. I told him it was all under control." Ron went back to shuffling his papers. "But he did say he wanted to talk to me after you got settled in. Do you know anything about that? I just assumed that it had something to do with you being on light duties, but...?"

"Dunno." Mike punched the keys on the keyboard to log in, prescription bottle of pills staring at him seductively.

"Those things are addictive, you know."

"Apparently. I haven't taken my morning dose yet. Waited until I got here. Not supposed to drive—"

"And you're back on full duties?"

"Like I said, I got shit to do." Mike popped a couple of pills from the bottle into his mouth and took a swig of his coffee.

"Suit yourself, but nothing is more important than your health."

* * *

"Who are all of the fashionista octogenarians sitting on the rad out front?" Amanda's voice pulled Mike's glazed-over eyes away from the screen he had been staring at. "You look like shit, Mike. What the hell are you doing here?"

"And good morning to you, Detective Sergeant Black." *Fuck! How long have I been staring at the damn computer? And when did Ron leave?*

"Seriously, Mike, go home. You don't look well. There's not much bruising left, but there's probably still a lot of internal swelling going on."

"I'm good. Cleared. Ready for work."

"I've already got one body on the go. I don't need another. Seriously, you do *not* look well. Where's Ron? I'll get him to drive you home."

"I'm good. Besides, I probably have to go to Court."

"Yeah, the boss told me." Amanda stopped as she noticed Mike's blank look. "What? You think I'm just pulling in now? It's almost eight o'clock. The morning is practically over. I got here before seven and that was after I did my 5k run and got my two kids off to school. At least," Amanda looked at the time on her phone, "I hope they're on their way now. Haven't heard differently, so…. Anyway, popped upstairs to see Landon. Helluva nice man. Thought he might be a little out of his depth here, but he seems to be exactly what this district needs right now. Ran into Ron. Hadn't planned on it, but given the looks of you, I'll get him to take over for a bit. And I'll call Calloway later. Let her know that you're in no condition to testify before she recalls the jury." She winked at Mike. "But she would already know that, wouldn't she?"

"Unlikely. Haven't spoken to her for a while."

"Trouble in paradise, Romeo?"

"She's *not* my girlfriend. Never was. Never will be. We just have a lot of cases together."

"Whatever you say, Mikey. It's all good with me if you want to keep her on the down-low."

"Okay, that's enough." Mike pushed himself away from his desk and walked over to the coat rack to grab his coat.

"Fair enough. Can you call our friend Brebeuf and tell him to keep the hell away from my crime scene? If I had a dime for every call I've had forwarded to me about a Tahoe seen in the area that comes back registered to him, I could buy myself even more shoes."

"Can I grab a coffee first?"

"Going for coffee? I'll come with you." Ron bounced back into the office.

"Hold up, Dream Team," Amanda pulled in the reins. "I've got a hallway full of beautiful people who just want to help. Don't care how you do it, but grab all of their names and let me know if anyone actually has anything useful to say before you move them along. Staff Sergeant at the front doesn't like having them there, apparently. Not my problem. Regardless, boys, be gentle. These are not your typical witnesses."

"Who is?" Ron replied, picking up a pad and pen. "We'll grab our coffees later."

Chapter Nineteen

11:23 a.m., Wednesday, October 10, 2018

"Nice neighbourhood," Mike remarked, staring out the passenger window as he cracked the opening on the plastic lid of his coffee cup to take a sip. "Guess that's what happens when you have a couple of lawyers' salaries to pay the bills."

"I suppose." Ron peered through the windshield as he looked for numbers on the mammoth homes, his coffee untouched in the holder just below the console. "Bet a cop and a lawyer's salary would do just about as good."

Mike glanced sideways at Ron before taking a more committed gulp of coffee. "She dropped by the house a couple of times. Nothing happened. Nothing."

"Well, that's not what I heard…."

"What? That I banged her right there on the living room floor with my son watching? Oh, and wait. My not-even-ex-wife was likely having furniture moved out while we were at it, right? What the fuck is wrong with you people?"

"No harm meant, Mike. You know how it goes. And at least these young kids think of you as capable. I mean, could be worse. They could have had you in a hospital bed in your living room with a catheter."

Mike grimaced. "We seem to have wandered a long way from home for a cup of joe, partner. Coffee shops in D-6 not good enough for you?"

Ron pulled the car over. "There it is." He nodded at a yellow brick house set back from the street. "Couple of doors down. Across the street. That two-storey over there."

"What are we looking at?"

"The Sobatics house." Ron withdrew his cup of coffee from its cradle, cautiously removing the lid before taking two long sips, pausing for a moment, then snapping the lid back in place and returning the cup to its home without blinking or taking his eyes from their target.

The two detectives sat staring a while longer at what would be an impressive façade in any other neighbourhood but seemed fairly average on this street.

"You know," Ron finally said, "I like the way they have those shutters on the front windows. Makes it look more, I guess, finished. And the house is big enough to do that. I always thought they'd look good on our house, but Marie..." His voice trailed off.

"She okay?"

"No, she's not. Hey, look at the garden along that side fence. I wonder if they do it themselves. Lilac bushes are so easy to grow, but they can really get away from you if you're not careful. And look at the way it's tiered. I like that look, but you have to have the space to do it. Our lot isn't wide enough. And people have their dogs running around off-leash and the damned things go all over the place. I hate that. Burned patches all over my front yard. Doesn't look like there are any burned patches on this lawn. Wonder why?"

"Dunno. Don't suppose the dogs here are any different from the dogs in your neighbourhood. So what's happening with her?"

"Maybe it's the owners. Doctors don't know. Seem to think it's a more aggressive cancer than they had thought. I'm not really a dog person, you know. Too much work. I bet they all have dog walkers around here. And gardeners. I mean, look at that lawn. Perfect. I've got grubs this year. Do you have grubs where you are, Mike?"

"I don't have a lawn where I am, Ron. Downtown, remember? So what are you going to do?"

"Might try some new treatment this latest specialist was on about. Not up to me. Whatever she wants." Ron reached down, feeling around for his coffee cup, eyes not moving from the house. "Going to pick up some grub killer after work. I'm not sorry we didn't have any children. Don't get me wrong. I like kids. It's just that, well, it never really worked out for us. Not like we tried anything extraordinary or anything like that, but we tried and nothing really happened. I don't know if Marie was as good with it as she said. Women are funny that way, aren't they? I mean, you think they tell us everything, but they don't, do they?"

"You're asking me?"

"I've known my wife for forty-nine years. Did you know that?" Ron took a gulp of his coffee and then fumbled to put it back in the holder. "I met her when I was five. First day at my new school. First week in Canada."

Mike glanced over at his partner.

"Born in the States. Dual citizenship. You didn't know that, huh? Came to Canada when my parents divorced. Mom had family in Montreal. Lived with them for a while. English-speaking, obviously. Anyway, met Marie that first day. Still remember, mostly because she punched me in the nose and broke my glasses after I told her she looked funny."

"You're a smooth operator, Ron Roberts."

"Yep. *My* mother went over to *her* mother's house with me and my broken glasses after school that day, demanding her mother pay to get them fixed. I don't know what came of it all, except that Marie became my new best friend. My only friend for a long time. Those Montreal kids are a tough crowd."

Then suddenly Ron pointed to the front door of their target, "Look! Someone's leaving." Without warning, he leapt from the car. Mike hastily pushed his coffee cup into its holder and bailed out after him.

A woman in her mid-fifties wearing yoga pants and an oversize shirt was just locking the front door as Ron approached her, careful not to step onto her property. "Have you got a moment, ma'am?" Ron called out from the sidewalk, flashing his badge at the woman. "We're the police."

"Oh God! Has something happened to one of the kids?" The woman leaned against the door frame, her knees almost gave out.

"No, it's okay. We just want to talk to you." Ron replied. Mike, now beside him, hadn't the faintest clue what his partner had planned.

"Yes, of course. I mean…" The woman unlocked the door and stepped inside while the two men approached the house but remained on the doorstep.

"May we come in?" Ron pressed.

"I'd rather you not," the woman said, regaining her composure. "In fact, no. How may I help you?"

"Just wondering if your husband is around."

"What's this all about?"

"Just wondering if we can speak to your husband."

"He's not in. He's— Who did you say you were again?"

"Roberts. Detective Roberts. And this is my partner, Detective O'Shea. From 6 District. We're investigating a missing person and we think your husband may be able to help us."

"I'm sure he would if he could, Detective. Detectives, that is. But he's not in. In fact, he's gone to Ottawa for a couple of days on business. If you have a card…?"

"Of course." Ron reached inside his coat and pulled one out. Mike stared past the woman into the house.

"I'll get him to call you when he returns." The woman stepped all the way back inside the house and began to close the door.

"That would be wonderful. Thank you, Mrs. Sobatics. You wouldn't happen to know anyone by the name of Sibby or Elizabeth M—?" Ron plowed on.

"No," she snapped coldly. "I don't."

"Perhaps your husband does?" Ron pushed forward just enough that she could not close the door without hitting his face.

"My husband has a very large social circle. He's a very…uh, social man. He's a politician, as I'm sure you know."

"Yes." Ron did not move back.

"And I'm a lawyer." The woman quickly looked Ron up and down, as if these words would make him disappear.

"Yes, we know that, too."

"My husband and I don't always move in the same circles." She peered out at the men, one hand now part way up the back of the door while the other was still wrapped around the handle, not yet pushing the door shut in Ron's face.

"I understand."

"I'll be speaking with Mr. Sobatics this evening. I'll be sure to let him know that you were around." She began to push the door shut.

Ron remained in place. "I'm sure you will, Mrs. Sobatics. When do you expect him home?"

"Likely by the weekend." Their faces were by now only a couple of inches away from each other and even closer to the door.

"*Likely?*" Ron asked, undeterred.

"He's made a lot of friends over the years living in Ottawa, Detective. There'll be a lot of catching up to do, I suspect. He drove this time, so I wouldn't be surprised if he gave himself a day or two to go fishing while he's away."

The need to explain his situation, the belief that she knew where he was and what he would be doing, the resignation in her voice: All were so familiar to Mike from his task force days and the many conversations he'd had with powerless women victimized by men who thought they owned them.

"So he didn't fly?"

"No, Detective. He took the Tahoe. Why are you asking?"

"Just curious." A half-smile came to Ron's face.

"Lovely. Now I have an appointment to attend to, gentlemen, so if you don't mind…?" The door closed another inch.

"Of course not. Thank you for your time, Mrs. Sobatics."

"Of course. Oh, and what was…is…your missing woman's name again? Just so I can tell my husband if he asks."

"Elizabeth MacDonald. He would know her as Sibby Mac."

"You seem awfully sure of yourself, Detective."

"Yes, I suppose I am. Enjoy your afternoon, Mrs. Sobatics."

* * *

"Bird in a gilded cage." The words rolled out of Mike's mouth as he fumbled for his seat belt.

"What?" Ron threw the car into drive and began meandering through the tony neighbourhood, scrutinizing the houses as he drove.

"*She's only a bird in a gilded cage, a beautiful sight to see. You may think she's happy and free from care—she's not though she seems to be,*" Mike's voice lilted as he recited the words to a song he thought he'd long forgotten. "My father used to sing it to my mother when I was little. *''Tis sad when you think of her wasted life, for youth cannot mate with age, and her beauty was sold for an old man's gold. She's a bird in a gilded cage.'* I think Dad was trying to remind Mom that she married for love."

"Does he still sing it to her?"

"Maybe in her dreams. She was widowed a long time ago." Mike adjusted himself in his seat, "Anyway, our Mrs. Sobatics knows that her husband cheats on her, and she probably also knows he's not just visiting 'old friends' in Ottawa this week."

"Agreed. Hey, look at that awning," Ron pointed to the front of a house as they drove slowly by. "So simple, yet effective. Very nice. And I'm thinking that they both know Sibby Mac. I wouldn't be surprised if Mrs. S. suspects or even knows that he has something to do with her murder."

"You think she knows that much?" Mike took a swig of his coffee, his face screwing up in disgust as he spat the now-cold liquid back into the cup.

"If she's held it together for this long, she's not a foolish woman. She knows what he's about and has made it her business to know every step he takes because that's the only way she can stay prepared to do damage control to keep her...what did you call it?...*gilded cage* intact."

"Impressive, Ron. I had no idea that you had such insight into the psyche of the weaker sex." Mike rolled his window down, then pulled the lid off the cup and chucked the disgusting brew out the window.

"I don't. Marie and I have been watching a lot of those morning talk shows lately."

The car jerked as Ron came to a full stop at the stop sign.

"Sounds pretty awful." Mike snapped the lid back on the cup and leaned towards Ron to replace it in the holder.

"Yes, it is." Right hand on the wheel, left hand on his lap, Ron stared straight ahead as the car started moving again and he squeezed out the words he did not want to say.

"She's dying, Mike."

Chapter Twenty

9:05 a.m., Thursday, October 11, 2018

"I think ye had better get out of bed, Michael. There's people here to see ye."

As his mother backed out of his bedroom, Mike fumbled in vain for his cell phone. After spending a few seconds orienting himself to the unexpected daylight shining through the sheets he'd thrown up to replace the drapes that no longer hung in the windows, he found his watch.

9:05 a.m.

He set the timepiece down in disbelief and then picked it up to look at it again. The hands still indicated 9:05. *Shit! How did that happen??*

"And ye'll be putting some clothes on, to be sure. There's a lady present!" Mary-Margaret hollered back to him as she made her way back down the stairs.

Shit. Shit. Shit. Where the fuck is my cell phone? Shit!

Mike stumbled into a pair of pants that he picked up off the floor and struggled into a shirt that he found on the back of the chair. Then he rushed headlong down the stairs towards the voices in his living room.

"Ah, there's our Michael," his mother graciously announced, standing in the middle of the room so that she had a full view of the stairs while being able to face the guests seated by the window, the requisite cups of tea and plate of biscuits before them. "Yer friends, Ronny and, I'm sorry, what's yer name again, luv?"

"Amanda," the detective sergeant replied.

"Amanda. of course. Such a lovely name. Ronny and Mandy are here for ye, son."

Mike fumbled to tuck his wrinkled shirt into his pants before realizing that he had not lined the buttons up properly with their buttonholes.

"No worries, Mike. Just glad you're not..." Amanda paused, her eyes shifting over to Mary-Margaret, whose own eyes were staring at the tiny woman expectantly.

"Dead," Ron concluded, looking like a father indulging a daughter's tea party whims as he juggled the fragile cup in one hand while trying to keep the saucer with its spoon level in the other.

"No. But certainly dead to the world was our Michael." Mary-Margaret reached out and and relieved Ron of the saucer that appeared to be only seconds away from eluding his grasp and placed it on the table in front of him. "Ye might know, I was up at 4:30 this mornin' to make Michael his breakfast when I heard a terrible noise coming from his room. Of course, I didn't want to intrude, but I had to sort it out."

"Of course, you did, Mom." Mike rubbed the sleep from his eyes, his embarrassment fighting with a rising impatience with his mother.

"Michael!" Amanda softly chided him while smiling up at Mary-Margaret as only one mother can smile at another.

"Well, yes. And so," Mary-Margaret continued with her story, "I stood outside his door for a good ten minutes and when I heard nothing but this terrible racket—"

"You mean my alarm, Mom?"

"Well, if that's what ye are wakin' up to every mornin', no wonder ye are such an ogre! It was horrible." Mary-Margaret glanced at Amanda and Ron for affirmation on the evils of alarm clocks before returning her attention to her son. "Anyway, I saw that phone of yers buzzin' and barkin' and ye not movin', so I gave ye a shake just to make sure—"

"That he wasn't dead?" Ron interjected with a smile, then took another sip of tea.

"Exactly what I was thinkin', Ronny. And then Michael, when ye told me to *feck off…"* Mary-Margaret dramatically put her hand to her chest and threw her head back in mock horror. "It was at that point that I determined that ye weren't dead, but probably needed the rest. Given that it's been only… how many days since that madman practically bashed yer brains in, and here I am only tryin' to keep ye alive, with ye runnin' off tellin' yer doctor some half-baked story about bein' the full shilling."

"So you just let me sleep?"

"I did just that, Michael. Ye have been stompin' around here like a narky old bear, and I thought—"

Mike held a hand up to stem the onslaught of words. "Mom, I'm fine. Yes, my head hurts. But that doesn't mean you can just let me sleep in and not go to work." His temple was beginning to throb.

"I beg to differ, me son. I made the right decision. And the world, as we know it, has not stopped. Another biscuit, Mandy? Such a beautiful name. And such gorgeous hair. Yer mother must have cursed ye as a girl, though, havin' to comb it out every morn and night?"

"Yes. In fact, she did. And no thank you, Mrs. O'Shea—"

"Oh, call me Mary-Margaret, me luv. No one but the servicemen at the Church call me Mrs. O'Shea." Mike could tell from the rising colour in his mother's cheeks that she was pleased that anyone would consider such a respectful formality anymore.

"Mary-Margaret, then. Thank you, but no. I've probably already had too many biscuits for one day."

"Ach, I'm not seein' it if ye have, dear. There's hardly an ounce on ye. But what do I know?" Mary-Margaret glanced disapprovingly at Mike. "I'm only a mother. Maybe ye can talk some sense into this one, Mandy. As thick as two short planks is our Michael some days."

She glanced at her watch. "Oh my! Look at the time. Ye will have to excuse me while I get me arse in gear. I have to get over to Sally-next-door's to walk the dog. Yappy wee thing, but I've been takin' it for walks goin' on seven years now. She's a stewardess is our Sally-next-door, and at her age, too! Well, I'll leave ye to it then. Lovely meetin' ye both. Such nice friends, Michael. Ye are very lucky. But don't push yerself too hard!"

* * *

Eleven missed calls since 6 a.m. Three from B. Calloway. Five Unknowns, but likely Ron calling from the station. One from a number Mike recognized as Amanda's cell.

And two from the Courts. *Shit. Time for Mom to go back to her own place.*

Mike tossed the cell phone on the dresser. He finally was able to shower.

Downstairs in the living room, Amanda, not wanting to waste any time, was hunched over the laptop she had retrieved from the car, scanning the most recent uploads, while Ron, equally disciplined, was jotting down some notes about the previous day in his memo book.

"Question," Amanda's head popped up over the laptop screen. "Did you and Mike happen to speak to Katherine Sobatics yesterday?"

"As a matter of fact, we did." Ron looked up from the pad in his hand. "Why?"

"That's exactly what I was going to ask you."

"Well, we were in the area—"

"I call bullshit, but continue."

"And she happened to be coming out of her house."

"And so you and Mike thought you'd pounce on her?"

"Well, no. Not exactly."

"Then what, exactly?"

"Well, we just thought—"

"Highly unlikely—"

"That, since we were all there—"

"Ron, please stop talking. You and Mike fucked up. You had no right or reason to speak to anyone, and now you've tipped off our main...no, correction...our only possible suspect."

"I think you're being a bit harsh, and what about Brebeuf? He's still looking pretty hinky," Ron countered. "Listen, Mandy—"

"Don't. The only person who still gets to call me Mandy is my sister and now, apparently, Mike's mother. Regardless, what the *fuck* were you thinking, Ron?"

114

"Honestly, I don't know. We were out for a drive, I ended up in front of the Sobatics house, his wife walked out, and I just thought we might as well have a word."

"Well, that *word*, as you so eloquently put it, may have set us back big time. You know how nobody likes writing warrants, Ron? Well, now that Sobatics knows we're looking at him, he's gotten himself lawyered up, and I can't get near him without briefcases full of them."

"Oh."

"Yeah. Lawyers lawyered up. Not pretty. I can almost explain away the behaviour of Mr. Brain Injury upstairs, but I expected a bit...no, a lot more from you. Unless this is how you roll, in which case, get the fuck away from my case."

"I made a mistake. I'm sorry."

"I don't have time for this, Ron. I've got rogue reporters writing shit about my deceased, the Feds calling the chief to ask why we haven't made an arrest, and now a team of lawyers wanting me to disclose everything I have on an ongoing investigation. Until we get this shitshow under control, just do what I ask, okay?"

She cocked her head at the sound of Mike singing in the shower upstairs. "And please, tell me that's not *Bohemian Rhapsody* that he's singing?"

Her cell phone rang. "Yes," she turned her attention to her phone. "Amanda Black speaking."

While Amanda was giving the Crown what he needed to negotiate a plea bargain in a case scheduled for trial the following week, Ron thought about his wife. She would be at the hospice now. He should have taken the day off to go with her, but Marie said she didn't want him there. She said it would be easier for her to manage without having to look at him. He knew she was lying. She wanted it to be easier for him. And it wasn't. He should have been there, helping her arrange her end-of-life care.

"Are you intending to be single for the rest of your life, Mike?" Amanda asked, her phone call ending just as she spied Mike coming down the stairs.

"What?" Mike looked down at himself. "I wore this yesterday, and it was okay."

"Well, you either slept in those pants or you left them crumpled up overnight in a place I don't even want to imagine. For the love of God, Crumply-Pants, pull yourself together. And unless you want to stay single— and unpopular—for the rest of your life, never tell a woman, *any* woman, that you're wearing yesterday's clothes. God, I hope Ms. Calloway knows what she's in for."

"Fuck *off*, Detective Sergeant."

"There is no rank in Homicide or in the world of dating advice. Point taken. Ready, Ron?" Amanda slung her laptop case over her shoulder. "You'll be taking over the team meeting at 10:30. I've got a conference call at 10:45 with my sister and her care team that I can't reschedule. Don't worry. While we were waiting for Sleeping Beauty here to…uh, beautify, I made some notes of the things I want you to ensure get done."

Ron gave Mike a disapproving look. "If that's what we were waiting for, then we should have waited a bit longer, I'd say."

Chapter Twenty-One

10:30 a.m., Thursday, October 11, 2018

"I see a couple of new faces here, but I'm assuming you all know each other, so we don't have to waste time going around the room," Amanda announced, her entrance into the Major Crime office quieting the hum of voices from the dozen or so men juggling steno pads and coffee mugs stained from months, years in some cases, of constant use and sanitary neglect. She commandeered one of the less cluttered desks. "Now I know it's tight in here, but since you guys don't seem to want to come to me, I'll have to come to you. Pull in a couple more chairs so that everyone can sit. No sense standing."

Amanda flipped open her laptop and waited for it to connect to the overtaxed station server while a few officers disappeared in search of more chairs. The rest leaned against the walls of the room, gazing indifferently at the detective sergeant. Mike had secured a chair beside Amanda by virtue of favour more than rank, while Ron remained standing, ready to assume Amanda's place once she left for her conference call. Checking the time on her screen as patiently as her nature would allow, Amanda recalled the words of her dentist and made a conscious effort to not grind her teeth while she waited another few minutes for the crowd to settle down enough for her to begin the briefing.

"Preston McAfee, Foot Patrol," the spit-polished uniform announced, responding to Amanda's nod.

"I know who you are, Preston. What have you got for me?" Amanda said, noticing Ron rolling his eyes as some of the more grimy old-clothes officers slouching against the wall chortled.

"Oh. Yes. Sorry, ma'am. Detective Sergeant, ma'am. I mean…" Red-faced and flustered, the earnest young officer, the only man in the room without a coffee, buried his face in his memo book and carried on. "I spoke to three people from the neighbourhood who came to the front desk. Detective Roberts detailed me at approximately…."

Preston quickly thumbed his way back and forth through a series of pages in his memo book, stopping only after a chorus of even louder chortles erupted, this time seeming to come from the entire room. Amanda shot a disapproving look at the officers. Ron just looked down, shaking his head.

"The detective sergeant hasn't got all day, guys. Listen up!" Mike hollered out before quietly addressing the young officer. "An overview is good enough, Preston. Don't worry about the times."

"Spoke to a Douglas Haliday, husband of Matty…Matilda McKinley," Preston soldiered on, a look of relief and gratitude flashing across his face, "who stated that he has known the deceased—"

"Missing, presumed deceased," Ron corrected.

"No, I'm good with deceased. That's why I'm here, Sunshine," Amanda interjected, her voice notably sharp. "Homicide Squad, remember? You gotta be cold to get my attention these days. Go ahead, officer."

"F-for approximately twenty-six years," Preston stammered, glancing at Amanda and then Ron before refocusing on his notes. "Described her as a very generous, fun-loving…"

A few mumbled comments came from the assembled cops.

"…neighbour. Never any problems. Very involved with the community. Well-liked…"

"I bet!" a deep boozy voice called out to another round of laughter.

"…never married, no kids, entertained frequently…"

A couple of whistles and a clear 'bow-chicka-bow-bow' transformed the atmosphere of the investigative briefing into that of the two-bit strip joint around the corner from the station just before the day's headliner mounted the stage.

"…and sat on a number of boards…"

"And faces…!"

"Okay, that's it!" Amanda shouted. "The line you crossed is way back there."

Except for a bubble or two clunking its way through the ancient radiator and a few uncomfortable coughs, the room was instantly still. A few more moments of feet shuffling and the sound of men sipping their cooling coffee passed before Amanda continued.

"Gentlemen, we have all read the papers. We have all seen the news. We are all aware of what sells. And some of us in this room," Amanda made eye contact with as many of the officers as dared look up at her, "have personal knowledge of how what is written and what is the truth are not necessarily the same thing."

A few of the men looked down sheepishly at their feet, while others looked up at the ceiling. Having made her point, Amanda nodded to Ron to take over, snatching up her steno pad as she left the room.

"Thank you for the update, officer," Ron said. "Next?"

There was a slight murmur in the room as the door closed behind Amanda before another officer read out a list of possible suspects in a series of daytime break-and-enters near the area of the homicide. Ron directed the officer to ensure that every one of these suspects could be eliminated for the homicide.

"Any signs of a body?" Mike asked.

"I got a call in to my man at the morgue," a burly old-clothes officer whose stained T-shirt barely covered his belly said before scratching his unkempt beard. "He's got nothin', but he's put the word out. Gonna give me a call if a Jane Doe turns up anywhere across the country."

"Spoke to a few people who knew her from her charity work. Definitely a high flyer," a much younger old-clothes officer piped up. "This gal knew how to pull in the bucks, I tell ya. All aboveboard. No bullshit. Got more pics of her steppin' in and out of limos with guys who look like they have a lot of cashola than I got of my kid."

"I spoke with a girl down at St. Mary's. They fuckin' love her there," a fit, modestly hip old-clothesman stated. "Said she runs cooking classes or something for new moms a couple of mornings a week. Teaches 'em how to feed their kids healthy. A lot of 'em there also know her from the soup kitchen."

"Get their names?" Ron asked, his eyes fixed on the pad of paper he had been jotting notes on.

"Boss, there have to be over a hundred or more bums at every meal."

Ron looked up. "Well, sounds like you have your work cut out for you then, doesn't it? Until we can say otherwise, every one of them is a potential suspect. Think full, frank, fair."

"Fuuuuck," the officer replied, but not before he received an elbow or two from the men on either side of him.

"Anyone else?" Ron looked around the room before focusing on a particularly scrawny young officer who was pecking away feverishly on the tiny keyboard of the tablet balanced on his knees.

"Nerdster," the burly old-clothes officer called out to his colleague. "He's talkin' to you."

"Huh? Oh, yeah. Found the site she used to find guys to, uh…" No one dared make a sound, despite Amanda's absence.

"…hook up with 'sugars.' For men and women with money looking to have sex with each other. Men and women, men and men, women and women, any combination thereof. No strings. No complications. So the site says, anyway."

Ron waited patiently for Theodore 'Nerdster' Weinstalk to continue. While he had been in the same recruit class as Preston McAfee, Weinstalk's advanced computer skills opened doors to opportunities that McAfee never even knew existed. This was likely Weinstalk's saving grace, given his apparent inability to embrace—and, in fact, his complete indifference towards—the strong police culture.

"Nerdster!" Billy-Bob prompted.

"Right. Sorry." The young officer mumbled as he pushed the metal frame of his heavy glasses back up his nose. "It would appear that the deceased used an algorithm of sorts for connecting with her targets."

"What the fuck are you talking about?" a voice demanded.

Weinstalk continued, unruffled. "Which is to say that the site was visited every Friday between 1 a.m. and 2 a.m., at which time, it would appear, the deceased connected with her...uh...targets. Clever timing, considering that more new profiles, on average, are uploaded on Fridays between 12:58 a.m. and 1:37 a.m. than at any other days or times of the week."

"Do we have names and addresses?" Ron asked.

"Names, yes. IP addresses, of course."

"Of course," another voice muttered.

"But actual physical addresses, not so much. If I understand correctly, she hosted. She wouldn't need their geographic coordinates."

"Fair enough. Thoughts, Mike?" Ron, who was a self-admitted technological troglodyte, deferred to his partner.

"We're going to have to get warrants for those IPs," Mike directed. Everyone in the room groaned. "No shortcuts. I don't care if you know a guy who knows a guy. This is a homicide investigation, and we can't afford to fuck it up."

"Fucking Nerdster!" An officer sitting beside Weinstalk grimaced, then gave the young officer a spirited smack to the head.

"Timing on that, anyone?" Ron threw the question out to the room.

"Couple of days, maybe?" the well-groomed hip officer suggested.

Both Mike and Ron looked dubiously at one another.

"Fuck that!" the burly old-clothes officer shouted. "I'll get typin'. We'll get 'er done by midnight. C'mon, Nerdster. This dinosaur needs your ed-ja-ma-cated word skills." Billy-Bob pushed his way past the well-groomed officer towards the door, drawing the scrawny computer geek along in his wake. "Step into my office and we'll chat. But first, I gotta take a dump. Check ya later, dicks. And hugs and kisses to your lady boss." With a wave of his hand that culminated in the finger thrown up behind him, the burly officer and the scrawny computer geek disappeared from the inner sanctum.

"Well," Ron glanced over at Mike before clicking his pen closed and addressing the rest of their ragtag team. "I guess that ends our briefing, gentlemen."

Chapter Twenty-Two

4:27 a.m., Friday, October 12, 2018

"Huh? What the…? Mom, what are you doing here?" Mike jolted awake.

"Just checkin' to make sure ye are not…" Mike's mother gently fluffed his pillow.

"Dead?"

"Well, perhaps. Ye know, I used to put a mirror under yer nose when ye were a baby, just to make sure ye were breathin'." She smiled at her clear recollection of those times from decades gone by. "I did that with all of me babies. At the time, yer father, God rest his soul, used to say I was daft, but ye know, we've had more funerals for wee ones than I'd care to recall since I've been at the Church."

"And you thought it would be a good idea now because…?"

"Well, mostly because I didn't want to hear that infernal racket bellowin' from yer room while I'm tryin' to get myself set for the day. I have no idea how Max sleeps through that."

"He's on the third floor, Mom. And I usually wake up before…" Strains of Metallica shattered the air. "…that goes off."

"Well, that's not healthy, either. Wakin' up before yer alarm."

"*You* woke me up!"

"I don't know, Michael," Mary-Margaret continued, not missing a beat. "This police work and murder sounds like a terrible job. Ye shall not make old bones at this rate."

"I guess." Mike could feel his head beginning to pound. *It's not the injury. It's her.*

"Oh, and while we're at it. I was just thinkin', as I was readin' a book last night that Max gave me… Couldn't sleep for love nor money. Don't know why. Wound tighter than an eight-day clock, I was. Anyway, this book, I was thinkin' that it would be something' our Sibby Mac would read."

"Mom," Mike groaned, "she's not *'our Sibby Mac'* and she's dead. She doesn't read anything anymore."

"And how do ye know she's dead, luv? Have ye got a body? What if that pervert has just kidnapped her and is holdin' her as a sex slave somewhere?"

"What?" Mike pulled the blankets up over his exposed chest, suddenly very self-conscious.

"What 'what'? Ye read about it all the time, Michael, these high flyers and their perversions. What if yer Mister Monster Man has kidnapped her and all the while we're sittin' here snug as bugs, our wee Sibby Mac is being held captive?"

"Granny?" Max sauntered into Mike's bedroom.

"Ach, what a tired wee lamb ye are. Get yerself back up the stair to yer room and off to sleep, luv, while I get yer Da ready for work. Ye see, Michael," she chided, pulling her son to his feet, "I was right. That racket ye call music is enough to wake the dead."

Definitely time for her to go home, Mike decided on his way down the hall to the shower.

Squirting the last of the liquid soap Carmen had left into the palm of his hand while the sharp spray of the shower stabbed at him, he considered the possibility that Sibby Mac might still be alive. What then? *Exigent circumstances and an easy workaround to a warrant? Brebeuf has already placed himself at the scene. Store security tapes put Sobatics pretty damned close, except close isn't good enough. A photo lineup might place Sobatics at the house, but what if the two of them are in it together?*

He closed his eyes as the hot water beat down on his face, recalling what experience had taught him: Sex or ego are the only two motives for murder, and there's usually a very thin line separating the two. *Maybe Brebeuf got tired of being her eunuch. Maybe she turned Sobatics down. Either of them—or both of them—could have killed her. Or have her stowed away somewhere. If we can convince a judge that there's a chance she's alive, we wouldn't need a warrant to get into the back of either Tahoe to look for some DNA.*

Mike turned the taps off and reached for a towel as he stepped over to the vanity, leaving a trail of watery footprints behind him. He wiped the steam off the mirror, then splashed some water onto the shaving cream puck before briskly swirling it into a frothy lather.

Regardless, somebody other than Brebeuf had to have seen the vehicle that took the trunk with her in it, dead or alive. It's a tight neighbourhood with even tighter streets. No parking allowed. Heavily monitored. We already know Brebeuf was there. Check to see if any parking tickets were issued for Sobatics's Tahoe. Easiest way to place it at the scene.

Mike coated the stubble on his face with the foam before scraping it away quickly with his razor. *Shit.* He had nicked his chin. He recoiled at the sting as a circle of blood expanded in the shaving cream. Reaching over to grab some toilet paper, he pressed a tiny piece to the wound, struggling to overcome the urge to dab and look. *Fucking Amanda is right. Gotta pick up my game. Okay, so call Parking. Run both plates.*

He succumbed and looked at the cut. The bleeding continued. He tore off another square and reapplied it to his chin. *Check witness statements.* He looked over at the bright digits of the clock that shone through the steam coating the rest of the bathroom surfaces. *Already 5:03. Shit.*

* * *

Mary-Margaret looked up from the pot on the stove. "Where do ye think ye are goin', mister?"

"Work. Gotta go. Thanks, Mom. Love you." Mike grabbed the coffee she had poured for him and gave her a peck on the cheek.

"What about yer rollies, then?" she called after him with a piercing whisper, mindful of Max sleeping two floors above them.

"Max'll eat 'em. I bet he loves them just as much as I do. See you later."

* * *

Amanda listened to Mike's idea and the rationale behind it. "Hmm, interesting theory, but I'm not sure about its practicality. Let me give Polermo a call and get him to look a little closer at the luminol report. He'd be the one to convince a judge that she may still be alive despite the overwhelming evidence suggesting otherwise."

Amanda pressed a single button on her cell phone before leaving a brief message. *Of course, she would have the chief coroner on speed-dial,* Mike thought.

"I honestly shudder to think of that woman, or any woman, for that matter, being held with no demands having been made." Amanda's eyes locked with Mike's, knowing that they both shared first-hand experience with true evil. "Given the evidence I saw, I did not allow for the possibility that she was other than dead. I may have let my ego get in the way, Mike. Horrible mistake for anyone to make, especially a Homicide investigator. Especially me."

"You didn't know."

"No, I didn't. But I believed that I did. And that may end up being my cross to bear."

"It happens to the best of us."

"And what if she wasn't dead when she was hauled out of that house, Mike? Blithely saying that it happens to the best of us doesn't cut it."

Mike searched for words. Amanda Black was a good investigator. No, a great investigator. He knew it, and so did she. He thought of what he had just said: *We all make mistakes? Not everyone is great every day? It's going to be okay? Fuck, Amanda's right: Homicide doesn't work that way.*

Amanda cleared her throat. "On the upside, we can place a Tahoe registered to a numbered company owned by Sobatics right in front of the house. Got ticketed last Thursday at 11:35 a.m., right before Brebeuf dropped by and saw the man at the door. If and when Polermo says that she could still be alive, we'll put out an alert on the vehicle and go from there. Great work,

Mike."

"Uh, it was my mother," Mike mumbled.

"Sorry?"

"I can't take the credit. It was Mom. She was the one who thought that our victim might still be alive. She believes that Sibby Mac is being held for sexual purposes, but that's another story."

"Interesting. How much does this Sally-across-the-moors pay your mother to walk the dog? Let me know and I'll double it if she'll come work for me. She can have your desk."

Her cell phone rang. "Amanda Black speaking." She paused. "Wonderful. I owe you a dinner. No. Don't. My treat. Somewhere nice." She glanced over at Mike. "Somewhere my disheveled colleague here would never be allowed. God, Mike, can you at least pretend to make an effort? Okay, Doc. Thanks. Talk soon."

Amanda hung up the phone, a huge smile on her face.

"That was quick," Mike said.

"I swear that man sleeps with his files. Says he's good with the possibility that she could still be alive. Get a photo of the model of Sobatics's Tahoe and the plate number out to every copper in the province. Send it to Quebec, too. And tell our guys that there's a bottle in it for whoever brings it in to me," Amanda commanded, referring to the age-old tradition of rewarding good police work with booze.

"Oh sure, the doctor gets a fancy dinner, and the actual workers get a jug."

"Not all men are created equal, Mike. Make sure you tell Brebeuf to keep away from the scene. He's been chatting up the neighbours, apparently. If he keeps it up, I'm going to have to arrest him for obstruct or else seriously consider that he was the man at the door, given that no one else saw anyone. Which reminds me," Amanda slowly looked Mike up and down, "if you're going to get anywhere with Crownie Calloway, you really need to pick up your game."

"Fuck! The trial—"

"Has been put over until Monday. I called and spoke to Bridget to let her know that you were in no shape to testify. Truth be told, I need you more than she does right now. Regardless, she said there was some issue that had to be clarified for the jury today that wouldn't require your attendance."

"What a shitshow," Mike grumbled.

"Honestly, Mike, between having to manage you, my kids, my husband, my parents, my sister, and the job they actual pay me to do, it's a wonder anything gets done around here. Okay. Let's get back to work. We've got a missing woman to find. Oh, and send your mother some flowers from me. And tell her that I said that she's lovely. And likely a helluva lot easier to manage than you are."

Chapter Twenty-Three

1:30 p.m., Friday, October 12, 2018

"I've got a mom and her kid coming in for an interview in a few minutes," Mike sighed as he looked out the filthy window in the investigative office.

Ron looked across his desk at his partner, taking a break from writing up his memo book notes. "What interview?"

"From the Sanderson press release. She's one of about a dozen or so parents who have called and want to talk."

"Does Amanda know about this?"

"Doubt it."

"Hmmm."

While it was generally not in Mike's nature to take an investigation personally, Ron knew how important the Sanderson one was to his partner, so he refrained from reminding him that he had been told—ordered, in fact—to put everything else on hold pending the conclusion of the MacDonald case. Finding himself an accessory, however unwilling, to Mike's insubordination, Ron instead offered his assistance.

"I wasn't expecting a boy. A little boy."

Ron nodded sadly in agreement.

"If you can keep Amanda at bay for me…" Mike adjusted his suit jacket as he hauled his tired body up and away from his desk, blank DVD and steno pad in hand. "I swear, I lose a piece of my soul every time I talk to one of these kids."

"Want to go for a beer after work?" Ron offered. "Not a whole night of drinking. Just a beer or two?"

"Yeah, I would. See you in a bit."

* * *

"Jacob. That's a great name. Do they call you Jake or Jacob?" Mike smiled warmly at his interviewee, whose tiny shoulders were visible above the table across from him only because of the cushion he had been given to sit on. Mike then acknowledged the boy's mother, whose weathered eyes betrayed her broken heart.

This little boy, with his fluorescent yellow polo shirt, elastic-waist jeans, and slip-on sneakers, whose legs were flailing madly midair under the table, would be known as Victim #1.

"What happened to your *face*?" The boy seemed to simultaneously back away and move towards Mike.

"Jacob!" his mother remonstrated, offering a quick apologetic glance to Mike.

"It's okay, Mom," Mike assured the woman, knowing that he actually had two victims in the room. "Got into a fight a while back. You should see the other guy."

"Whoa!" The little boy's eyes widened with admiration.

"Right now though, Jacob, I need to ask you some things. Okay? Do you know why you're here?"

"To talk about Greg?" The boy looked down at the table and began fidgeting with the plastic dinosaur he held in his perfect little hands. Mike remembered when Max's hands were that tiny.

"Put that down, Jacob." The mother grabbed the toy from her son, slamming it on the table away from him with more force than Mike was sure she had intended. "The nice detective is trying to talk to you."

"Mom!" the boy squawked in moderate protest before his tiny body crumpled into itself, making him seem even smaller.

"Yeah. To talk about Greg. How do you know him?" Mike cut to the chase, his eyes not moving from the little boy.

"From soccer." Jacob's eyes were fixed on the now-empty space in front of him, his mouth pouting, his hands fidgeting under the table.

"Is he on your team?" Mike was glad he had chosen the more traditional interview setting instead of the comfier couch where such delicate interviews usually took place. The table that separated him from Jacob and his mother provided a safe buffer for the boy. For Mike, too. But no matter where they sat, Mike had done enough interviews like this to know that there would be nothing soft about the questions he had to ask or the answers he was going to hear.

The boy looked up at Mike. "No, silly, he's too *old!*"

Mike looked at the boy's mother, who pulled her son to her in a hug. To be expected. *He's only a child. A small boy, likely a young seven. She blames herself. She should have been there. Should have known. Should have... But she didn't. And now she's sitting in a police station, another adult judging her for what she allowed to happen.* At least, that's the narrative that Mike knew was likely plaguing her now. No matter how many times, no matter how many ways he tried to absolve them of blame, Mike knew that every mother felt this way. Hopefully, this one would go for the counselling Mike had suggested for her. Some did, some didn't. It was a crapshoot. You never knew which ones would and which ones wouldn't. *All we can do is try.*

"I said *don't!*" The boy jerked himself away from his mother before acquiescing to her touch, all the while not making eye contact with her. *Passive. Compliant. Detached. All of the qualities that made him a good little boy...and an excellent candidate for grooming by the likes of Gregory Sanderson.*

Only a dozen more interviews after this, hopefully. Until the next wanker comes along. Meanwhile, let's just get this one over with.

"Is he a coach?" Mike continued.

"No." Jacob had retrieved the dinosaur from the other side of his mother and resumed fidgeting with it. She made an attempt to take it back, but Mike waved her off with a tiny flick of his hand.

130

Whatever gets you through this is okay by me, little buddy. At least, you're not drunk or stoned, like the older ones will likely be.

"Well, if he's not a player and he's not a coach, how do you know him from soccer?"

The boy looked up incredulously at Mike, saying nothing.

"You're gonna have to help me out, here, buddy. I'm not a soccer player, so I don't know how these things go."

A few minutes passed in silence, with Jacob alternately plucking at the dinosaur and picking at his well-manicured fingernails, wondering, Mike knew, whether or not he could trust this man sitting across from him. In spite of himself, the boy snuggled up against his mother, who instinctively enveloped him in her arms. Her voice finally broke the silence. "He was always at the games. I thought… No, we all thought he was a parent from the other team, but—"

"Hang on a minute, Mom." Mike raised his hand slightly. "I'd like to hear what the big man here has to say."

"I don't want to talk about it anymore," Jacob said angrily. He might have pushed himself away from the table if his feet could touch the ground, but suspended on the chair as he was, all that was left for him to do was to fold his arms and drop his chin down to his chest.

"How come?" Mike deliberately made himself sound more like a kid being denied a second dessert for some unfathomable reason than a police detective trying to elicit information from a child who had narrowly escaped the game.

"Because." Jacob's tiny head nodded defiantly.

"Jacob…" the boy's mother began, fearing that the investigator would give up and that all of this upset would be for nothing.

"It's okay, Mom. Just give us a minute," Mike reassured her, nodding at his young associate. "Man-to-man, Jacob. You good with that, buddy?"

The little boy looked up at Mike.

"You got a job?" Mike's eyes narrowed as he put his elbows on the table and leaned in towards the child, giving him his best Mean Detective stare.

"No!" The boy laughed.

"So what do you do with your time?"

"I go to school." He stared back at Mike.

"What grade?" Mike sneered. It was that, he knew, or break out laughing.

"Two."

"You like it?" Mike tilted his head slightly.

"No." The boy mirrored Mike, putting his tiny bare elbows on the table, chin in his hands.

"Why not?"

"Because it's stupid."

"Jacob!" The boy's mother sounded mortified.

"Mom!" Mike held his hand up again.

"Sorry." She sat back, withdrawing from the verbal jousting match.

"You play any instruments, Jacob?"

"Guitar."

"Any good?" Mike pulled out his best interrogation voice.

"Pretty good," the boy countered, not breaking eye contact with Mike, chin now out of hands, preparing to go face-to-face with the detective.

"You in a band?"

"Not yet."

"Gonna be?"

"Probably."

"Can I come and see you when you are?"

"No," the boy mumbled, almost inaudibly. He broke contact with Mike, his eyes immediately dropping to look at an invisible spot on the table in front of him.

"Why not?" Mike's voice dropped to an equally soft tone.

"'Cause I don't want you to."

"Does Greg watch you play soccer, Jacob?" Mike carefully leaned a bit closer, considering that the span of his hand was likely the same size as the little back that was beginning to softly shake beneath its fluorescent yellow shirt.

"Yeah."

"And then what?" *Come on, little guy. We can get through this, me and you.*

"He sometimes gives me stuff."

"Like what?"

"Like popsicles."

"Why does he give you popsicles, Jacob?" *Gotta be clear with these kids,* Mike reminded himself. *You only get one shot. One clear shot.*

"Because I let him."

"Let him what?"

The little boy looked up at the detective, eyes starting to water. *Stay with me, Jake. Stay with me.*

"Let him touch my pee-pee."

"You mean, like your penis?" *Do not show surprise. Or disgust. Or anything. Let the kid talk. And please, please, please stay quiet, Mom.*

"Uh-huh."

"What does he touch your penis with, Jacob?"

"His mouth."

"Okay." *Fucker. You fucker. You herpes-infected fucker. This kid, too?* Mike took a deep breath in through his nose. *Pull it back. Calm. Be calm.* "Do you know how many times he's touched your penis with his mouth?"

"I dunno. Maybe this many times?" Jacob held out both of his hands, all of his fingers exposed. For the first time, Mike noticed a tiny bit of dirt under one of the boy's fingernails.

"Is that ten times, Jacob?" Mike clarified for the audio portion of the interview.

"I dunno."

"Jacob isn't very good with his numbers," his mother apologized. "I'm trying to get extra help for him at school."

"I am so!" Jacob protested with grand indignation.

"No worries, Mom." Mike smiled warmly at the woman, who was visibly holding back tears. "Does Greg only give you popsicles if you let him touch your penis with his mouth?"

"Uh-huh."

"Do you only get popsicles if Greg gives them to you?"

"Uh-huh." Jacob looked accusingly up at his mother.

"My husband, Jacob's father, has been in and out of work and—"

"It's okay, Mom." *You've done nothing wrong,* Mike wanted to add. *It happens to kids from all walks of life. It's not your fault.* But the camera was running and Mike couldn't say anything more. This was a victim interview. Clean. Clear. As pure as an interview with a seven-year-old could possibly be. No second chances. No missteps. Especially not for this case. Mom was just going to have to soak in her own feelings of inadequacy for a bit longer.

"I always bring juice and snacks from home." She pulled her son tight against her.

"Mom, it's okay. It's not your fault." *Minor digression. Understandable, considering the circumstances. Shouldn't cause too much trouble in court. What the hell else could I say?*

"Stop it!" Jacob suddenly hollered at his mother, jerking himself away from her attempt to console both of them. "I *hate* you!"

Shit, shit, shit! Mike was taken aback. *Gotta get this train back on track or I'll lose whatever else there is to tell.*

"Okay, Jacob. I can see that you're a bit…upset with Mom," he began. "I'm wondering if, maybe, there isn't something more going on?"

The little boy stared intently at Mike. Mike stared back. The two blinked at each other. Mike arched one of his eyebrows. The little boy furrowed his. Mike arched his other eyebrow. The little boy jerked back slightly.

"Are you a real cop?" the boy finally asked, straight-faced.

"Yeah." Mike replied, equally deadpan.

"Then show me your gun."

Mike leaned back slightly, pulled his suit jacket open without moving any other part of his body, and revealed the issue Glock pistol that he had strapped to the side of his body.

"Cool!!!" The boy nodded approvingly.

"Are you a real kid?" Mike leaned in, squinting his eyes.

"Yeah!" The boy laughed, revealing the missing baby tooth on his lower jaw.

"Then tell me what flavour of popsicle you like."

"Blue."

Mike's eyes narrowed. "That's not a flavour."

"Greg says it is."

"What does Greg know?"

"Lots," the boy said protectively.

"Like what?" Mike tossed his head back slightly. *Fucker has this kid, hook, line, and sinker.*

"Like how to make me feel good."

"Oh God," the child's mother softly whimpered.

"How does he make you feel good?" Mike plowed on, not taking his eyes off the boy.

"Like this." Jacob opened his mouth and stuck out his tongue.

"What does that mean?" Mike casually asked. After years of running trials like this, he knew how extraordinarily high the burden of proof was in demonstrating that the child clearly knew what was being asked of them in an interview.

And so the little boy, in his tiny fluorescent yellow polo shirt and elastic-waist jeans, his hair fantastically askew, proceeded to explain how Greg Sanderson performed fellatio on him. He told Mike about how Greg had performed fellatio on other boys on the team, and on other boys on other teams. He knew about this because Greg had told him. And had also told him about how other boys got more than popsicles if they let Greg's friends perform fellatio on them.

This little boy, whose feet did not touch the ground, whose fingernails, no matter how lovingly scrubbed, continued to have dirt under them, told Mike how Greg had offered him extra popsicles if he let other men Greg knew put their fingers in his bum. Like a child telling about a recent adventure, the boy told Mike that he said no because that was just poopy and gross.

"Is that what you told Greg?"

"Yeah."

"What happened after that?"

"Nothing. He just stopped giving me popsicles."

"And touching your penis?"

"Yeah. He said he was going to give the popsicles to other boys."

"How did that make you feel?" Mike asked, speculating that the actual interview was concluding. *Surely to God there isn't more.*

"Sad."

"Why sad?"

"Because Greg's my friend."

"Yeah?"

"Um…no, not really."

"Why is that?'

"Because after that, he never even waved to me." The boy looked down at his hands.

Shame. He feels shame. And here I am: part investigator, part social worker, part tough guy, part healer, part dad looking at a kid who could be mine. 'And what would ye say to yer own son, Michael?' I don't know, Mom, I don't know.

"Is there anything else you want to tell me, Jacob?"

"Are you mad at me?"

"No."

Jacob was kicking his legs back and forth ferociously under the table, his little body rocking madly.

"You're a good guy, Jacob. And your mom loves you."

"He told me that something bad would happen if I told anyone." The kicking stopped, and the tiny body seemed to go limp. But for the sniffling that was just beginning, Mike would have thought the child had stopped breathing.

"Like what?"

"I don't know." The boy put his head down on his folded arms on the table, now audibly sobbing.

"You're talking to me now, and nothing bad has happened." Mike leaned forward so that his chin almost rested on the table across from the child.

"Yeah. But you're a cop. And you have a gun."

"Yeah. That's right. I *am* a cop. And I *do* have a gun." Mike sat up and leaned back. "But nothing bad is going to happen anyway. You know that, right?"

Slowly, Jacob lifted his head, his skinny little arm reaching up to wipe away the flood of snot and tears that had accumulated on the soft baby face.

"O-okay." The boy's reply was hesitant, but it gave Mike hope.

"You're are a brave man, my friend." *Is that the beginning of a smile I see?*

The little boy began to mirror the detective's posture again, sitting back in his own chair.

"I talk to a lot of people in this room, Jacob," Mike went on with a smile, "but not many guys have the guts to sit across this table with me and be as strong as you've been."

"Okay." Jacob sucked back the last bit of snot as he took another swipe at his face with his arm.

"And I bet you play a wicked axe."

"Yup!" The little boy nodded vigorously.

"Tell you what," Mike said, looking quickly over to the boy's mother and then back to Jacob, "I'm gonna give Mom my card. It has my phone number on it. Do you have a phone?"

"No, not yet." Jacob looked over at his mom hopefully.

"We've talked about this before, Jacob. Your father and I think you're still too young to have your own cell phone," she advised firmly while still looking for approval from Mike, who nodded back at her.

"Reasonable. Okay, then. Tell you what. When you start your band, get Mom to give me a call, and I'll come and see you play."

"You gotta buy a ticket, you know. No comps."

"Okay, I think I can swing it. But don't make your shows too late. I have to get up early for work in the morning."

"That's okay. I have to go to bed by 7:30 anyway."

"Deal. Been an honour to speak with you, Jacob."

Mike stood up and extended his hand across the table. The little boy reached his tiny hand out, allowing it to be swallowed up in the detective's hand, choosing to hold Mike's hand rather than shake it.

As Mike watched them leave the interview room, he saw a definite spring in the step of both mother and son as they walked away.

May God have mercy on your soul, because I sure as hell won't, he thought, jaw tightening as he thought of Gregory Sanderson and all the other little

Jacobs. And of Malcolm. And Chelsea Hendricks. And Sal.

Chapter Twenty-Four

Even on a bright afternoon, a pub can hold many secrets: a heart broken and finally laid to rest at that table, a job secured at another, a lonely soul searching for its mooring at the bar, a rite of passage observed in the corner booth. The Blind Pig was no exception. Older men were over there, on their way home from work, just popping in for a pint and a smile from the pretty servers. A group of young people sat in the corner, here to begin a night that will be spent elsewhere, celebrating something or anything. One or two women can be seen now in the dim lighting by the bar with men clearly known to them from work: mismatched, professional obligation.

"I suppose you're not really drinking?" Ron asked Mike, oblivious to the server standing by their table with her early-shift smile glued on, blouse buttons undone as low as the hour deemed appropriate.

Mike smiled up at the young woman. "I don't think one will hurt either way."

"Suit yourself. I'll have a pint of Grolsch." Ron handed the beer menu to the server without looking up. "You, Mike?"

"I'm sorry, sir, we don't have Grolsch on tap. The only Dutch beer on tap is Heineken." The server returned the menu to Ron, her attention drawn over her left shoulder to the table by the door where a group of young men were grabbing their jackets from the backs of their chairs, the pitchers of beer she had just delivered to them emptied, no sign of payment in sight. "Do you want a pint of that?"

"Well," Ron looked disdainfully down his nose at the menu "I suppose—"

"A pint of Guinness," Mike interrupted, his eyes following the server's. He stood up and shot a cautionary scowl at the boys that resolved itself once they dug deep into their pants pockets and deposited some bills on the table. Oblivious to the potential dine-and-dash, Ron passed the menu back to the server, who nodded thankfully at Mike and turned on her heel to retrieve the boys' payment on her way back to the bar.

"I don't think she was looking to make our beer order her career, Ron."

"Well then, maybe she's in the wrong business. Anyway, that's not why I invited you out this afternoon. There's something I want to discuss with you." Ron rapped the knuckles of both hands on the table and stared straight at Mike.

"Great," Mike sighed, looking away. *Be kind, lad,* he heard his mother saying. *He's makin' an effort.*

"As you may or may not know, I am not well-liked at the station. No, no, it's true." Ron came to as close to a conciliatory tone as Mike imagined him capable of producing. "I know it, and it doesn't bother me. I've never given much weight to popularity and, truth be told, I don't really care. The only reason I'm telling you this is so that you don't go thinking that what I am *actually* about to tell you has anything to do with what may or may not be going on at the station."

Mike blinked a couple of times.

"I have always been a loner," Ron continued. "Even as a child, I was a loner. I'm telling this to you because I don't want you to think that *that* has anything to do with what I'm about to tell you, either."

"This better be good, Ron," Mike said, waiting patiently to taste the beer the server had just plunked down in front of him.

"It is. Cheers." Ron took a sip of his beer. "To police work and all those who do it well."

"Sláinte," Mike responded, welcoming the familiar flavour of his Guinness while waiting for Ron to get to the point.

"As I've told you, Mike, Marie has been having some health issues. Serious health issues. Now before you get all gushy on me, she and I are prepared for the worst. Wills made years ago, everything in order. *That's* not what I brought you here to talk about." Ron took a gulp of beer. "As a result of her medical issues, I've been going to counselling. Now don't jump the gun on this one. Nothing to do with us, Marie and me, I mean. Sure, we've had our ups and downs, but we've pretty well figured out how to maneuver through those storms. What the counselling was about, and don't laugh, is happiness."

Mike took a couple of mouthfuls of beer. His head was beginning to pound.

"I know. Apparently, happiness is important. But *that's* not what I brought you here to talk about."

"For chrissake, Ron, I'm going to be done this and ordering the next before you get to the point. What's up?"

"Well…" Ron took a huge gulp of beer. "Apparently, I am clinically depressed."

Mike looked down at his empty glass. "Does it matter?" he finally asked, not knowing what else to say.

"Perhaps. Because now I have to go to *more* counselling to deal with this so-called clinical depression that I have had all my life, which means I don't know any different." He took a more refined sip from his glass.

"Okay."

"So why would I go to counselling to fix something that I didn't even know was broken?"

"Because maybe you'll actually be happy?"

"I *am* happy. Or as happy as I get, apparently."

"In that clinically depressed way you have." Mike lifted the empty glass to his mouth, hoping for one last drop of Guinness to materialize. When it did not, he set it down on the table, anticipating another one. "Great. Then stay the way you are. Nothing saying you have to go to this counselling, is there?"

"Well, that's the real issue. You see, Marie and I didn't *choose* to go to counselling to begin with. When I asked the boss a few weeks back about taking a couple of hours off, he asked why. I thought he was making conversation, so I told him. Next thing I know, he's sending me to counselling."

"Can he do that?" Mike looked around for the server.

"No. I called the union, and they said I don't have to go. So I didn't. And because I didn't make the appointment to begin with, I didn't bother cancelling it."

"My friend and I will have another pint," Mike told the server as she passed by carrying a tray of rocks glasses full of whisky.

"So the day after I didn't go to this appointment someone else scheduled for me, I was updating the boss on one of my occurrences and he advised that I *had* to go, as in he ordered me to go to see the departmental shrink."

Mike refocused on Ron. "And they found out that you're depressing. I mean depressed."

"Exactly." Ron took a couple of gulps of his beer, eager to continue with his story.

"Fair enough. And...?"

Ron brought the glass up to his mouth again but did not drink. "They are suggesting that I consider retiring." Quick gulp.

"What?"

"Well. Not in so many words. Just that I ought to consider developing 'outside interests.'"

"That's a lot different from retiring, Ron." Mike rocked his empty glass on the table.

"I suppose. But I do have a lot of outside interests."

"Like what?"

"Well, Marie and I—"

"No, I think they mean *you*." Mike clasped his hands behind his head, raised his elbows above his head and stretched his back before dropping his elbows to the table, refocusing on the man who had just made him his new and likely only confidante. "*Your* interests. Outside of Marie."

"I know you've been married a few times, Mike, so no offence intended, but—"

"Twice. I've been married twice, Ron." Mike stared at the server flirting with the bartender. *Oh, sweet Jesus, that Guinness would come in very handy right about now.*

"Twice. Well, that's twice as many times as I've been married. Anyway, point is, after a while, *your* hobbies and interests become *hers*."

Mike looked back at Ron. "What is Marie interested in, then?" *Breathe. Find your bubble of hope, or whatever the hell the last therapist called it, and breathe.*

"Lots of things. She goes to yoga on Monday nights, volunteers at the book bank a couple of times a week when I'm on evenings or midnights, writes pieces for this wellness publication at work. Things like that."

"And what do you do, Ron?" *This is God givin' ye a chance to give back, Michael,* he could again hear his mother's voice saying. *The poor soul is lookin' to ye for guidance.*

"Well, I like to cook."

"Cook what?" *Be kind, Michael. The wee lamb is reachin' out to ye,* her voice echoed.

"Dinner. You know, when Marie's at yoga. Or if she's caught up at work."

"That's not a hobby, Ron. That's called keeping yourself alive. I'm thinking the concern here is that you have no life outside of work and Marie, and work—and sorry, Marie —will end, sooner rather than later."

"That was a bit abrupt."

"What about a pet? Have any pets?"

"No, I don't like them. Too much work."

"Try a hamster. Or fish. Fish aren't too much work." Mike caught the eye of the server and motioned her over to the table. "That second round, please."

"I had a dog once," Ron reminisced.

"Sorry, I'm just cashing out. If you don't mind?" The server held out a plastic tray with a tab on it, waiting for one of the men to take it. Ron pulled his wallet out and, without taking the tray, put a bill on it, dismissing the woman.

"Got hit by a car. Killed instantly upon impact." Ron gulped back the last of his beer, slamming the empty glass down in front of him.

"What about our beer?" Mike beckoned to the server disappearing behind a door marked Employees Only. *Fuck.* "Listen. There's nothing wrong with being depressed, if that's where you're at, but there might be a problem with having your whole existence wrapped up in another person, unless you're a fourteen-year-old girl who lives vicariously through the shit she sees on social media, and even then… You know what I'm saying?" Mike felt his patience rapidly slipping away.

"I suppose. In fact, I suppose I asked you here this afternoon to tell me just that."

"You're a weirdo, Ron. You know that, right?" Mike nodded warmly at their new server, taking the pints from her tray before she even had a chance to set them down on the table. "Sláinte mhaith." He took a healthy gulp, and then felt the vibration of his phone in his suit pocket. He took another gulp before retrieving the phone. "Shit. Amanda's called and left a message."

"Hey, Crumply-Pants. Boys have the Tahoe and the driver: Sobatics's youngest. Looks remarkably like his dad. Don't know if you're interested, but I could use the help. Give me a call or just make your way back to the station. If you run into Roberts, bring him along. Tried to get a hold of him as well, but there's no cell phone number on file for him here at the station and he's not picking up at home. Thanks. Amanda. Amanda Black, just in case you weren't sure. Talk soon."

"Drink up, Chuckles. We gotta get back to the station." Mike began to chug his beer.

"But we've been drinking." Ron stared at the glass in front of him.

"Are you new?"

"We could always just leave the beer behind."

"Again I ask: Are you new?" Mike quickly polished off his pint and fumbled for his wallet.

"I've got this one, too. I'll go back to the station. I've just had one. You just go on home and get some rest." Ron pushed his untouched pint away and laid a couple of tens on the table.

"Thanks for the beer. And no thanks to heading home. I'm not missing this."

"And *your* outside interests are…?" Ron winked at Mike as the two men hurried out the door, Ron adjusting his fedora to shield his eyes from the late afternoon sunlight.

Chapter Twenty-Five

9:20 p.m., Friday, October 12, 2018

"Where is my son?" A woman looking classier than most of the Friday night bail-outs demanded, the glass door into the dingy foyer of the police station barely having had a chance to close behind her.

"Sorry?" the uniformed officer asked, looking up at the clock on the wall just over the woman's head, wondering if his relief would be late again tonight.

"My son. I want to speak to my son."

"It's okay, Mom. I'm done," Russell Sobatics said, feeding his belt through his pant loops as another uniformed officer half-pushed him out through the shit-brown metal door to the women's left.

"You didn't say anything, did you?"

"What? That Dad set me up? That he's been fucking around on you with every piece of ass he could get his hands on? No. Why would I do that?"

"Don't forget your property." The officer who had led the young man to freedom tossed an open plastic bag onto the counter, its contents tumbling out. Russell scrambled to retrieve them.

"Stop talking, Russell. Let's go." Katherine Sobatics arched her back and threw her shoulders back, assuming the authoritative stance acquired years before in her law-school training.

"Kaitlin is picking me up." Without looking at his mother, Russell scraped some coins up off the counter and shoved them into a front pocket of his baggy jeans before retrieving his cell phone, wallet, and expensive watch his parents had given to him the previous year for his eighteenth birthday.

"Speaking of piece of ass," Katherine murmured.

Ignoring the cops behind the counter, Russell defiantly confronted his mother while his pudgy fingers punched at the face of his cell phone. "Why do you defend him, Mom? He's a pompous jerk who treats you like shit. Always has. Always will."

"If you're not coming home with me, let's at least get out of here!" Katherine said under her breath.

"Got everything, Russell?" Amanda smiled brightly at the feuding pair as she made her way from the back investigative office towards the front counter, a steno pad in hand. "And you must be Mrs. Sobatics. Glad you're here, actually. Saves me a call. A vehicle registered to your husband's company has been impounded. Shall we notify him or you, Russell, when we're done with it?"

"You didn't have to speak to them. You know that, Russell," Katherine, ignoring Amanda, advised her son, just as she would a client.

"Not like I had a choice," Russell grumbled. "Practically tore me out of the Tahoe, said they'd—"

"What did they offer you? Never mind. We'll talk outside." Katherine's attention switched to Amanda. "And I will be awaiting a call about the vehicle, officer. I hope for your sake that you have a warrant to seize it and another to search it."

"Detective Sergeant. Detective Sergeant Black from Homicide," Amanda corrected, extending her arm across the counter to the woman. "And we do have sufficient grounds."

"Really? Now I'm curious." Katherine had her best lawyerly smile firmly affixed to her face. "Homicide. You said you were from Homicide?"

"Yes, Homicide. Would you like to come around the counter here and we can talk? I can buzz you in."

"I don't think so, no. Clearly, you have my contact information. If you or your officers want to speak to me—or my family—then you can call me.

Otherwise, we'll wait to hear when my husband's Tahoe will be returned."

"Oh, we'll certainly let you know, Mrs. Sobatics. But I hope you have something else to drive. It might be a while."

"What are you saying?"

"Mrs. Sobatics, are you sure you don't want to come around and maybe have a little chat in private?"

Weighing her options, Katherine glanced over the chipped countertop at Amanda and then at the uniformed station duty operator and the civilian clerk behind him, both of whom appeared to be missing only buttered popcorn and overpriced pop to complete their evening entertainment. She straightened her back and pursed her lips before glancing over at her youngest child. "I'm sure my son has nothing to do with whatever you're investigating."

"Don't look at me, Mom." Peering out into the darkness of the residential street on the other side of the filthy window, Russell spat out a piece of fingernail he had been chewing on. "It's Fucknuts you should be worried about."

"Russell!" Katherine admonished, simultaneously recoiling and posturing. "Wait outside. Now, Detective Sergeant, as you may or may not know, both my husband and I are lawyers."

"Yes, I'm well aware of that fact."

"My oldest son and daughter are lawyers as well."

"You must be very proud."

"What I'm trying to say is..." Katherine stopped and looked over at the uniformed officer who had been staring at her, clearly enjoying the theatre that was unfolding before him, "that my son, Russell, clearly did not understand his rights to retain and instruct counsel. He clearly felt some sort of duress if and when he gave you anything remotely resembling a statement. Whatever he may have said—"

"Mrs. Sobatics, I'm well aware of who you, your children, and your husband are because I'm investigating a homicide. That's what I do. I'm a *homicide* investigator. Right now, I'm looking at the SUV your son was driving as a potential crime vehicle. I was hoping your son could help me understand how that vehicle fits into my investigation. As it stands now, however," Amanda bluffed, "I'm going to have to wait for my forensics people to tell me what your son may already know, at which point, I will be speaking to your son again. Or your husband. In the meantime, I would suggest—"

"Is this where you try to dazzle me with your misunderstanding of the law by telling me that you'll arrest me if I don't stop asking questions, Detective Sergeant? Please. My husband and I are both—"

"Lawyers. Yes, I know. And right now, your son and you and anyone else who has access to that vehicle are also persons of interest in my homicide investigation. Govern yourself accordingly, counsellor." Amanda turned on her heel and disappeared down the hall leading to the investigative office, a low whistle of admiration from the duty officer at the front desk following her.

* * *

"Forensics?" Ron looked up from his computer screen over at Mike, his ears pricking up at the sound of the phone ringing.

Equally as anxious, Mike grabbed the receiver after the first ring, scrabbling with his other hand to find a pen and a scrap of paper amid the piles of photocopied officers' notes and press releases on his desk.

"Did you say Forensics?" Amanda echoed, rounding the corner into the D office at her usual breakneck speed.

Mike affirmed with a nod, the voice on the other end of the phone just beginning to relay information to him.

"Who is it? Is it Amy? Tell me it's Amy. God, I love that girl."

Mike nodded again.

"The persistence of a bloodhound, that one," Amanda smiled over at Ron, who looked up from the notes he had been writing up. "I once had a dog, you know," he said. "Thinking about maybe getting another one."

"Don't. Too much work. Goldfish. Get a goldfish. Much easier." Amanda glanced around the filthy office before plunking herself down at one of the cleaner desks, although not before sweeping the remnants of someone's lunch or what could just as easily have been crack cocaine residue off the desk's surface.

"I suppose." Looking over at his partner scribbling madly, Ron refocused on the investigation. "How did your interview go with…the son, was it? You know the mother said her husband had the Tahoe in Ottawa, right?"

"Yeah. That's okay. Just another piece of the puzzle. The kid was great. Good kid. A bit slow, but not enough to be concerned about. Hates his dad." Amanda started to type her badge number and password on her keyboard. "Which is a bonus for us. Wasn't too pleased with the officer who arrested him. Who was it, by the way? I believe I owe him a jug."

"Ricky Jergensen." Ron let the words hang in the air, knowing his dislike for the pompous constable was equalled by Amanda's.

"You're fucking kidding me, right?" Amanda's jaw dropped, the light from the freshly awoken computer screen accentuating her stunned expression.

"No, I'm not. They punted him from old-clothes back to uniform a couple of weeks ago," Ron explained, referring to the common practice of punishing officers by transferring them back to front-line duties in response to disciplinary issues. "Don't think he's too pleased to be back in… How did he put it that night? *'The monkey suit writing traffic tickets for a living'.*"

"Is he the only copper in this district?" Given Jergensen's well-known questionable ethics, Amanda found herself considering the potential legal arguments that would likely ensue from what she had originally believed to be a legitimate traffic stop.

"Well, at least he shaved. And he's covered up most of his tattoos. So how did it go with Katherine Sobatics?"

"You mean Mommy Dearest? As well as can be expected." Amanda momentarily diverted her attention to the flashing prompt on the screen. "That *is* my password, asshole." She looked back at Ron. "Technology. Great when it works. I hope Russell's girlfriend did come to pick him up because, otherwise, Mama will be grilling him silly to find out what Daddy's done this time. Though I doubt this is the first time her baby's been thrown under the bus by his father. Strange breed, these rich people."

"So what did *he* have to say?"

"I'll wait till Crumply-Pants gets off the... Oh, good, you're done. And?"

"Some scratch marks on the tailgate. Look fairly new. Could be caused by dragging something in or out. Found some hair in the back of the vehicle itself. Might be human, might not be. Amy thinks she's probably found blood. Took a swab. Just taking a look at it now before sending it and the hair strands out to the lab with a rush on them."

"So that means we won't know definitively until sometime tomorrow or Sunday, depending on how backed-up the lab is. Shit!"

"Amy's willing to state that the hair's human."

"Love her. Simply love her," Amanda almost burbled with delight, an emotion remarkably rare among homicide investigators. "And you know what the best part of all of this is? She won't make any noise about it. Just a small notation in her memo book, and that'll be it. Makes life so much easier in court."

"So you're willing to go on the *possibility* that it's human hair?" Ron's eyebrows arched disapprovingly. "That would never happen in Traffic."

"Pfff," Mike commented. "How many murder charges did you lay in Traffic?"

"Dozens of death-related charges, in fact. Investigated them start to finish. Alone. There are no huge budgets with discretionary funds or officers reassigned for traffic death investigations. Just old-fashioned police work. So, what did the kid say?"

"Good kid. Looks a lot like his father. Wow. No paternity test needed there. Too bad the old man's such a shitty dad," Amanda mused. "Apparently, they're a family of brainiacs, except for our boy. Not stupid, but not law school material. Anyway, young Rusty is kind of the black sheep of the family. Scraped through high school. Daddy pulled some strings and got him in as a clerk at City Hall about a year and a half ago and never passes up the opportunity to remind him of it. Kid lives at home. Hangs out with a girl he met at work about four months ago. Plays hockey every Friday night in a beer league. Daddy lets him take the Tahoe if he's not using it, which is more often than not because the old man flies to Ottawa most weekends."

"Like this weekend?" Ron asked.

"Yep. Did not take the Tahoe. Probably sitting in the garage when you two were at the house. Anyway, according to our boy, Daddy is snuggled up with the girlfriend in their regular suite at the Fairmont as we speak. Mom knows, according to Rusty, but for whatever reason—"

"Half of everything is still half," Ron pointed out.

"She turns a blind eye to it all, and they're still together. Anyhow, last Thursday, Rusty gets a phone call at work from Daddy. Daddy never calls his son at work—"

Mike winced. "He doesn't call him Daddy, does he?"

"No. He calls him Fucknuts. Mom refers to him as Daddy, and, for the sake of this discussion, I prefer Daddy over Fucknuts."

"Fair enough. Carry on."

"So, Daddy calls Rusty at work and asks him if he can do a favour for his old man."

Mike interrupted. "This is going to end badly, isn't it?"

"Yep. Daddy tells Rusty that there's the old steamer trunk full of books from the basement in the back of the truck."

"So we're thinking our victim is dead now?" Mike picked up a retractable pen from his desk and began clicking the end cap until he broke the spring.

"Seems likely, yes. Anyway, deal is if Rusty wants to use the Tahoe Friday night, he has to drop the trunk off at the dump first."

"Easy peasy."

"You'd think. Except our boy isn't the shiniest lure in the tackle box. He forgets about the deal until he goes to put his hockey bag in the back just before the game and sees the trunk sitting there."

"Oops!" said Ron.

"Right. Sonny Boy piles his bag on top of the trunk and goes merrily on his way to hockey. Game ends, bag goes back in with the trunk, Rusty and a buddy stop off for a few cold ones at the bar around the corner from the arena, our boy drops off his buddy, drives home, takes out the bag, and then leaves the Tahoe in the driveway with the suspect trunk still in it."

"Nasty." Mike winced again.

"Next day, Rusty wakes up to Daddy shaking the daylights out of him as soon as Mommy Dearest has left the house for her Saturday spa day. Our boy is already feeling poorly from the multiple beers he consumed the night before—"

"And drove home after, as you've noted." Ron, always the traffic cop, sniffed disapprovingly.

"And drove home after. By the way, guys, don't think I didn't notice that you've both been drinking. Might want to rinse with mouthwash before going anywhere else. Regardless, now little Rusty has got Daddy screaming at him to get rid of this trunk. So he hauls himself out of bed and gets to the dump on Bermondsey just before they close at noon, so he says, and tosses the trunk."

"Pretty heavy. You'd have to drag that thing out the back," Ron suggested.

"Scratch marks on the bumper, remember? We need to find that trunk, guys. Contact the dump. Find out when it was last cleared out and where they took the garbage. If it's been shipped off to a landfill, find out which one and then search the whole thing right down to the tiniest fragment of lint. If they haven't cleared the dumping station out yet, you'll have an easier go of it. All you'll have to do in that case is sift through the mounds of trash until you find my trunk."

"Who?" Ron examined a piece of fluff he'd just picked off of his tie with disdain before flicking it at the floor, where it could reside camouflaged amid the dirt of decades of sporadic cleanings and waxings.

"You two. I'll put a call in to our warrant guy and get him typing."

Mike threw his head back and groaned. "You're kidding, right?"

"Do I look like I'm kidding?" Amanda blinked a couple of times, looking from Mike to Ron. "Hopefully, we'll find out in a few minutes whether or not the trash has been moved. I'll get the warrant written and signed in a couple of hours, and you'll be able to get through it all before they open tomorrow morning so we don't have to close them down and do a whole media thing."

Mike rolled his eyes.

"Don't suppose either of you boys know how to use a backhoe, do you?"

"I do," Ron advised.

"Of course, you do," Amanda smirked.

Her cell phone rang. After a brief exchange on the phone, she wished the two detectives good luck. "That place is huge. A few thousand square feet of ground. Maybe fifty or sixty feet high. Call me when you find the trunk."

Chapter Twenty-Six

11:15 a.m., Saturday, October 13, 2018

Mary-Margaret met her son at the door. "And look what the cat's brought in! We were just startin' to worry about ye!"

"We?" Mike slurred, blurry-eyed with fatigue.

"Bridget and I. We were just thinking we should call the police and report ye missin'."

"Bridget?"

"Good morning, Mike." Bridget waved self-consciously from her seat by the window.

"She just this moment popped by to see ye. She says it's to discuss some case or other, but I've been around the block a time or two, Michael!" His mother winked knowingly. "I've just got a kettle on. Go shower, and I'll get us all some tea. Ye smell worse than a set of tires after a car bomb, me son." Mary-Margaret took a breath, her entire face puckering in mock disgust.

"I was at the dump all night."

"Shooting rats?" Bridget grinned.

Mike felt his mood becoming increasingly fouler than his smell. "Looking for a body."

"Would that be our Sibby Mac?" Mary-Margaret inquired.

Mike shot a look at his mother, who immediately realized that she was treading on the wrong side of confidential information. *The police department is not unlike the Church, really. So many secrets,* she had always said. "That must have been a night worth not relivin', me son. Did ye find this body of yers?"

"No." Mike tried to spit out his disappointment and disgust.

"Well, a good hot shower and a strong cuppa will do ye a world of good. I'm sure Bridget and I would love to hear all about it, regardless."

Bridget started to stand up. "You know, I really ought to be going."

"And me with a kettle on? Not a chance. Sitcheedoon, young lady, and pay no attention to me ill-mannered son. He's actually a very nice lad, once ye get past all his faults." Mary-Margaret's gaze lovingly followed Mike up the stairs. "Don't worry about me. I'll be making meself scarce once ye start with yer *professional* chatter. Years of workin' at the Church have taught me not to stick me nose in places it has no business bein'. There's things even I don't need or even want to know, given what little Michael has told me about the work ye and he do. Ach, the kettle's screamin' for me. Give me a minute, and I'll have yer tea."

Left alone in Mike O'Shea's living room, Bridget couldn't help but feel that she was intruding. Aside from seeing him at those horrendous annual Christmas parties she'd felt obligated to attend, she really didn't know Mike outside of work. The time Bridget saw him at the hospital was just coincidence, and she was sure he didn't remember it anyway. Checking her oversize purse for nothing in particular, she concluded that it would be best to decline the tea and go home.

"Shower and an hour, my ass," Mike yawned as he came down the stairs in a pair of clean jeans and a button-down shirt, his hair still wet and slicked back. He hated this practice of short turn-arounds in homicide. "All I want to do is sleep."

Mary-Margaret marched out of the kitchen carrying a tray bearing a plate of golden-brown buns, three cups with matching saucers, and a crystal milk and sugar set. "Michael, ye will feel better after having a cinnamon bun. Fresh out of the oven. Ye as well, Bridget."

Mike looked questioningly at the tray. "Where did we get these?"

"I had Max bring them from home mid-week. Ye can't serve tea to company in those ratty old mugs ye have in your cupboards, luv. Tell me she took the good china, too?"

"I don't know what she took, Mom," Mike replied, more interested at the moment in his tea than with whatever his soon-to-be ex-wife had left him with.

"I think I should go," Bridget apologized, declining the tea.

"Nonsense," Mary-Margaret countered. "Ye have gone to all the trouble of callin' someone in to watch yer father. Michael, did you know that our Bridget takes care of her elderly father? What a lovely girl. Perhaps one day, ye shall do the same for me. In any event, the least ye can do now, son, is look lively. Ye can sleep all afternoon and all day tomorrow. Max and I will make our own way to Church. Not like it would kill ye to darken the door yerself. What parish do ye belong to, Bridget?"

Bridget pulled down the bottom of her skirt as she fumbled to stand up.

"Our Michael doesn't believe and all. He's still angry about his Da," Mary-Margaret continued, causing Bridget to sit down again. "Blames God and the Church when, if he'd give it half a thought, he'd realize that it was God, or the belief in God, that put meals on our table after his Da died, God rest his soul. Anyway, Michael, just because ye have become a heathen doesn't mean yer son shouldn't have some religious training. Try a bun, Bridget."

"Yeah, church is pretty cool, Dad." Wearing only a T-shirt and barely decent boxer shorts, Mike's son leapt into the living room from the fourth stair up. Somewhat embarrassed, he thrust his hand out to the unexpected guest. "Whoa. Sorry. Hello, I'm Max."

Bridget stood up, equally embarrassed, and shook Max's hand. "Bridget. Bridget Calloway. A pleasure."

"For the love of God, my child, get yerself up those stairs and put on some clothes. That's no way to greet company. Michael, what kind of a house do ye run here?"

"No, it's me. I'm sorry," Bridget fumbled.

"Max, put some clothes on. Smarten up," Mike barked.

"Sorry, Dad." Blushing furiously, Max beat a hasty retreat up the stairs.

"That is no way to speak to the boy. He's obviously embarrassed enough," Mary-Margaret admonished her son before turning apologetically to Bridget, motioning her to sit back down. "It's not the young lad's fault, luv. His mother left Michael to raise the lad on his own when our wee Max was just an infant, dontcha know? And then Michael's second wife just now leaves, and the wee lamb is motherless again. Ach, it's a wonder he's doin' as well as he is, poor wee soul. Good thing Granny's here to keep things goin'."

Mike closed his eyes, doing his best not to allow the irritation welling up inside of him to spew out.

Bridget stood up again, breaking the rising tension between mother and son. "I really *must* go."

"No, no. Please stay." Mike waved his hand around vacantly. "I'm sorry. It's okay. What can I help you with, Bridget?"

Hesitating momentarily, Bridget sat down for the third time since she had arrived. "The Sanderson case."

"Right."

Mary-Margaret's ears pricked up.

"We need to wrap it up, Mike. The jury can't stand down for a whole month. I've spoken to the judge personally and asked him if he would give us two days next week and—"

"Wait, I thought he hated you."

"He does. But he loves justice."

"Oh my, look at the time." Mary-Margaret sprang up. "And me with buns coolin' and more bakin' that needs doin' for tomorrow's dinner. I'll just be in the kitchen if ye need anything, luv. Luvs."

Mary-Margaret gone, Bridget said with a smile, "Your mother is adorable."

"Maybe we could hook her up with your father," Mike muttered.

"Well, she'd better hurry. He's terminal, remember?" Gallows humour was one of the few coping skills Bridget had left.

"Oh. No, I didn't remember. Sorry." In fact, Mike remembered very little of the night Amanda had rushed him to the hospital and Bridget had just happened to be there with her father. "But I do recall you telling me that I was the best detective on the planet."

"No, wasn't me. Must have been Amanda, and she was likely referring to Ron. I actually think I may have told you to fuck off." Their familiar banter seemed to be putting Bridget at ease.

"Wouldn't be the only woman to have said that to me."

"I don't doubt it, Detective. So. Sanderson. Trial. Monday. Can you be... What was it: 'bright-eyed and bushy-tailed' by 10 a.m. on Monday?"

"Are you asking or telling?"

"Telling. And I'm surprised that you have to ask." The sparkle came back to Bridget's eyes.

"Okay. What else do you need?"

"I need you to focus on just the issues before the court. I know you think there could be other victims, but—"

"I don't think. I know," Mike corrected. "I had a little guy in for an interview this..." Mike looked down at his watch and then corrected himself, "yesterday afternoon. He was very clear about what Sanderson did to him. We've likely got a few dozen victims. And I'm absolutely sure they are tied in to the same ring that got hold of Chelsea Hendricks."

"That was almost fifteen years ago, Mike," Bridget sighed, typing on the laptop that she had brought with her.

"Same fuckers running it from the top."

"I'll want to hear more about that later, but for Monday, I *really* need you to focus on our little girl."

Mike nodded with resignation.

"And I think you need to know..." Bridget hesitated. "She's back at Sick Kids Hospital. She tried to hang herself Thursday afternoon. Luckily, one of the women in the shelter happened to go into the wrong room and saw her in time to cut her down. It's not looking too good, though, Mike. She's on life support."

"Shelter?"

"Yes. Dad is on a court order not to be around his daughter, and that puts Mom in a bad spot."

"Me or the kid, right?" Mike recited the all-too-familiar ultimatum.

"Yep. And Mom chose her daughter. So..."

"Jesus."

They both sat in silence for a moment, Mike staring ahead of him in

159

disbelief while Bridget looked on helplessly.

"Why am I hearing this from you?" Mike finally said, annoyed. "This is my case. I should have been the one telling you all of this."

"Because you've been off work. Injured. In the line of duty. Remember? Messages haven't been getting through to you. Maybe you haven't been checking. Maybe they haven't been left. Whatever the case may be, it's okay, Mike. I've been following up."

"But she's *my* victim. He's *my* accused."

"Let it go. I've got this one."

"But—"

"I know you've done your best, Mike. You always do." Bridget leaned over and placed her hand on Mike's knee. "The system is flawed. That's not your fault. You can only do so much. I'm sorry."

"Not your fault, either. Apparently, it's nobody's fault that this shit keeps happening." Mike shook his head and leaned back in a big stretch. *After all of these years, all of these stories, all of these endings, you'd think it would get easier. How many more victims are there? And how many more ropes? Fuck.*

"Listen, I'd like to stay and go over a couple of things for Monday, but I'm looking at the time and I only have the caregiver until one. I really do have to run, but maybe we can talk on the phone later this evening? After you've had some rest, maybe?" Gathering her laptop and her purse, Bridget stood up.

"Yeah, sure. Let me get the door. And, um, thanks for telling me. In person. I really appreciate it."

"I'm sorry, Mike." Bridget turned to face him, only to find herself standing a little closer to him than she thought she should be. "I know how hard these cases are on you."

"No. It's okay. I mean… Yeah, it's…okay. Thanks."

"Monday morning will be okay, Mike. I really have no need to call tonight." They walked the few steps to the front door. Mike pulled it open.

"Yeah. You bet. And, uh, say hi to your father for me." Mike stood awkwardly at the open door, wishing he had given her a hug.

"I will," Bridget called back over her shoulder as she walked towards her car parked in front of the house.

Mike closed the door behind her, frozen with fatigue yet still aware of the smell of her light perfume hanging in the air.

"She gone?" Max's voice called down from the second-floor landing.

"Yeah." Mike stood by the door, intentionally breathing in Bridget's scent for a few moments before walking back into the living room.

"She's hot," Max commented as he sprang past Mike on his way to the kitchen.

"I work with her, Max," Mike countered. *And she's probably got the caregiver for the day and is off for fancy bistro lunch with some up-and-coming superstar defence lawyer. Whatever. We just work together.*

"So? She's still hot." Max reiterated before disappearing into his grandmother's domain.

"Yeah, she is," Mike mumbled, shuffling up the stairs to his bedroom.

Chapter Twenty-Seven

8:49 a.m., Sunday, October 14, 2018

"Michael. It's Mandy. On the phone for ye. Wake up, son." The familiar gentle yet persistent shaking of his shoulder reminded Mike that his mother was here. Still.

Mandy? Who the hell is Mandy?

"Here, take the phone, luv." Mary-Margaret passed him the cell phone he'd left on his nightstand. "I turned it off yesterday so ye could get some sleep. Turned it back on just a few minutes ago. and now it's ringin' like the bells of St. Mary's on Christmas mornin'. Surprised ye could sleep through it. I'm just on me way out and thought it must be important, so I picked it up. Good thing, too. Here."

Mike took the phone from his mother with a nod, his mind still foggy.

"Yeah?" he exhaled into the device as he pressed it to his sleep-fuzzy head.

"I swear no one but your mother and my sister *ever* calls me Mandy. And why is your mother answering your phone? I've been trying to get a hold of you since yesterday. Anyway, we may have found the body."

Mandy. Amanda Black. Okay. Found the body? You're kidding me. Just went through a million shitty diapers and tons of smashed drywall and—

"I believe we have found the trunk," Amanda continued.

"Huh?"

"Up north, in a garage. Rusty took it to the dump, like he said, but one of the guys who works there pulled it aside and then took it to his cottage and

162

left it in his garage for a week, and here we are. I'm just heading over to the morgue to see if it's Sibby Mac. Can't imagine it wouldn't be. How many trunks have dead women in them?"

Mike sat up in bed, swinging his legs out from under the warmth of the comforter to get up. "What are you talking about?"

"Got a call from the Orillia O.P.P. last night. Guy with a cottage up there called in to say he found a body in a trunk he got from a kid at the Bermondsey dump. Apparently the guy works there and saw our boy, Rusty, dragging the trunk out of the back of the Tahoe the previous Saturday. Thinking he could use it at the cottage, this guy pulls his own truck around, and the two of them slide the trunk from the Tahoe into the back of our guy's truck. When our guy mentions that it's awfully heavy for an empty trunk, Rusty tells him that it's full of his old man's books. Our guy doesn't really have time to ask questions and takes it at face value, mostly because he knows he'll lose his job if he gets caught taking stuff from work, whether it's garbage or not."

"Would have been nice if Rusty had mentioned this guy in his statement." Mike grimaced, scratching what he was sure were fragments of shitty diaper out of the creases in his scruffy face, still smelling rotting garbage despite having showering the day before until the hot water ran out.

"Yep, would have been, but he didn't. Have to ask why later. And after practically breaking his back getting the trunk off his truck up north, our guy figures he ought to pop it open to see what he's got, but his wife thinks she's going into labour. Turns out she's not, but they decide to come back to the city anyway, and they don't go back up to the cottage again until last night. Both he and mom-to-be notice a pretty rank smell coming from the garage, which causes our guy to take a look inside the trunk. When he opens it, he sees what he believes to be a dead animal wrapped in Saran wrap, but after a second look, he realizes it's not and calls the local constabulary."

"Poor bugger."

"Likely not a pretty sight. Fortunately, the boys from the detachment had the sense to seize the trunk as one big package before having it shipped to the coroner's here in Toronto. Polermo called me yesterday afternoon to advise that they were backed up because of that flu epidemic in the seniors' home and wouldn't be getting to it until this morning, which worked out well for me. Damned family stuff keeps getting in the way of listening to the dead speak. Anyway, I'm on my way to the morgue now."

"Hmm." Mike stood up, feeling much stiffer than he'd thought he'd be. He took a few seconds to get his balance, waving his mother off when she moved in to help.

"Shit! Now that's two nice dinners I owe him. People are going to talk, Crumply-Pants. Listen, I tried to call you all yesterday afternoon, but your phone just kept ringing until it went to voicemail. Where were you?"

"Apparently asleep." Mike was shocked as he looked at the time on his watch on the nightstand.

"This is the big league, Mike. I need you to keep your phone turned on and you to be available until we're done. Anyway, we're opening the trunk at ten. No need for you to be here when we do, but I will need you to get hold of Ron. He doesn't answer his phone either. What is it with you guys? Don't know. Don't care."

Mike felt his head starting to ache again.

"You two are going to write up a warrant for the cameras at the dump after you check the video notes of the interview I did with Rusty Sobatics. I want from about twenty minutes before he said he got there until about half an hour after the dump closes."

Mike groaned. "What happened to your warrant writers?"

"Where you been, Sleeping Beauty? Triple homicide yesterday. Active shooter in a mall beats old lady in a trunk every time. Anyway, a jury will want to see the kid's vehicle actually coming and going. We'll also want video of the dump employee's vehicle coming and going like, say, at the beginning and end of his shift, so write the warrant up for the whole day. Unless they can see it on a screen, the average person won't believe it. Disappointing when real crime has to imitate crime fiction to be believed. Fascinating times we live in, Mike. Simply fascinating. And make sure that all the 'i's are dotted and the 't's are crossed. I imagine Rusty's lawyered up pretty damned tight by now. And make sure the warrant also includes the receipts from the dump for the Tahoe."

Mike struggled to keep the phone to his ear with one hand while he hopped around his room attempting to put his pants on with the other.

"After that, I'd like you to get a good still of Rusty from his booking hall tape along with a picture of his dad. You can probably pull a fairly recent one of James off the Internet. Rusty looks a lot like his father, and I want to make sure we have the right Sobatics in our sights. Are you with me, Mike?"

Mike sat down on the bed, still half-asleep and having to admit to himself that his balance was insufficient to permit him to dress standing up. *Autopsy at ten? At night? Since when do they do autopsies at 10 p.m.? And where is Mom going at this hour?* Mike squinted at the sun shining through the sheets he had covering his bedroom windows. *Holy shit. Is it Sunday morning? Did I sleep from yesterday afternoon until...* He looked again at his watch on the nightstand. *Nine a.m.? Fuck!*

"Mike?"

"Yeah, I'm here. Go ahead."

"Good. So get Ron. Wait. Can you drive yet?"

"What?"

"Forget it. I'm just outside your door now. Come out, and you can drop me off at the morgue and head to the station with my car. The autopsy should be done by eleven. We'll say noon because we have to get the body out of the trunk, and that will take some time. You know what? I'll call you when I'm ready to be picked up."

What the fuck?

"Meanwhile," Amanda continued relentlessly, "get those pictures ready for me. We still don't have enough to arrest, but I'm thinking we can do a photo lineup with your buddy, Glen Brebeuf. Maybe give him a call and see if we can get him in this afternoon or first thing tomorrow morning at the latest. You and Ron can deal with Brebeuf. Okay, your mother is walking towards the car. I'm going to hang up."

Tomorrow. Monday. Bridget. Sanderson. Trial. Jury. Kid on life support. Shit.

"Wait!" Mike objected. "Ron's gonna have to cover this on his own. I've got court."

165

"Like hell you do. You're mine until the end of the month, remember? Hang on." Amanda's voice got considerably louder. "Yes, it is a glorious morning, Mary-Margaret."

"But—"

"No, thank you. I'm just here to pick up Mike." He could hear Amanda's voice wafting up from downstairs and as well as on the phone.

"Listen, Mike," Amanda's voice was directly in his ear now. "I've got a murderer on the loose, and I've got you on my team. Like I said, you are mine every day until at least the end of the month. I don't care what you two love-bugs do at—"

"Bullshit, Amanda, it's not like that. She came by to say my victim on that child abuse case tried to kill herself. And that the trial was back on for Monday and I'd still be required. Likely on Tuesday as well."

The phone might as well have been dead for all the response Mike got from Amanda.

"Okay," Amanda finally conceded, knowing that even she could not trump a judge. "I guess we'll just have to work around you. Get downstairs as quickly as you can. I'm inside your house now. Your mother won't let me leave without having one of her biscuits. How is it that you're not obese, Mike?"

Mike was about to reply when the phone clicked off.

Too close. This is all getting too close. Ever since she got here, this house has turned into a circus. Time for Mom to go home.

* * *

"Well, at this point, Mary-Margaret, I have strong reason to believe that the body in the trunk is that of Sibby Mac," Mike could hear Amanda saying gently as if it was his mother on the receiving end of what cops referred to as a compassionate message.

"It's just such a terrible thing. And so disrespectful." Mike visualized his mother wiping her nose with a tissue as he made his way downstairs.

"What I'm going to look at now is just the shell of Sibby Mac. Whoever she was is gone." Amanda rubbed the older woman's shoulder.

"Oh, I know it. I've been around death quite a bit, luv, what with Michael's Da and me work at the Church," Mary-Margaret sniffled. "It's just that, well, truth be told, I don't think I've ever really gotten past me Jimmy's death. That would be Michael's father. He was only thirty-two when he died. Accident at work, don't ye know?"

Mary-Margaret shook her head as she wrung her hands, looking over at her son coming down the stairs. "I remember that morning like it was yesterday." She slumped in the chair by the window, looking up at Amanda, continuing with the story as if it was the first time she had told it. "He had such a terrible headache when he woke up that day. 'Jimmy, me luv,' I says to him, 'why don't ye just have a lie-in this mornin'? Ye are always goin' nineteen to the dozen. It won't kill ye to stay home one day.' Ach. Those were my exact words, dontcha know? He said he had to go. Union meeting after work. He was a big union man, my Jimmy. Always looking after everyone, just like ye, Michael." Mary-Margaret's pale blue eyes looked over at her son as she reached for the hand he instinctively held out to her. "So in he goes, and next thing I know, there's that knock at me door. And me with four wee ones. Michael is my oldest, and he only thirteen at the time, God bless him." She squeezed Mike's hand. "Ach. I'm sorry, Mandy. I shouldn't be botherin' ye with all of this. Ye have got yer own troubles, I'm sure, and here's our Michael still lookin' like a bag of hammers, just like his Da did that mornin'."

Mike leaned down and kissed his mother on the forehead. "I'm okay, Mom. Don't worry. But we have to go."

"It's such a shame, this murder business," Mary-Margaret continued. "I would have liked to have known our Sibby Mac, I'm sure. Ye may believe I'm daft, Mandy, but I came up with a list of reads I thought she might have liked. Ach, listen to me. Too late now, anyway, isn't it? Will there be a funeral mass, then?"

"I suppose." Amanda looked over at Mike for direction. He shrugged.

"Well, if they're needin' a spot, the Church is always there. Speakin' of which, I'm already late." With surprising agility, Mary-Margaret seemed to sprint from her chair towards the front door. "And, Michael, don't forget dinner tonight. Paul is bringin' his new *special friend*."

"You mean boyfriend, Mom?"

"Yes. His new boyfriend. So be on yer best. I'll be saying a prayer for ye in Church today, son, and lightin' a candle for our Sibby Mac, God rest her soul." Mary-Margaret hollered up the stairs, "Max, meet ye in the car!"

Eyebrows raised as grandmother and grandson headed off to Church, Amanda asked, "Anything I need to know, Mike?"

"No. You probably know too much already." Mike pulled his trench coat from the hall closet, and putting it on, ushered Amanda out the door.

Chapter Twenty-Eight

4:57 p.m., Sunday, October 14, 2018

"The man's an artist," Amanda gushed.

"You're sick." Mike winced in the sunlight as he manoeuvred the unmarked car into the tight parking lot behind the station.

"Watching a pathologist peel back plastic wrap without disturbing the skin is a stunning sight. Hands of a sculptor, that Polermo. Simply brilliant."

"You are one weird chick."

"Welcome to my world. Did Brebeuf come in, and was he ruled out as involved in any way?"

"Uh-huh. Ron had a hard run at him."

"Good. I'm going to need him to positively ID the body then. I'm satisfied that I just saw Elizabeth MacDonald, but the judges prefer having someone else make the call. Let's set that up sooner rather than later. You'll be taking him. He likes you. How about a photo lineup?"

"Done. Ron had it ready when Brebeuf came in. Positively picked out Sobatics Senior as the man at the door."

"Great. Warrant for the vehicle done?"

"Uh-huh. Be executed tomorrow at seven a.m.. Time for a chat with Sobatics?"

"Give me a couple of minutes to freshen up and grab a coffee. Damn. I should have had you pick one up for me."

"Do I *look* like I do coffee runs?"

"Beneath you, Crumply-Pants?" Amanda winked.

"They're not crumply," Mike objected, looked down at his suit as he unbuckled his seat belt. "I just got this back from the dry cleaners."

"Shit. It's almost six. I was supposed to call Tony to remind him to pick up some diapers. Shit."

"Oh?"

"Adult diapers. For my sister. Quadriplegic. Shot in the neck during a botched robbery twenty years ago. You probably remember the case. Randy Valencourt was the shooter."

"That was your sister?"

"Yep. She's just starting to have occasional incontinence issues because the caregivers aren't doing the manual emptying at the same time every day, and my parents can't do it anymore. Talk about adding insult to injury. Never mind. Wait here while I go use the ladies' and then we'll—"

"It's Sunday."

"Yes, it is."

"We have to go to dinner"

"What the hell are you talking about?"

"Sunday dinner. Every Sunday. Barring death—your own. Mom's rules."

"You *are* kidding me."

"Nope."

"Well," Amanda considered, much to her own surprise, "our deceased is…deceased, but I'm not going to let this fucker slip through my fingers so that you can have some roast beef and Yorkshire pud with Mom. Maybe Ron and I will go."

"It's corned beef and cabbage. Always corned beef and cabbage."

"You're serious, aren't you?"

"Family first, remember?"

"Yes. Someone else's family, not your own. Shit, Mike. Okay, I really gotta pee. And call Tony. And find Ron. Don't worry, we'll all work around your schedule, princess."

"It wouldn't hurt you to grab something to eat yourself," Mike suggested, reminding Amanda that she had been on the go since before nine this morning.

"Maybe Mom could whip something up for Ron and me, then," Amanda huffed.

"No problem. Table's always set with two extra places. Just be kind about my family, okay?"

"I was kidding."

"I wasn't. While you're doing what you need to do, I'll give Mom a call and let her know. Any food allergies?"

"What fucking planet am I on?" Amanda got out of the car and slammed the door shut.

* * *

"Well, look who it is, everyone! Michael has brought Mandy and Ronnie from work to dinner. And this is why I always have places set extra, just in case ye were thinkin' I'm a bit off my nut, Jorge. Sitcheedoon there, Michael, at the head of the table where yer Da used to sit when he was alive, God rest his soul, and let Ronnie sit in yer place. And ye come sit here to me left, Mandy. I'm doubtin' we'll see Peter this evening. Doesn't even know where ye live now, does he, Michael? We'll leave that spot across from Ronnie as it was, just in case we have an unexpected guest. Have ye heard from yer Bridget, Michael? Good thing Katie and Ahmed aren't here. Had to get Max to pick up Sally-next-door's card table as it is. Reminds me of the old days when ye and Paulie and Richie used to sit off on your own. D'ye remember that, luv?"

"But what am I thinkin'? Let me introduce everyone. This is me daughter, Theresa, and her husband, Alan."

"Everyone calls me Teaszy. I blame Mike."

"And this is their son, Paulie, and his friend—"

"*Boy*friend, Gran," Paul quickly corrected.

"Boyfriend. Sorry, me lamb. Paulie's boyfriend, Jorge."

"What happened to Rob?" Mike asked.

"Ugh. He's a troll!"

"Off," Teaszy said.

"Again," Alan added, in case Amanda and Ron, the two newcomers, required clarification around the well-known on-again, off-again status of Paul's particular relationship with Rob.

Ron looked at Jorge. "You know, Jorge, you look very familiar."

"He looks *old*," Max mumbled under his breath.

"Lab tech. CFS," Jorge replied, ignoring Max's comment. Amanda's ears pricked up.

"Right, of course," Ron said. "And you're—"

"Dating Paul. Yes. He's very *mature* for his age." Jorge looking lovingly across the table at his much younger boyfriend.

"You mean you like much younger men," Alan muttered.

"And I suppose *you* don't enjoy the company of younger women," Jorge replied, then with a quick look over at Alan's wife, continued, "if you weren't otherwise, and quite luckily, I might add, taken."

"Don't be shy, Mandy. Make yourself up a plate. It's boardin'-house style here."

"Thank you. And what is this?"

"Boiled cabbage."

"Welcome to Ireland West," Mike said.

"And how is our Sibby Mac?" Mary-Margaret asked.

Amanda smiled politely. "Quite dead."

"Ach, it's a terrible thing, this murder and all."

"We're investigating a murder, are we?" Jorge piped up.

Leaning across the table towards his new lover, Paul gushed, "I bet you have some stories to tell."

"Well, I have seen my share and—"

"Good thing our Katie isn't here." Mary-Margaret interrupted. "She'd be squirmin' in her seat by now. Always was the sensitive type."

"Where is Katie?" Teaszy asked.

"Oh, God knows. Off to New York. Or London. Or maybe even Paris. She and Ahmed have been so busy with the magazine lately."

"My aunt runs a woman's magazine," Paul told Jorge, who nodded politely.

172

"She doesn't *run* it, she *edits* it," Max corrected.

"Whatever."

"So how long have you been dating my nephew, Jorge, is it?" Mike asked.

"We've just started."

"Met at the Leather Ball," Paul added proudly.

"Paulie," Alan groaned.

"What, Dad? Too butch?"

Teaszy cut in. "That's enough, Paulie. So you work with the police, do you, Jorge?"

"Not exactly. No, I'm the fellow they send their seized items to in hopes of finding a hair or—"

"A sperm sample?" Paul winked at Jorge, ignoring a look of disapproval from his father.

"Yes, sometimes a sperm sample, my pet."

"Would you like anything else?" Teaszy asked Amanda, wanting to change the topic.

"Take more of the corned beef, Mandy. It may be a bit on the cold side, but I can always chuck it in the microwave for ye. She didn't take *that*, did she, Michael?" Mary-Margaret asked. "Had to bring over all me own pots and pans, I did. Michael's previous wife took everything."

"Microwave is built in, Mom."

"Just as well."

"Are you working on the MacDonald homicide?" Ron asked Jorge.

"I don't recall off the top of my head."

"That's because you're full of thoughts of me, aren't you, lover?" Paul said from across the table.

"Discretion has never been one of Paulie's strong suits," Mike advised Amanda.

"Reminds me of my own dinner table," she reassured him.

"Michael was sayin' ye have children, Mandy," Mary-Margaret said, though Mike had never said anything of the sort.

"Yes. Two daughters."

"Easy wee ones, girls, but more than a handful when they're older."

"Aren't you a bit…uh, old to be dating my nephew?" Mike asked, looking closely at Jorge.

"Michael!" his mother remonstrated.

"Head injury. Doctor says I may not have a filter," Mike said with a smile.

"As if you ever did," Teaszy smirked.

"Thank you, Mike," Alan cut in. "Finally, someone around here has the balls to say what we've all been thinking."

"Alan!" Teaszy fired from across the table.

"And we all know it sure ain't you," Paul muttered.

"Paulie!"

"You might think so, but—" Jorge began.

A cell phone rang.

"Oh shit," Amanda glanced quickly over at Mary-Margaret. "I mean, shoot. Sorry. Can you excuse me for a moment? I've got to take this."

"Of course, Mandy. There's hardly any privacy in this house." Mary-Margaret looked disapprovingly at Mike and Alan. "Ye can pop into me room up the stairs there, if ye would prefer?"

"I'm good," Amanda reassured, stepping into the kitchen instead.

"I'm so sorry for our Michael's behaviour, Jorge. And Paulie," Mary-Margaret began, "ye and Jorge are both welcome at me table any time."

"But this is *my* table," Mike reminded his mother, although he did see her point.

"Not on Sundays! Now, Ronnie, we've heard not a peep out of ye. How is yer wee missus? Michael says she's having a tough go of it these days."

"Yes, well—"

"I know how you feel, luv. It's a tough row we hoe some days, but ye'll come out of it. Both of ye. I've been addin' ye in my prayers as of late."

"Thank you, but I'm not so sure—"

"Don't say another word, Ronnie. Just look at our Michael over there. Left for dead not how long ago, and now he's at the head of the table. Ach, there ye are, Mandy. Everything' alright?"

"Yes, fine. Thank you. Just a call from my mother."

"Yer mother, was it? Well. Ye see, Michael, ye are not the only one—"

"Mom, don't start."

"I'm just sayin', me luv."

"No, I'm quite familiar with involved families," Amanda said. "My kids have practically lived with their grandparents at various points in their lives."

"It's the shift work, isn't it? Terrible for families. And must be so hard for a mother."

"Mom!"

"I'm just sayin', Michael, from what little I've seen since I've been here, ye are hardly home. And ye are the father. I can only imagine how hard it must be on wee ones when it's the mother who is gone."

"Yes," Amanda conceded. "It has been challenging."

"And is everything' okay, then, Mandy?" Mary-Margaret's questioning circled back around to the phone call.

"Yes. We're just having some issues with my sister's caregivers these days."

"I blame the government for that. They cut back on everything' without a moment's thought about who they're hurtin', don't they? Just the other day, I was talkin' to Sally-next-door, whose own mother was in one of those homes until she died, God rest her soul, and—"

Mike cut in. "Mom."

"I am just tryin' to show ye people that I am in the know," Mary-Margaret advised with a no-nonsense look around the table. "And what kind of care does yer sister need, luv?"

"Mom, I don't think we need to interrogate our dinner guests."

"It's okay, Mike," Amanda reassured her colleague before returning to Mary-Margaret's question. "A lot. She's in a wheelchair."

Mary-Margaret looked stricken. "Oh, my luv. Was she born...?"

"No. She was twenty-four when she got caught in the crossfire of—"

"Jesus, Mary, and Joseph!" Mary-Margaret crossed herself.

"Is that why you became a cop, Mandy?" Paul asked.

"I was already a cop when it happened," Amanda replied, unsure how to advise Paul that her name was Amanda, not Mandy, without embarrassing Mary-Margaret.

"How long ago was that?" Jorge asked. "Sounds vaguely familiar."

Amanda looked a little more closely at him. "Coming up on twenty-one years."

"There was no conviction in that case, was there?"

"No."

"How does that happen? Surely to God there must have been witnesses?" Mary-Margaret asked.

"Cops must have fucked it up," Alan suggested.

"Alan!" Teaszy kicked her husband under the table.

"No. Forensics fucked up." Amanda looked down at her lap in a moment of reflection.

"I believe, if memory serves correct, that we were in the midst of moving facilities at the time and a few things got misplaced." Jorge said hurriedly.

"Eww, moving. Not like I haven't lost a pile of *my* shit every time I move out of that asshole Rob's place," Paul offered, clearly trying to defuse the rising tension.

"Then stop moving in with him," Alan commented, absently scraping the tines of his fork on his empty plate.

"Stop it, Alan," Teaszy hissed.

"No wonder Richie moved to Hong Kong." Paul glared at his father with disgust before looking over at his new boyfriend. "Wanna move to Hong Kong, Jorgie? I hear the boys are very pretty there."

Jorge smiled warmly at Paul. "Not as pretty as you, I'm sure."

Amanda spoke up. "And one of those things Forensics seem to have misplaced was the bullet that ended up in my sister's neck."

"Well, that wouldn't make or break a case if it had been properly put together, surely?" Jorge sounded defensive.

"No, you're right. It was the box with the gun and the dozen or so other boxes full of bloodied clothes belonging to the person Mr. Valencourt actually killed that kind of tipped the jury in favour of the accused," Amanda said, visibly trying to keep her emotions in check.

Mary-Margaret walked in from the kitchen carrying plates of dessert. "Soda bread pudding, anyone?"

"That looks delightful," Jorge said.

"It's not," Paul cautioned. "It's made from stale bread. Don't eat it."

"Paulie, is that any way to introduce your friend—"

"Boyfriend," Paul corrected his grandmother again.

"Boyfriend, then, to the *rich* traditions of our family?"

"Ronnie? You look like you could use a sweet." Mary-Margaret placed a plate in front of Ron before he had a chance to say anything.

"Teaszy'll have some, I'm sure," Alan commented.

"Not before Mandy. Here ye go, luv." Mary-Margaret placed the other plate in front of Amanda before returning to the kitchen to get more dessert.

Amanda took a polite spoonful of the rich pudding. "I'm sorry to cut this short, but we do have to get going, boys."

"Absolutely." Mike got up without touching the plate his mother had just placed in front of him.

"Then eat quickly, me son," Mary-Margaret ordered. "Ye'll waste away if ye are not careful."

"I'll eat his, Mary-Margaret," Alan offered.

"I hardly think *ye* need it, Alan," she shot at her son-in-law. "Don't think we haven't noticed that ye've put on a fair bit of weight over the last few months. If ye are goin' to get laid off, then ye are goin' to get laid off. No sense eatin' yerself into an early grave. Michael and Teaszy's Da, God rest his soul, was a worrier. Not a fleshy-looking fellow like ye, mind, but he was much younger when he died."

"Alan's not getting laid off, Mom."

Mary-Margaret turned her attention to Paul's boyfriend. "Well, he's not union, so there's no sayin' what might happen. Jorge, despite our Paulie's warnin', have some dessert. And if ye don't like it, I'm sure our Alan over here will eat it, won't ye, then?"

"I'd say Jorge is as likely to explode as I am," Alan snarked. "He's no youngster, is he?"

"I find his rolls very, very sexy," Paul purred.

"I think I'm going to barf," Max advised.

"Max!" Mike admonished.

"No, seriously. I'm going to barf." Max sprang from the table and bounded up the stairs to the bathroom.

"Please tell me this happens in your house, too," Max said to Amanda.

"Pretty much, yep. Just with girls."

Mary-Margaret sat down with her plate of dessert. "Ye're lookin' a little overwhelmed there, Ronnie. Everything okay?"

"I'm an only child."

"Ach. And ye with no children to call yer own, isn't that what ye were sayin', Michael? Such a sad state of affairs."

"Mom!"

Ron looked around the table at the gregarious but increasingly unruly family. "It's alright, Mike. I'm fine."

Amanda ate her last spoonful of pudding. "Thank you for the lovely dinner, Mary-Margaret, but I've got to get these boys back to work."

"No coffee? I know how much our Michael loves his coffee. I can make one…what did ye call it the other morning, son? 'For the road'?"

"I'm sure we're all fine, but thank you."

Chapter Twenty-Nine

7:58 p.m., Sunday, October 14, 2018

"The care he took to wrap her body was odd, I have to say. Almost obsessive. Like he didn't want her to rot," Amanda mused as Mike drove the unmarked police car into the Sobatics's upscale neighbourhood. "This car really is a shitbox, isn't it?"

"I guess it is when you look at what's parked in some of these driveways."

From the back seat, Ron piped up. "You know that as well as kings and queens, the Egyptians mummified people they considered to be sacred. Maybe this guy was trying to make a statement."

"Maybe it was some elaborate sex thing that went wrong," Mike suggested.

"You kiss you mother with that mouth?" Amanda looked over at Mike in disgust. "I think our killer just took a lot of care and effort to dispose of this body, which all went to shit when he left the actual task of getting rid of it to his most incompetent child."

"What a weirdo." Mike said as he ran his tongue over his teeth to clear away any remnants of dinner.

"Well, we'll soon find out, I suppose." And almost before Mike had a chance to put it in park, Ron hopped out of the car and sprinted up the front steps to the Sobatics house.

Mike and Amanda followed. Mike reached forward to land the signature cop knock on the door before stepping slightly behind Amanda, the lead investigator. Ron stood firmly on Amanda's left, also slightly behind her.

"Do you have a warrant, officer?" Katherine Sobatics asked, staring coldly at the officers.

"Detective Sergeant," Amanda corrected, cutting to the chase, not at all in the mood to suffer the arrogance of this woman lightly. "I believe your husband has been involved in the death of Elizabeth MacDonald, Mrs. Sobatics. Right now, I'd like him to come to the station with me, without a warrant, without handcuffs, without the world watching. I think that's reasonable, don't you?"

"You don't seem to be an overly reasonable woman, Detective. And I was addressing the gentlemen behind you."

Mike stepped in with a slight apologetic look at Amanda, realizing that Mrs. Sobatics likely preferred dealing with men. "As my boss here said, no, we don't have a warrant yet. We thought maybe you'd prefer to save face."

"A bit late for that, isn't it, Detective? You *are* a detective, aren't you?"

"Yes. As is my partner here." Mike pointed at Ron, who was frowning disapprovingly at the whole situation. "However—"

"Very dangerous, being a detective, I'd imagine. And sexy. Is your life dangerous and sexy, Detective…?"

"O'Shea. Mike O'Shea." He had seen that look, heard that tone of voice far too often over the past few months of his marriage. Taunting. Disdainful. Drunk.

"Mike O'Shea. And your colleague…?"

"Detective Roberts." Ron stepped forward, holding out a firm hand.

"Clearly, Detective O'Shea is the Good Cop. You must be the Bad Cop, Detective Roberts. And you?" Katherine turned her attention back to Amanda. "Must be the Bitch Cop. Funny, I don't remember that in any of the cop shows I've seen. In answer to your earlier question, there's really no point in my letting you in. My husband is not here."

"I'm sure he's not, Mrs. Sobatics," Amanda stated. "We'll be back with a warrant. I can't promise you that we can keep the media at bay much longer."

"Big scoop, Detective Sergeant? Going to make chief detective inspector with this arrest?" That Katherine had been drinking, and probably heavily, was becoming increasingly obvious.

"I doubt it, Mrs. Sobatics. Your husband's standing in life means very little to me. I deal with death. Murder. Homicide. That's why I'm here now, but I can see that we're wasting our time. Come, gentlemen. Let's get that warrant done."

"Aren't you going to leave one to watch the door? Make sure no one escapes? Maybe eyes on all the windows?" Katherine mocked, her boozed-up body swaying with her words.

"Oh, don't worry, Mrs. Sobatics. I've got my bases covered. This isn't my first rodeo." Amanda turned on her heel. "Come on, boys."

"Detective O'Shea?" Katherine called. Mike turned back. Ron froze. Amanda did not turn around, choosing instead to glance over her shoulder. "Change of heart. Come in. Bring your friends."

Mike entered the house, Ron and Amanda behind him.

"Don't worry about your shoes. The housekeeper will be in at seven tomorrow morning. Every morning except Sundays. James hates dirt. Even the dirt he creates himself. A drink?"

"Thank you, no." Mike smiled. *Sad, really.*

"Don't mind if I do then," Katherine half-laughed. "Would you mind pouring me one, Detective?"

Mike paused. Had he been on his own, he would have, and likely would have had one with her. *Just creating rapport. Use what you've got.* With Amanda here, though, he thought twice. And with Ron present, even pouring this woman a drink was out of the question; sharing one with her would have been absurd.

Katherine's eyes locked momentarily on Mike's. She knew his game. "Never mind, then. I'll get my own. Won't be the first one tonight, but I guess you can already tell, can't you? Trained investigators? Ha! I'm a lawyer, you know. Used to be pretty damned good. Criminal. Defence. But don't hate me, honey."

She turned to Ron and smiled superficially. "I have no interest in your world now. Used to. Loved it. You know, I was Kate when I met my husband in law school. Became Katherine when I was called to the bar. Became Mrs. Sobatics when I married James. And then I was Jimmy's or Chloe's

MAN AT THE DOOR

or Ashley's or Russell's mom. And now I'm just the reason James leaves other women's beds. What do they call you when you're at home, Detective O'Shea?"

"Mike."

"Not Michael?"

"Only my mother calls me Michael."

"I think I'm the only one who calls my baby Russell," Katherine sighed. "So, you're here about my husband, are you? He's in Ottawa. Again. I can give you the address where he's at, if you'd like. *And* the name of the woman he's likely fucking as we speak."

"That won't be necessary," Mike said. No matter how many times he saw it, the abject loneliness of a woman like Mrs. Sobatics always got to him. Ron cleared his throat, standing awkwardly just inside the doorway. Amanda continued to let Mike take the lead, hoping he wouldn't be seduced by an act that she also had seen many times before.

"Oh, don't worry, Mike. I'm not ashamed. I know what my husband is like. Everyone knows." Katherine took a big gulp of wine. "He hates dirt, but he sure can throw it in your face. Sit."

Mike sat down in the chair that Katherine had pointed to.

"The rest of you, sit. Somewhere. Anywhere." Katherine gestured broadly at the tastefully decorated living room as she set herself down carefully on a chair across from Mike. "This isn't new. James and his women, I mean. Started just before we got married. Terms of engagement, I suppose you'd say. I loved him. God, what a fool I was back then. Are you sure I can't offer you anything, Mike?"

"I'm sure. Thank you."

Tell me he's not falling for this bullshit, Amanda thought, then glanced over at Ron, who was sitting and trying not to fidget on one of the only hard-backed chairs in the beige room. *Thank Christ I've got Ron with me.*

"I was very supportive when he decided to go into politics. Supportive of everything he did. Thought running for office was better than running after skirts. And I had three children by then. Not a lot of leverage, you know. At least, that's what I thought. Do you have children, Mike?"

"One. A boy."

"So easy, one. Little did I know that the world of politics provides an even bigger arena for chasing skirts for men like James. We moved to Ottawa. I hated it. My children hated it. I moved back to Toronto with the children. Tried to kick-start my career. It was hard back then. A woman in law, three kids, more or less on her own." Katherine looked over at Amanda. "You're like me, Detective Sergeant. You know what I'm talking about. It's still hard, I suppose. Unless you have the 24/7 nanny. I didn't want that. Not for my children. So I just kind of gave it up for a while."

Ron, with nothing to contribute to the conversation, looked around the room. *Clean. Crisp. Not warm, but well decorated, if you like that kind of thing. Marie would like it. Maybe just a bit too showy. No. Marie likes our house. She's happy. She'd like that fireplace, though.*

"And then Russell came along." Katherine got up to pour herself another glass of wine, tipping the bottle towards her impromptu company, all of whom politely declined her offer with a head shake. "James wanted me to have an abortion. Didn't fit into his schedule, he said. I was in Toronto. He was in Ottawa. How was my pregnancy going to interfere with his schedule? I obviously decided to go through with it. James considered Russell to be some sort of pet project I had developed an interest in. As if he had nothing to do with it. Did your wife want more children, Mike?"

"I don't know, but this is—"

"I know, all about me. At last, I've found a man who will make it about me. Sorry," Katherine smiled, noting Mike's uneasiness. "Was that sounding too desperate? No one likes a desperate woman, particularly if she's over thirty. Isn't that right, Detective Sergeant?" Katherine glanced over at Amanda, then turned back to Mike.

"It wasn't until the papers started reporting James's affairs that I put my foot down. At the time, my older three were at an age when they could read, as could their friends. It's one thing to know; it's another to have everyone else know. But who the hell was I fooling? Everyone else *did* know. But at least it hadn't been in print. Until then. So James came home. To be with his loving wife and children, so said the papers. Ha!"

She emptied her glass with one hard swallow. Watching, hearing Katherine Sobatics pouring herself out to him made Mike wonder about his own mistress: the Job. Was that why Carmen left?

"He was like a caged animal when he came back to Toronto. The drinking. The abuse. Oh yes, he was abusive. *Is* abusive," Katherine corrected herself, almost seeming to sober up for a moment. "Mostly verbal. A few drunken brawls, but I think I held my own on those. And then he just started to drift back to Ottawa. To his women. To her. I know who she is but I don't really care."

Ron tried to stifle a yawn. Amanda looked over at Mike. Mike rubbed the scruff that was growing on his face.

"So, you ask yourself, why am I wasting my time listening to this pathetic, lonely old girl who is well past her best-before date?" Katherine leaned back, a self-deprecating half-smile on her face. "Because you're right. I did know Elizabeth MacDonald, and so did my husband."

Mike's ears pricked up.

"Women like me, empty nesters with no career or husband to speak of, become philanthropists. Do charity work. Raise funds for the arts. Go to fancy galas wearing all the jewelry our philandering husbands give us after each discovered indiscretion. And that's where I met Sibby."

Ron perked up.

"She and I sat on a few fundraising committees together. Real crackerjack. I think that's what they call women like her: bright, funny, fashionable, thin. Available. Everything James would want in a mistress. A bit older than his usual, but she played him well. Unlike the perky thirty-somethings he usually landed, she made herself unavailable to him. I knew—everyone knew—that he was trying to *fuck* her," Katherine spat out the word, "and I would laugh at him every time we came home from a dinner that she was at and he'd have that abandoned puppy look you men always get when you can't get laid. God knows he wasn't fucking me."

Amanda and Mike looked at one another.

"I knew he'd been sniffing at her and been turned down. Good on her. At least somebody stood up to him." She stood up to drain a final glass of wine out of the empty bottle before placing it back reluctantly on the mantel. "Well, that's a shame, isn't it? Must have a leak in it. I'd open another bottle, but I hate drinking alone."

Mike watched Katherine attempting to hold onto her dignity, knowing that she was hoping he would take her up on her earlier offer of a drink.

"Well, coffee, anyone?"

"I think we're all good, Mrs. Sobatics," Ron spoke up. Having completed his assessment of the living room, all he wanted now was to get back to work.

"Oh, look. Bad Cop speaks! Suit yourselves, then." Katherine sat on the edge of her chair, closer to Mike. "You know, Mike, James and I have been sleeping in separate bedrooms for over ten years. That's a long time without sex. At least, for one of us."

Mike would have felt sorry for her if he actually believed she had been celibate that long.

"Kinda hurts when your husband puts more energy into wooing some society woman than trying to satisfy you. And kinda hurts when he seems more upset by her rejection than by you locking your bedroom door behind you, you know."

Sex and ego: the only two motives for murder, Mike reminded himself.

"But at least she had the courage to tell me that she'd told him to piss off. Sibby phrased it more eloquently than that, but I knew what she meant. Ten years, though, Mike. That's a long time for a woman to go without sex."

Mike glanced over at Amanda, who was rolling her eyes.

"So now the question is: Did my husband kill her?" Katherine completely shifted gears. "Who the hell knows. Why would he? Not like she's the only game in town. Not like he isn't *fucking* his whore right now." She paused. "That was harsh, wasn't it? I apologize." She now looked squarely, almost defiantly, at Mike. "No, I don't think he killed her. I don't think he'd have the guts to."

As her words faded away, Katherine seemed to sink back into the alcohol-enhanced solitude that Mike assumed she had honed over the years.

"Why don't you think he would have had the guts to kill Elizabeth

MacDonald?" he finally asked.

"He's a coward," Katherine sneered without looked up. "Always has been. That's really why he doesn't leave me, you know."

Ron cleared his throat, uncomfortable with such raw emotions.

"He's afraid." Katherine thrust her chin out at Mike. "Afraid of what I know and what I might say. At least this way, as long as I stay locked away in my bedroom, his secrets are safe. If he was going to kill anyone, it would be me."

Mike looked over questioningly at Amanda, whose eyes had never left Katherine.

"Don't think I haven't thought of that? Why do you think I lock my bedroom door at night? To keep my husband from coming in to make passionate love to me? Ha! That would be rich, wouldn't it?" Katherine looked longingly at the empty bottle of wine. "No, I lock my door to keep my husband out. If he is a murderer—and I'm not saying he is—then he would do it while his victim was asleep. Because he's a coward. But he didn't kill Sibby Mac."

"How can you be so sure?" Mike gently pressed.

"Because he wouldn't know what to do with a woman's body if his dick wasn't in it."

Mike, Amanda, and Ron all glanced at one another.

"Oh my," Katherine chortled. "There I go again. Sorry, kids. God, I wish I had more wine. But that would explain why you think he had Russell dump her body, wouldn't it? Leave a boy to do a man's work. How convenient. How cowardly. How...Jimmy. He *hates* when anyone calls him Jimmy. But that *shit* would throw his own flesh and blood under the bus. The child he never wanted. The child he never wanted me to want."

She stood up abruptly. "I think you and your friends need to leave now, Detective O'Shea."

Mike rose as quickly as Katherine did. Amanda and Ron followed suit.

"I know that nothing I have said can be used against my husband," Katherine stated, now seemingly totally sober. "I also know that that bastard will likely be home sometime late tonight, after he gets the smell of that woman in Ottawa washed off him. Needless to say, I won't be waiting up for him. I'll be sleeping behind my locked door. But you'd know all that with your eyes on the place, wouldn't you, Mike?"

And with that, Katherine unceremoniously ushered the three detectives to the door. "I think it's time for you to leave. Thank you so much for stopping by."

Chapter Thirty

I t had been a very long day with too many moving parts. Mike's entire body ached almost as much as his head as he carefully parallel parked his truck near his house for the second time that day. He had told Amanda that he'd write up his notes in the morning, but he had a steno pad with him and planned to jot down a few notes before going to bed.

The house was quiet. Max was probably watching something on his computer in his room, and Mary-Margaret would be asleep in what was quickly becoming *her* room. The leaf from the dining room table had been removed, the chairs replaced, and the kitchen made spotless. Thankfully, and most important of all, the house was silent.

Mike looked in the kitchen cupboard for a coffee mug but then spotted a half-empty bottle of Jameson and decided that a whisky might be in order. It had been a long time since he had written up with a jug beside him. Recalling his days in the Juvenile Prostitution Task Force with a slight smile, Mike reminded himself that he wasn't thirty anymore. He poured himself a moderate shot and made his way to the dining room table.

To you, Katherine, Mike raised his glass before taking a healthy sip and thinking back to their conversation.

A bright woman with a stalled career, three small children, a philandering husband, and another child on the way that said philandering husband wanted nothing to do with. Could not have been easy for her. But there she was: While he's living the high life in Ottawa, she's at home in Toronto. She eventually builds a life for herself and her young family, but it doesn't include him. And why would she if he's banging enough women to make the news? He must have been pretty overt about it in addition to being profligate: He wasn't the first and he certainly wouldn't be the last guy to be screwing around on the government's dime.

So she pulls the plug. Brings him home. Does his behaviour change? Unlikely. It was easier for him when he didn't have to sneak around, so he slides back to his old stomping grounds. But they still present as a couple for photo ops at the requisite gala events and fundraisers.

And then he stumbles across Sibby Mac. But she's Katherine's friend, and friends don't fuck friends' husbands. Sometimes they do, but in this case, no. But he's got an itch that he wants his would-be paramour to scratch. He's persistent. She's resistant. Worlds collide. She's dead. And he gets the kid he never wanted in the first place to dispose of the body. Is it to ruin the kid or to get back at his wife one more time?

Wait. How does Katherine know about the body? She *did* say her husband had Russell dump Sibby Mac's body, didn't she? How did she know it was a body the kid was dumping? Did the kid tell her? Did the kid even know that there was a body in the trunk? It would have been pretty awkward to stuff even a slightly built old woman into the trunk on his own. Did the old man get his kid to help him? Hell, is the kid somehow involved in the actual murder?

As he made his way back to the kitchen to grab the bottle of Jameson, Mike pulled his cell phone from his pocket and dialed Amanda's number.

"Detective Sergeant Amanda Black," her not-as-chipper-as-usual voice answered.

"It's Mike. Did you tell the kid that he dumped Sibby Mac's body?"

"Mike? Oh. Right. Sorry, half asleep. No, I didn't. Why?"

"How does Katherine Sobatics know then?"

There was a pause. Mike took a gulp of whisky. He could visualize Amanda reaching for the omnipresent pen and paper by her bed.

"I don't know. How does she know?"

"Did you mention in the interview that a body was in the trunk?"

"No."

"So if the kid didn't know what was in the trunk at the time, and no one has told him since, is she just connecting the dots or has Fucknuts told her something?"

"I don't want to bring the kid back in until we have something solid, Mike, and I'm sure as hell not arresting her if I'm not in a position to convict or leverage. I need to find some lawful workaround."

"You think the kid might know more than we thought?"

"No, I mean I'll go over the video of the interview in the morning just to be sure, but he seemed genuine. And I don't believe anyone said anything about a body, specifically Sibby Mac's body, in the trunk."

Mike poured himself another shot. "But the kid knew it was about a homicide. And it's been in the papers. And I'm thinking Katherine Sobatics is not the most discreet woman on the planet."

"No, but it sounds like she's spent a lifetime being protective of her children, especially Russell. Leave it with me. I've made a note to look into it first thing tomorrow. I'll keep you posted. And we've still got to do the positive ID. Maybe you can get our complainant, Mr. Brebeuf, in and take him to the coroner's office tomorrow?"

"Sure, boss." Mike grunted, the thought of having to spend any more time with Glen Brebeuf striking him as enjoyable as sitting in a room with either of his ex-wives. He clicked the phone off and emptied the glass in front of him, enjoying the burning sensation flowing down his throat.

It felt good to be back doing real police work again.

190

Chapter Thirty-One

7:45 a.m., Monday, October 15, 2018

M ike unlocked the passenger door of his unmarked police car. "I appreciate you coming in like this, Mr. Brebeuf." "It can't be easy for you."

"Glen. Call me Glen. And this isn't the only thing that I'm going through hasn't been easy for me."

"Oh?" Much to his dismay, Mike took the bait. He had hoped for a quiet drive to the morgue this morning.

"I've left my wife, Detective."

"Oh." Mike pulled out of the parking lot.

"Yes. Sibby Mac's death has reminded me that life is too short to waste on something you don't want."

"Sounds a bit harsh."

"Not really. The wife. The kid. The SUV. The house with the picket fence. That wasn't my dream. That was hers."

"Who is 'her'?" Mike tried to sound interested but his mind was more focused on getting this ID out of the way and getting to court for the Sanderson trial than it was on Glen Brebeuf's petty little life.

"Sibby Mac. I think she was just trying to be kind by telling me that I wanted all of that. I don't think she meant anything by it. I think she just didn't want to hurt me."

"So she had you get married, have a kid…" *This is going to be a long day.*

191

Let's just get in, make the ID, and get out.

"And a dog," Brebeuf added, looking absently out the passenger window.

"And a dog. Only to have you turn around and walk out on them later? Doesn't sound too kind to me. Have you met my soon-to-be ex?"

"Sorry?" Brebeuf looked at Mike.

"Never mind," Mike muttered. "You were saying?"

"I don't think I was supposed to walk out."

"So why are you?" *Is anyone supposed to walk out?*

"Because the only thing keeping me there was Sibby Mac."

Stopping for a red light, Mike stared at his passenger. "I don't follow."

"As long as I was safely married off, she would let me come over once a week for lunch. I don't think she'd have me if she thought I still loved her the way I do."

"You're an interesting man, Mr. Brebeuf." Mike pressed down on the gas pedal as the traffic light turned to green.

"Glen. Call me Glen."

"Sure. Glen." Mike snapped back into his professional role. "So, before we take a look, let me tell you what you're going to be seeing. Once we get inside the building, we'll be going down the hall to your left. They know we're coming, so they'll direct us to a room off that hallway that looks kind of like a living room."

"Got it."

"You and I will go in, and you will see a big-screen TV on the wall. You can sit or stand. When you're ready, I will push the remote and a live feed of a body on a stretcher will fade in and out on the screen."

"Okay."

"A sheet will be over the body, so you will likely see just the head and shoulders. What I'm asking you to do is to tell me if you recognize the person you are going to see."

"What do you mean? It will be Sibby, won't it?"

Not bothering to answer Brebeuf's question, Mike continued. "You can let me know if you need to see the image again, or if you need to see more of the body or something specific if you're not sure. I'm going to warn you now,

192

Glen, while the body is in pretty good shape from a pathologist's perspective, this individual may not look exactly as you would expect. Keep in mind that it—"

"It *will* be Sibby, though, right?" Brebeuf insisted.

Mike scanned the street for a parking spot. "I can't say for sure, Glen, but if it is—"

"What do you mean: *if*? Do you mean to say I'm just going to look at some random body?"

"Glen, listen to me!" Mike almost shouted, and then lowered his voice. "She will not look as you remember her. There has been some trauma to the body, but they have done their best to make her appear as close to how she would have looked in life. Are you ready?" He parked and looked over at Brebeuf.

"I am."

Mike got out and walked around to the sidewalk, hesitating as he considered whether or not to take Brebeuf's arm as he watched the man fumble his way out of the car. He decided against it. *If nothing else, I can at least leave this guy with his dignity.*

Inside the morgue, the two men made their way to the viewing room down the hall from the security desk at the front. As his nose began to twitch, Mike wished that he had mentioned something about the slight odour of decomposing bodies that managed to seep into the public area. Then he realized that with the amount of cologne Brebeuf was wearing, it was unlikely the guy even noticed.

In the viewing room, Mike picked up remote control for the TV screen, letting his right hand drop casually to his side. When Brebeuf nodded to go ahead, Mike pressed the button with his thumb, his eyes glancing at the screen to ensure that it was operational, then settling on Brebeuf.

The image was clear. Camera angle was good. A tight headshot. Fade in, fade out. Mike had the timing down pretty well, knowing from experience just how long to leave the image on screen to get a response one way or the other. Some investigators just left the image up there, but Mike liked to keep things neat. The circumstances were usually pretty ugly if a body ended up here for identification, and the bodies often showed it. No need to have to look any longer than necessary, particularly for family or friends.

Recalling the kitchen where he had seen the drops of blood that had not been wiped up, Mike figured Sibby Mac had been beaten to death before being wrapped up and jammed into the steamer trunk. Even though the body had had sufficient time to start rotting, it looked surprisingly good now. The plastic wrap must have kept her head together and maybe delayed the decomposition process. Any blood on her face would either have stuck to the plastic and come off when the body was unwrapped or been rinsed off during the autopsy. She didn't look bad at all.

Not like the old days, when we had to bring the family right into the room with the body. Had mothers collapsing over the remains of their murdered daughters almost every time. What a fiasco that was.

"That's her."

"Her?"

"Sibby Mac. Elizabeth MacDonald. That is the body of Elizabeth MacDonald. Can we leave now?"

"Of course. And thank you, Glen."

They drove back to the station in silence. After making an ID, Mike usually spent time discussing when the body would be released from the morgue and how to proceed with funeral arrangements. Today, he did not. He thought instead of his time with the Juvenile Prostitution Task Force and Susan Ramsden, one of the mothers who still called him on the anniversary of her daughter's murder, sitting beside him in the passenger seat. He could hear her quiet sobs in his head as clearly as if she were actually sitting beside him now. There were no cameras or TV screens in the morgue back then, and it had been hard to disguise the viciousness of the murder. They had a pretty good idea who did it: The slash marks on her body suggested that she had been one of Malcolm's girls. But there was not enough to arrest the bastard, even if they could have found him.

Back at the station, Mike parked, and the two men got out and stood awkwardly beside the car as officers carrying duty bags hustled in and out of the marked scout cars parked around them, preparing to begin or end their shifts.

"So that's it then?" Brebeuf asked.

Mike shook off his memories and led Brebeuf past the officers and in through the back door of the station. "Yes, that's it. I'll keep you posted on the progress of the investigation. We're going to need you when the matter comes to court."

"No," Brebeuf corrected, stopping just inside the building. "I mean is that it between you and me?"

"You and me?"

"Well, yes. I mean, I get that we're not friends or anything, but do you think we could grab a coffee or something some time? I'm planning on selling the house once we get this separation thing going, and I'm likely going to move back downtown. I never was a suburbanite, Detective. Not me. I like action. I was thinking that I'd rent a condo or something down here and, well, you know. Maybe we could hang out or something like that?"

"Hang out?" Mike repeated as he escorted Brebeuf along through the tiny hallway towards the front of the station.

"Not hang out exactly, but maybe grab a coffee. I know you like coffee. All cops like coffee, don't they?"

"Yeah. Sure. Okay." Mike opened the door leading to the waiting area of the station.

Brebeuf turned to face Mike. "You've been very kind, Detective. And very understanding. You've helped me move from a very dark place in my life to where I am now. Thank you for that."

They walked into the waiting room. Neither man moved for a moment, although to Mike's mind, Brebeuf was standing far too close for comfort. He cleared his throat, then opened the outer door of the station and motioned for Brebeuf to leave. "I hope that things work out for you, Glen."

"Thank you, Detective," Brebeuf replied almost happily. "I think they will."

Mike smiled, trying not to shake his head in disbelief as he watched Brebeuf get into his car and drive away, giving a quick wave and a brief honk of his horn.

Then Mike looked down at his watch and hustled down the hall to pick up his notes for court.

Chapter Thirty-Two

10:13 a.m., Monday, October 15, 2018

The jury had fallen out of love with Bridget Calloway. In contrast, Mike O'Shea, with his solid evidence and no-nonsense responses to the annoying defence attorney and moody judge, was still looked upon favourably. The significant delay in the trial necessary for his recovery from the well-publicized assault on him had bought the prosecution a bit more time, but now listening to the radiators banging to life in the cold courtroom and waiting for the ancient furnace to kick in was proving to be too much, even for these twelve ordinary people.

"Take your mind back to the events of February 14th of last year, if you can, Detective." Unable to tell whether the coolness she felt in the room was due to the autumn air or to the indifference of the jury, Bridget stood beside the lectern and focused on Mike. "As you've previously stated, you were at the Hospital for Sick Children with the victim, Jessica Sanderson, correct?"

"Yes." Mike nodded to the judge who was tapping away on his laptop.

"Was there anyone else with young Jessica at that time?" Bridget stepped slightly away from the lectern and her notes, inching closer to the jury.

"Her mother and," Mike paused just long enough, he hoped, to create some interest in his testimony, "her newborn son."

A collective gasp came from the jury box.

"Her newborn son," Bridget repeated, acknowledging Mike's timing with a slight smile before stopping herself for a moment to glance over at the jury.

"Very good. And does this son of hers have a name?"

The defence attorney half stood and asked in a bored tone, "Relevance?"

"I think it will be easier for the jury to follow along if we can refer to the baby by name instead of referring to it as… Was it a boy or girl, Detective?"

"Boy."

"Referring to him as the 'baby,'" Bridget suggested cheerily in distinct contrast to the defence attorney who seemed fatigued. She moved back behind her lectern.

"Very well, Ms. Calloway," the judge acquiesced without slowing his typing or looking up from the screen. "Continue."

"And…" Bridget looked down at her notes and then up at Mike, smiling as if this was the first time she had spoken to him all morning. "Did Jessica Sanderson's baby boy have a name?"

"No." Mike looked down at his fingers, noting the indentation of where his wedding band had been. "Not at that time. She—Jessica—did not know she was pregnant until she was actually in labour."

Another gasp came from the jury box. Mike glanced over and saw one of the more matronly jurors shaking her head, while one of the men glared daggers at the accused man sitting boldly beside his attorney.

"But her mother was there, correct? Surely *she* would have known?" Bridget walked over to where the jury was sitting, contorting her own body to mimic the appearance of a pregnant woman, her face twisted in a look of complete disbelief.

"No. My victim just thought she was getting fat. Wore baggy clothes." Mike kept his face and voice steady. He was the supporting actor to Bridget's lead in this tough final act.

"And never went for a single ultrasound or doctor's appointment?" Bridget stood by the jury, hand dangling on the front of the jury box, just as a singer would lean on her accompanist's piano.

"No."

"Must have been terrifying for the child." Bridget spoke to the jury, shaking her head just enough to indicate sadness, but not enough to annoy the judge. Or so she hoped. "So there you have them: Jessica, her mother, and Baby Sanderson." Bridget quickly swung around, her glance scanning the accused before focusing on Mike. "Did you or anyone else call for Children's Aid at this time, Detective?" Bridget was leaning against the jury box now, intentionally creating the illusion for the jury that she was asking the questions that every man and woman in those seats wanted to know.

"Not at that time, no. The call hadn't been made yet."

"And whose call was it to make?" Bridget began to nod slightly as she looked around her, ensuring that her jurors were onside with her questions.

"I object!" This time it was Gregory Sanderson himself who jumped up.

"Sit down, Mr. Sanderson," the judge snapped impatiently at the accused, slamming down the top of his laptop before redirecting his overall annoyance towards the accused's lawyer. "Mr. Reiner, please control your client. And Ms. Calloway, could you please keep your summer-stock theatrics out of my courtroom?"

"Of course." Bridget strode back to her lectern, glancing at the jury for their response as she went. "While you didn't make the call, Children's Aid would have to be called at some point after the baby had been born. Why would a social worker need to be involved so soon?"

Reiner leapt up, tossing his pen down on the table and pushing some strands of gelled hair back into place with his other hand. "Objection. Witness cannot testify to Children's Aid protocol."

"Did you two go to theatre school together, Mr. Reiner? Strike that remark from the record. Detective, please continue," the judge directed.

"The victim in this matter is also a child and falls under the mandate of Children's Aid," Mike said. "And the decision to place her son in foster care had been made during her labour."

"While she was in labour. And why foster care and not adoption, Detective?"

Reiner rose slightly from his seat while carefully placing his pen down on the paper in front of him. This time, his hair stayed in place. "Objection. Witness cannot testify to this!"

"Ms. Calloway?" The judge looked at Bridget.

"Fair enough. Allow me to rephrase. Who made the decision to place the child in foster care?"

"The parents."

"Parents meaning…?" Bridget looked down at the papers on the lectern, pen in hand, as if she was going to write down Mike's answer.

"Her mother. And father. The accused. There." Mike pointed.

"But the baby technically belongs to Jessica so…?" Bridget tilted her head slightly to one side, hoping that she was clarifying a concern the jury might be having, still mindful of the judge's caution about theatrics.

"The decision to put the child up for adoption must by law be delayed until the mother is capable of informed consent," Mike explained, sensing that despite her exceptional sensitivity to such things, Bridget might be overstepping this judge's patience, and he wanted to get his information out before the judge shut them both down.

"Which means when she's an adult?

"Your Honour?" the defence moaned.

"Rephrase, Ms. Calloway."

"I have no further questions, Your Honour." Bridget made some final notations on the paper in front of her before she turned the floor over to her colleague.

Reiner took ownership of the lectern by placing his own stack of papers on it. "Officer O'Shea. You investigate a lot of crimes, don't you?"

"Yes. That's my job. I'm a detective."

"And you've been a police officer for…?" Reiner asked without making eye contact, instead shuffling through the papers in front of him.

"Twenty-seven years."

"That's quite impressive, Detective. And you are quite dedicated to your work, I assume?"

"Yes, I am."

"In fact, you almost got yourself killed, as we are all likely aware, apprehending a murder suspect just a few weeks ago." Reiner looked over at the jury, carefully to make eye contact with an elderly man in the back corner and the young woman sitting directly in front of him, both of whom he was guessing would be sympathetic to Mike's experience.

"Well…"

"No, that's very brave of you, sir. I commend you and thank you for your service. As someone who works in this city and is raising a family here, I am very thankful that there are men and women like you out there, keeping us safe." He waited for the jury to nod their approval. "Now, as a detective with almost thirty years' experience, I would assume that you know something about DNA. Would that be fair to say?"

"Yes, it would be."

"So much so that you have mentioned in your evidence that my client, Gregory Sanderson, and his daughter, Jessica Sanderson, and her son all share the same DNA, correct?"

"Correct."

Reiner wheeled around to face the jury. "Imagine that! A father, daughter, and grandson sharing similar DNA. Is that at all unusual, Detective?"

"No."

"Did you rule out anyone else as a possible—forgive my insensitivity, Your Honour—sperm donor?"

"No."

"I see. Now let's take our minds back to February 23rd of last year, nine days after Jessica had her baby." Reiner's eyes became steely cold as he looked at Mike, but his tone seemed to warm as he turned to speak to the judge. "For the record, they ended up naming him Jerome, Your Honour."

"Hrmph." The judge looked impatiently at the lawyer before him, twiddling a pen between the fingers of one hand, resting his face in the palm of the other.

"Detective, I'd like you to explain to me how you came to know that Gregory Sanderson, my client, had the herpes simplex virus." A jeering tone replaced the earlier warmth in his voice.

Flipping through the pages of his memo book to find the exact date, Mike began, "I have a notation here."

"Maybe I can help you out, officer. You didn't know." It was impossible for the biting tone of Reiner's voice to have been lost on anyone in that courtroom. Before Mike had a chance to respond, the defence lawyer pressed on. "In fact, you still don't know. Because, in fact, Jessica Sanderson contracted herpes from someone else. Isn't that correct, officer?"

Mike stopped flipping the pages to look directly at the lawyer in front of him. "No, that is *not* correct."

"So you are telling the court that it is not possible that Jessica Sanderson could have contracted herpes from anyone but my client."

"Not likely."

"Not likely, you say. Not a very solid answer, is it? In fact, I'm sorry to say," Reiner placed his hands on either side of the lectern as he leaned in towards Mike, "Jessica couldn't have told you who gave her herpes because she was a sexually active young lady. Isn't that a fact, officer?"

"No, it is not."

"Is that so?" Reiner released the lectern to consult his notes. "Well, you mentioned earlier today that the complainant in this matter, Jessica Sanderson, is on life support, correct?"

"Yes."

"And that she and her mother had been residing in a women's shelter as a result of court-imposed non-contact restrictions on my client?"

What the fuck is he trying to say? That it's the court's fault—my fault—she tried to kill herself?

"A non-contact restriction on your client *and* the victim, yes," Mike agreed. "But that doesn't mean—"

"I can't imagine, as a father, losing a child to suicide, can you, Detective?" Reiner was playing the jury for all it was worth. "Those teenage years, statistically the most dangerous years of a person's life. Terrifying thought as a parent, isn't it? Is there anyone in this room who would disagree with me?"

"Mr. Reiner, I would caution you to stick to your judiciary duties," the judge groaned, his tired eyes peering out through glasses smudged from being removed too many times in response to too many dubious courtroom antics.

"Sorry, Your Honour. I clearly digress. Strike those comments, please,"

Reiner directed the court recorder. He looked down at his notes. "You've worked quite a bit with young girls, haven't you, Detective, when you were in the... let's see, Juvenile Prostitution Task Force, wasn't it?"

"Yes."

"And these were girls involved in the sex trade, correct?"

"Yes."

"Any as young as ten or eleven?"

"Yes."

"So even without all of this research, from your experience, Detective, would it be fair to say that some girls, even as young as eleven, let's say, are sexually active?"

"Not the girls I've dealt with. No, not by choice."

"Really? Well, maybe not in your experience, but if Your Honour will refer to the materials I'm providing," Reiner handed a folder of documents up to the court clerk, "you will see that it's not unusual for an eleven-year-old girl to develop crushes, start having sexual fantasies, and actually actively seek out a sexual partner."

Mike looked over at Bridget, who was madly jotting something down on the pad of yellow foolscap in front of her.

Passing another folder of papers to the clerk, Reiner said, "I have here notes from the therapist Jessica had been seeing in the two years prior to the incident that has brought us here today. It would seem that Jessica expressed a strong interest in sexual activity that worried her parents, Cindy and Gregory Sanderson. Now, Detective, have you ever made a mistake?"

"Yes."

"Have you ever overlooked something?"

"Yes."

"By all accounts, though, you are a good, thorough, caring investigator. Would you agree?"

"Yes."

"But you didn't know, prior to perhaps just a few moments ago, that Jessica's mother never used her married surname, did you, Detective?"

"No." *Strike one.*

"So you wouldn't know that Jessica was also sometimes known as Jessica Jacobs, specifically with reference to any ob-gyn files, would you, Detective?"

"No." *Strike two.*

"Did you know that Jessica was sexually active?"

"Well..."

"Of course, Detective, you would know. She had a baby, didn't she?" Reiner turned momentarily to the jury with a deprecating grin on his face.

He turned back to Mike. "Let me rephrase. Did you know that Jessica Sanderson, aka Jessica Jacobs, had been sexually active with age-appropriate boys since the time she was about eleven years old?"

"According to my interviews—"

"Yes or no, Detective, if you please?"

"No." *Strike three and he's out!*

"And she did know," Reiner released the lectern and stepped back from it, ready to move towards the jury box, "that she was pregnant because she had told her mother three months before the baby was born that she had been missing her period. And that her mother had taken her to the doctor, who confirmed that she was, in fact, pregnant. Isn't that correct, officer?"

"Not that I'm aware of." Mike tried to keep his voice steady as anger welled up inside of him.

"And," the lawyer continued, throwing this comment over his shoulder as he sauntered towards the jury, "that she and her mother had been to the Children's Aid office a month prior to the birth of the baby, Jerome, to negotiate an adoption...or rather, fostering process within the family?"

Mike looked blankly at Reiner and the jury.

"Did you know that?" the lawyer asked Mike.

"No, I did not."

"It was, truth be told, my client who was the one who was unaware that his little girl was pregnant," Reiner informed the jury. A look of confusion swept through the box.

"That's not true," Mike stated flatly.

Bridget's eyes darted back and forth between the stunned detective and the defence attorney, as much bewildered by these allegations as Mike was.

She could feel the glare of the jury on her, as if she had somehow tried to dupe them with all of the evidence she had so meticulously presented over the past several months. There was nothing she could do at this point except to let this one play itself out.

"I have the Children's Aid records here, Your Honour." Reiner hustled back to the lectern. "Exhibit 3h for the record, I believe, Madam Clerk? And I have medical records for my client here. Exhibit 3i for the record. And I have a statement from Cindy Jacobs, Jessica's mother, stating that she knew her daughter was pregnant, had ensured regular check-ups with an ob-gyn, including ultrasounds, et cetera, here. Exhibit 3j for the record." Reiner extracted three folders from his pile and handed them, one by one, to the court clerk for filing.

Mike had to clutch his memo book to stop himself from dropping it as he watched the clerk accept the three folders from Reiner. *I spoke to Children's Aid. I subpoenaed all their files. Read through each and every page. Nothing about a visit from the mother and daughter.*

"You will note, Your Honour," Reiner said smugly, "that Jessica Sanderson is known as Jessica Jacobs. You *did* uncover that obvious fact in your investigation, didn't you, Detective O'Shea?"

Rookie mistake. Fuck.

"Detective?" the judge prompted, suddenly appearing interested in the matter before him.

"No, I did not."

"And what do we know about this baby? Rest assured, my friends..." Reiner waltzed back over to the jury box, as if he was rejoining friends at a social function, the smile on his face increasing with each step. "Jerome Jacobs, as he is known, is living with Andrea Sanderson, Jessica's aunt. I personally spoke to her last week, and she advises that the boy has four teeth, is almost walking, and is exceptionally fond of a stuffed rabbit named Binky that the woman known to him as his Aunt Jessica gave him when he was born."

What the fuck?

"It would appear that the picture that the Court has presented is very different from the truth, wouldn't you say, Detective?" Reiner smirked at

Mike, encouraging the jury with a casual gesture of his hand to join him in his joke.

Mike had given up on finding the right page in his memo book.

"Your Honour, I would submit to you that the matter that brings us here today—that has brought us here for weeks—is the result of the unintentional, albeit damning, words of a young girl who found herself in the unfortunate situation of an unplanned teenage pregnancy. For reasons we may never know, this clearly troubled young girl made the decision to create a damning but untrue story that she repeated to her mother, the police, and now to you, the jury, about who the father of her child is. And now Jessica Jacobs-Sanderson lies in a hospital bed on life support, which is the true tragedy before us today. Wouldn't you agree, Detective O'Shea?"

Mike glanced at Reiner in disbelief before looking at the jury, recalling the little boy with the plastic dinosaur he had interviewed last week, thinking about the numerous interviews with similar little boys and girls that he had lined up for the following weeks. Thinking, too, of the young girls on the stroll. And about how he knew they were all tied in to this accused. And how this accused was tied into Malcolm. And Sal.

"I believe the defence has asked a question, Detective," the judge prompted.

"No, I don't agree. My investigation—" Mike began, only to be interrupted by Reiner.

"Is flawed, Detective. You've been fooled. Duped. Hoodwinked. Not because you are a bad person, but because the complainant lied. I have no further questions, Your Honour."

Not waiting to be excused, Reiner quickly gathered up his loose papers from the lectern and rejoined his grinning client at the defence table, leaving layers of doubt in the minds of the jurors.

"Ms. Calloway?" The judge's eyebrows lifted.

"I have no further questions of Detective O'Shea," Bridget conceded as she rose from behind her table, chin up, back straight.

"Adjourned until after lunch then," the judge grumbled, getting up without further notice, leaving the court clerk to once again scramble to get everyone in the room on their feet before His Honour disappeared from his perch.

206

Chapter Thirty-Three

1:45 p.m., Tuesday, October 16, 2018

B ridget stomped down the hallway back to the Crown's office, purse squeezed tightly under her right arm, Crown brief crushed up against her body. "Reiner is a fucking asshole."

Taking long strides to keep pace with her, Mike admitted, "No, I did a shitty investigation."

Bridget continued to seethe, ignoring Mike's acceptance of blame. "That fucker could have stopped with the DNA argument. Or the sexually active one. Or the ob-gyn files. But no, he had to hammer it home in front of this judge to make me look as unprepared as possible. Fucker!"

"I'm not following."

"Reiner disclosed to me during the lunch break that he has been retained by Mark Johnstone."

"*My* Mark Johnstone?"

"Amanda Black's. You're one of the victims this time, remember? And Reiner seems to think that this judge will be presiding over that case, too."

"So he wants to make me look stupid and you to look...?"

"Incompetent. Did you know that he asked me out for drinks a couple of years ago?"

"Reiner?"

"No, the judge. We'd just finished a ten-week attempt murder trial. I had to take my father to the hospital. Not like I would have gone out with him anyway. And he's married, or at least he was at the time. Regardless, I'm not taking the case. I've already told my boss. For the first time ever, I'm going to pull the family-commitment card. Dad is too sick for me to commit to another long trial."

"Really?"

"Yeah. You know, I should have reported him to the Law Society back then. But I was young and naive." Bridget juggled the Crown brief so she could punch in the entry code. "Not like that was the first time a married man thought he could seduce me with a free drink. Nothing is free, Mike. My mother told me that a long time ago. Speaking of mothers, how's yours?"

"Great. Leaving soon hopefully." Mike thought about the upheaval Mary-Margaret was causing in his otherwise uneventful personal life, not counting, of course, his pending divorce.

"Her *Wee Michael* all better?" Bridget mocked, opening the heavy door that separated the Crown lawyers from the public riffraff.

"Something like that."

"So I guess I'll see you around?"

"Sure." Mike wanted to ask her to lunch but decided against it. Instead, the two stood awkwardly at the door to the Crown's office, acting like a couple of timid teenagers ending an early date.

* * *

Recognizing his home phone number, Mike grabbed the receiver of the ringing phone on his desk without taking his coat off or sitting down. He gave Ron a cursory nod of acknowledgment. "What's up, Max?"

"Ach, Michael," Mary-Margaret began, "it's yer mother. I'm sorry to be callin' ye like this, but I tried yer mobile several times and there was no answer." Mike pulled his cell phone from his pocket and saw that there were, in fact, several missed calls from a blocked phone number. *Shit.*

"Is something wrong, Mom?"

"Everything is fine now, son. I was at the hospital when I was callin', but don't worry. I'm home here now. A young fella from yer work gave me a drive. Lovely lad by the name of Preston. Says he knows ye. I tried to call Max, but the youngster's in school, of course."

"What happened?" Mike snaked out of his coat and deposited it on his desk, noticing that someone had replaced his desk chair with one whose seat was stained with spilled coffee or something much more sinister.

"I was walkin' Sally-next-door's wee pup at that leash-free park around the corner from ye, don't ye know, when it must have gotten startled and just plowed into me. Next thing I know, I'm on the ground, and me ankle is on fire."

"How big is this *wee pup?*" Mike spotted his chair by the grouping of desks just behind his, and kicking away the offending imposter, quickly swapped it out for his own chair. Ron, watching, shook his head in disgust at the overall condition of the dilapidated investigative office.

"No more than a pound. Well, no, that's not entirely true. Five or six pounds maybe. Anyway, doctor says it wasn't the size of the dog, just the way it came at me."

Mike was focused more on getting comfortable in his newly retrieved chair than he was to his mother's words. He was brought back to the matter at hand by a peal of laughter on the other end of the line. "What's so funny?"

"I probably shouldn't be saying this to ye, my son, but this won't be the first time it wasn't the size but the way it came at me that got me in trouble."

"Thanks for that, Mom." Mike looked across his desk and rolled his eyes at Ron, who was busying himself shuffling papers, trying not to eavesdrop. "So what happens now?"

"Well, I'm to go back in six weeks and they'll take this cast off and give me a walkin' cast, all things being equal."

"A cast?" Mike logged on to his computer, then noticed a sticky note affixed to the top right corner of the monitor.

"Well, I've broken me right foot, luv! Now don't worry about a thing. Max is going to take me back to me house tonight."

"Why?" Mike pulled the note down, glanced at it, then tightly crumpled it up and tossed it into the overflowing waste basket beside his desk.

"Because I want to be home. Amidst me own things. I've stayed long enough with ye. Life goes on, dontcha know?"

"Mom," Mike refocused, trying to shrug off the message on the sticky note, "you've broken your foot. You can't drive. You probably can barely walk. You are not going home now."

"Ach, I didn't think of that. It's the drivin', isn't it? How will I get to me yoga if I can't drive? But then again, I suppose I won't be goin' to me yoga if me foot is broken, will I? Well, that settles it. I'll get Max to drop by me place nonetheless to pick up some clothes I'll be needin'."

"What clothes could you possibly need, Mom? You have a closet-full at my place now."

"Well, I'll need me funeral dress and shoes and bag for starts. And then my—"

"Stop right there, Mom. Whose funeral are you going to?" Looking over at the trash basket, Mike considered the pros and cons of giving Amanda Black a call to let her know that Janelle Austin was asking about Sibby Mac's funeral. *Likely going to crash it. Vultures feeding off others' misfortunes.*

"Sibby Mac's, Michael. It's on Friday, and this is Tuesday."

"How do you know this? You don't even know Sibby Mac."

"Mandy told me."

"Who?"

"Mandy. The girl ye work with. Michael, yer memory seems to be failin' ye. Are ye sure ye shouldn't just pack it up for the day and come home?"

Mike shook his head, at a complete loss for words. Ron sent a questioning look across at him, having abandoned any pretense of not eavesdropping.

"I called her from the hospital," Mary-Margaret stated, and then when there was no reply from Mike, she continued slowly, spelling it out as if he were five years old again. "Well, she gave me her number the other day, Mandy did, and said to call if I needed anything. I couldn't get a hold of ye so—"

"So you called the officer-in-charge of a homicide I'm working on who also happens to be my boss at the moment?" Mike tried not to holler into the receiver or, more importantly, yell at his mother, but failed miserably.

Ron shook his finger disapprovingly at Mike. "Don't yell at your mother."

"Well, what else was I supposed to do?" *Oh shit, now I've put her back up,* Mike groaned to himself.

"Ye weren't picking up, and Max was in school. Who did I have left to call?"

"Oh, I don't know. Teaszy? Paulie? Someone other than Detective Sergeant Black?"

"Well, of course, we can think of that now, can't we?" Mary-Margaret muttered. "But at that moment, Mandy's name came into me head. She was at an autopsy when I called. Not at all like what we see on the tellie, she said. I told her I don't bother with that rubbish. The tellie, that is. Anyway, she was busy and suggested I call a taxi instead, and that's when I saw the young lad in uniform and I said to meself, 'Mary-Margaret, that sharp young man likely knows our Michael. Why don't ye go over and say hello?' And so I did. And he does know ye, too. And he offered me a lift. Lovely young man, that Preston."

"Mom…" Mike began. *Shit, why am I whining? I sound like a five-year-old.*

"Ye know, it's a shame Mandy is married to someone else. She'd make a fine wife for ye, Michael. When she and Ronnie were over for dinner on Sunday, I saw it, and I'm sure I wasn't the only one at the table who did."

"Mom!"

"In any event, I'm home here now at yer house, safe and sound, but I'm hangin' up me phone. All of this yammerin' you've been doing about the case and Mandy has made me forget to keep me foot up. Ta-ra for now, luv."

* * *

Paul Landon poked his head into the D office. "Got a minute, Mike?"

"Sure, boss," Mike replied.

"See you up in my office in two."

Ron rolled his eyes as he looked over at Mike. "Good luck!"

Then it was Mike's turn to roll his eyes as he walked past Ron to head upstairs to the unit commander's office.

* * *

"Sit down, Mike," Landon directed, at the same time adjusting his uniform pants as he seated himself behind his desk, the sound of a toilet still flushing in the background. "One of the perks of my job, I suppose. I can piss in a private bathroom. Can I get you a coffee?"

"No, thanks. I'm fine." Mike settled into the all-too-familiar visitor's wingback chair. "What's up?"

Landon stood up. "How well do you know Karl Hageneur?"

"Well enough. Why?"

"I have a sensitive issue here. No, wait. Let me start that again. As you know, this organization draws its strength from keeping up with the times." Landon walked around his desk to sit in the wingback chair next to Mike's.

"I'm going to cut to the chase here." He took a deep breath. "I need a good, strong partner for Karl."

Mike looked blankly at his unit commander.

"As I'm sure you know, Ron Roberts's wife is not well," Landon began again. "Ron has spoken to me in confidence, but I feel I can trust you, and you will find out soon enough if you don't already know. Ron is planning on retiring very soon."

Mike continued to stare blankly.

"You will need a new partner. This is Karl's last day with us as Karl."

"You lost me there, boss."

"Karl is going to take the next three months off. Combination sick leave and holidays. When he comes back, he will be Carla. He has self-identified to me and the Service that he is a transgender woman who is going to present as his...uh, her gender of choice upon his...that is, her return."

"Hmm."

"I thought that you would be the best person for *her* to work with upon *her* return and just wanted to let you know that, unless there are any reasons that I cannot imagine, *she* will be your new permanent partner when *she* returns."

"How good is *her* case prep?" Mike asked, mimicking Landon's emphasis on the female pronoun. He remembered the days when a woman—any woman—in the investigative office was an oddity, and it really didn't matter to him who his partner was as long as he or she pulled their weight.

"You know, I honestly don't know." Landon smiled, confident that Carla was right: Mike *was* the right choice.

"Has she had all the courses, or will I be working alone until she gets caught up?"

"That's a very good question." Landon went over to the door to ask his secretary to pull Hageneur's file, his step almost jaunty with relief.

"With all due respect, sir…"

"Paul," he smiled broadly at Mike. *I have* made the right choice. *Hot spit!*

"Paul, I'm swamped now. If I'm going to be on my own for the next three or four months, I need Karl…sorry, Carla to be ready to hit the ground running."

"Yes, of course." Landon nodded emphatically in agreement. The relief in his voice was palpable now.

"And it's not fair to her. I mean, if she hasn't got the qualifications, then this isn't the place for her."

"Well, that's the thing, Mike. Apparently, she will require some accommodation for medical reasons when she returns. As you know, we are mandated to accommodate…you know. Not that we wouldn't anyway."

"So why not leave her as a sergeant on one of the platoons? She can stay inside for a while. She knows that job. Why make it harder for her by putting her in a position where she doesn't have the training?"

Landon sighed heavily. "Well, that's the other thing, Mike." He sounded embarrassed. "I trust that all of my people would treat a fellow officer—or anyone, really—with dignity and respect, but some of us have a long way to go yet. I know that you will do the right thing."

"Hmm."

"Mike, I personally have no issue with Karl becoming Carla. It's none of my business. And darned good on her for being who she really is. It's just that—"

"It's okay, boss. I get it."

The unit commander gave a big smile of relief.

"It's just that I need a good partner. I've got the Johnstone homicide coming up. Black is the officer in charge of it, obviously, but that's likely going to involve a bit of court time, and I've got this kiddy-diddler investigation on the go. Lots of interviews to be done on that one. And then there's this Sibby Mac—"

"Who or what is a Sibby Mac?"

"Elizabeth MacDonald. Everyone calls her Sibby Mac." *Oh God, I'm sounding like my mother.* "Anyway, I've got a fuck-ton of work without taking into account the shit the guys bring in off the road every day. Ron and I can handle it, but if he's retiring—"

"Yes, he is retiring. Sadly." Landon fumbled with his pen.

"I'll make sure everything keeps running smoothly on my end, then."

"I'm going to speak to every officer in the station during parade over the next couple of weeks to outline what my expectations are, and I'm following that up with a trans community member coming in to speak to each platoon on their training days. Is there anything you think I'm missing here, Mike?"

"I don't understand. Like what?"

"This is all new to me. To us. To the organization. I've got the chief telling me I've got to make this work, but no one is telling me how to do it. I'm asking you, man to man, what else I can do?"

"Are you asking me how to manage a career move?"

"No. I've been given the opportunity to help another human being self-actualize. I'm asking you to help me make it so. My father was a preacher. I'm not a religious man, but I *am* following in his footsteps in terms of spirituality. I have been given a tremendous opportunity to help someone—one of my own—and I don't want to squander it."

"What does Carla want?"

"She actually asked specifically to work with you, Mike. She didn't say anything about you that I didn't already know or suspect. As well as being an awfully good detective, you're a good man. The people around here respect you. They listen to you. I need your leadership now. I can't order you or tell you to help me, but I'm sure as Hades asking."

"When does she leave?"

"I think she may be gone now. After she came in to tell me this morning, I told her to take the day or do whatever she wanted. She has the rest of the week off already, and then she's gone until the end of the year. I don't know if she's booked off or not. I can call her on the air if you'd like?"

"No, it's okay. I just wanted to wish her well. I imagine this is a pretty big deal."

"I imagine. You are a good man, Mike. But I shan't keep you. Detective Sergeant Black will be pounding on my door pretty soon if you don't get back down there to help her out." He stood to signal the end of the meeting.

Mike got up and shook the outstretched hand.

"I mean it, Mike. You're a good man. And I am tremendously lucky to have you. Thank you."

* * *

"There's a woman here to see you, Detective. I told her you were busy but...." Preston McAfee, standing behind the front counter in his crisp uniform and glistening boots, half-whispered to Mike coming down the stairs from Landon's office. Mike took a side-glance at the woman seated on the radiator cover picking at her scabby legs, recognizing her as someone he had known for a long time.

"What are you doing inside?" Mike turned his attention to the young officer.

"Hand. Hurt it making an arrest." Preston held up his bandaged right hand as evidence.

"Were you at the hospital earlier today, by any chance?"

"Yeah. I had to pick up some records for my injury report. Saw your mom. She's really nice."

"Thanks for driving her home."

"Oh, no problem, Detective. She's so proud of you!"

"I bet," Mike replied awkwardly. "Got your notes in for the Johnstone case? Detective Sergeant Black says the prelim is coming up very quickly."

"Already done. I saw Detective Sergeant Black already. She just came in from doing some press thing outside. She said you and Detective Roberts are working on another homicide with her. Is that your guy in the cells?"

Mike chuckled to himself. He wanted to say *no shit, Sherlock*, but being sarcastic with Preston was like shooting fish in a barrel. The kid was just so damned earnest. And eager. *If only all of the new kids were like him.*

"Mikey?" a broken, familiar voice called out.

"Good afternoon, Lisa," Mike casually replied, giving this shadow of a woman perhaps the only smile she would receive that day.

"Haven't seen you around lately. They told me you were off. You look like shit. You okay, hon?"

Mike made his way to the front counter, standing firmly on the cop side of the barrier. "A little busy, Lisa. You slept lately?"

"Fuck no, Mikey. You know better'n to ask me that! I got a fucking habit to support." Lisa laughed.

"So I see. Still on that shit, eh?" It was a rhetorical question. The ravages of crystal meth were obvious. Mike had known Lisa since his Juvenile Prostitution Task Force days. She was a good-looking girl back then. First pimp must have made a fortune off her before she got fucked up. They tried to get her back to her family, back to something real, but it was too late. Hard drugs and a series of violent boyfriends—johns and pimps—had become her family.

"Hey. Word is that Robby finally did a header. That true?"

"He slipped," Mike corrected. *Word travels.*

"Ha! They *all* slip, don't they? Georgia. Brenda. Baby-Girl. And now Robby. It's the lifestyle, man. The booze. The drugs. The johns. I guess it's the same for you guys, too, eh? Except no johns. Ha!" Lisa cackled, startling the middle-aged civilian station operator who had been watching the crack whore from behind her desk well behind the front counter. She rolled her eyes before turning her attention back to her computer monitor.

"I guess." *How the hell are you still alive with all the shit you've pushed and snorted?*

"You and Robby were the best, man. Remember when you two pulled fucking Strumpy offa me? 'Member him? Fucking asshole. We had a kid together, you know. Some fucking doctors in Forest Hill probably raising her now. Probably going to one of those all-girls' schools. All I gots is the ring he gave me, see? I wear it here to remind me of him." Lisa held up the middle finger of her bony left hand to display a chunky ring that, had it been plastic, could have come from a bubble-gum machine. Then she broke into a scratching frenzy. "Goddamn bugs under my skin, Mikey. This shit is killing me."

"I have to get back to work, Lisa."

"I know." Moment of lucidity. "I just wanted to see you. And say I'm sorry about Robby."

"Thanks. Take care of yourself, eh?"

Lisa bounced out of the station, higher than a kite. Mike turned to walk back to his office, doubting that she had a clue where any of her children were, much less one who might have been lucky enough to find her way into a family that would send her to an all-girls' private school.

Chapter Thirty-Four

5:03 a.m., Wednesday, October 17, 2018

Placing his cell phone carefully on the counter, Mike looked at his reflection in his bathroom mirror. Still half asleep, he rubbed one hand along his cheeks, trying to decide whether or not he wanted to start sporting a beard. Bridget thought beards made men look more masculine. *That is* what *she said, wasn't it?* But the habit of shaving was too strong, and he ended up giving in to it.

Then he made his way to the kitchen and was surprised not to see his mother there. While it was nice not to have to discuss the merits of a good breakfast every morning, he felt badly for her present condition. As he poured himself a coffee for the road, however, he began to feel more concerned about his own predicament. Mary-Margaret was not a young woman, by any stretch of the imagination. *Six weeks in a cast, that's what she said. And what if it doesn't heal properly? What if she can never go home to her own house?*

Mulling over the possibility that his mother would never leave, Mike quietly locked the front door behind him and nodded a polite hello to an early-morning jogger before settling in to put the truck in drive.

As the truck seemed to make its own way towards the station, he took a sip of the hot coffee, burning the tip of his tongue and cursing as he did every dayshift morning. But today was different. Stopping at a red light, he decided to vary his morning routine by switching on his turn indicator to head north instead of west.

The truck pulled up a couple of doors down from the Sobatics house. Maybe it was a subconscious yearning for his old plainclothes days when he would stake out an address for days, or maybe it was something else that brought Mike to where he was. Regardless, he turned the engine off and slouched down just enough to become one with the interior of the truck, or at the very least, to look as if he was sleeping as the trickle of housekeepers and nannies trudged by him towards their employers' homes.

No Tahoe. Still not returned or just in the garage? Or was it parked in the driveway in front of the mistress's house in Ottawa?

Mike looked down at his watch, taking another sip of the cooling coffee while rolling his window down a couple of inches. *5:58. Should be at my desk. Should head in now or give Ron a quick call to let him know where I am.*

He took another sip of coffee. *No. Hang tight.*

As he was fidgeting with his thoughts, a big SUV almost sideswiped him as it barreled by, the driver gunning for the curb just ahead of Mike. The Tahoe then cut across the sidewalk, barely missing a middle-aged woman carrying a large purse and a shopping bag. It came to an abrupt stop on the lawn several feet beyond where she had just walked.

The deep treads that would surely scar Sobatics's front lawn for several weeks to come were just the calling card Mike had been hoping for.

Falling back on his training, he suppressed the urge to leap out of his truck, waiting instead to see what the other vehicle would reveal. Within seconds, Mike saw the driver and lone occupant, the man he recognized from the photos as James Sobatics, practically fall out of the front seat, fumble to maintain his balance as he hit the ground, and then fling himself towards the front door of the house.

Pissed or stoned? Hell, maybe both.

Mike watched his mark fumble his keys in the lock, finally giving in to banging on the door with clenched fists. A light in an upper-floor front window turned on. *Must be Katherine's bedroom.* He saw the curtains shift slightly as he imagined whoever was in the room looked out to the street. A few moments later, he saw the front door open a sliver.

She's left the chain on. Doesn't want him in. Mike remembered her saying that her husband was a violent drunk.

Despite the otherwise peaceful morning air, Mike couldn't quite make out the words, but he knew by the tone of Sobatics's voice that this was not a happy homecoming. Mike watched the door close and then open enough for Sobatics to push his way in. Its forceful slamming causes the nearby newspaper delivery man to pause before hopping back into his car to carry on with his route.

Torn between his initial intention to remain a witness and his natural instinct to protect, Mike succumbed to the latter, his extensive experience with both drunks and domestics making him fairly confident that things would likely end badly for Katherine if he stayed out of it.

He slid quickly out of the driver's seat and ran up to the house. As he approached, his instincts were vindicated. He could hear Sobatics's bellows through the double-bricked walls. He couldn't quite catch what the man was saying, but the emotion was clear.

Reaching into his jacket pocket and coming up empty, Mike realized he had no means to call for backup. He had left his cell phone at home, likely on the bathroom counter. *Shit shit shit!* He considered knocking on a neighbour's door but figured this was the type of neighbourhood where nobody opens their door to a stranger, particularly at this hour in the morning.

A woman's scream cut short his thoughts. The time to call for backup was over.

Throwing his full weight behind his shoulder, Mike tried to break down the front door. He bounced off the door once, twice, three times. He tried once again, and the fourth time was a charm. Powered by adrenaline, he sprang off the splintered wooden door frame and into the house, careful not to stumble on the pieces of the deadbolt lock still spinning on the hardwood floor beyond him. Orienting himself to the sounds of the argument, Mike raced up the stairs to the second floor, oblivious to the burning pain in his shoulder.

He immediately saw that one of the bedroom doors had been pulled off its hinges and lay broken in the hallway between Mike and the screaming.

Dancing around the wreckage, he took advantage of the open doorway to pull himself into the bedroom, catching his left hand on one of the tattered hinges. The pain in his hand caught his attention long enough for him to bring it up to his face, allowing the blood from a significant gash to run down into the sleeve of his jacket. *Good thing I'm not wearing a wedding ring. I'd probably lose my finger.*

Not ten feet from where he stood, Mike could see Sobatics straddling his wife's body on the bed, one hand pinning her wrists against the headboard, the other around her slender neck.

"I...swear to...God," Katherine choked out, struggling to buck her husband off of her, "I never...meant for it...to go like...this."

"You fucking cunt," Sobatics spat. "You women are all just fucking cunts!"

Leaning away from her face, he shifted his weight so that now he was exerting more pressure on the hand around her neck.

"James...stop!" Katherine croaked out desperately as the pressure increased around her throat.

"Shut the fuck up, bitch."

Before Mike could move, Sobatics pulled his hand from Katherine's neck, and making a fist, smashed it into her face. Mike could hear the sound of breaking bones and crushed cartilage. He saw the blood gushing from her face.

It was more the element of surprise and Sobatics being off-balance than Mike's actual strength that allowed the detective to yank the raging man off his wife and onto the floor beside the bed. Mike saw how the pastel pillowcase under Katherine's now-motionless head was turning a crimson red, and the vivid image of Sal, his head blown apart and blood everywhere, flashed before his eyes. *Oh God, am I too late again?*

A roundhouse punch to his ribs brought Mike back to reality as Sobatics, still in a berserker rage, scrambled to get on top of him. Oblivious to the swelling in his shoulder and the pain in his torn left hand, Mike clutched his opponent's body, forcing Sobatics back down onto the floor, the blood from the open wound on Mike's hand now competing with the blood from Katherine's ruined face on Sobatics's shirt.

While neither man was in his prime, Mike was surprised at Sobatics's strength and agility. Based on the photos he'd seen of the former politician, he was under the impression that Sobatics was an average middle-aged man with little or no proclivity to hand-to-hand combat. Now he found himself wrestling with not only a drunk, but a drunk who, unlike Mike himself, likely went to the gym regularly.

As his adrenaline gave way to fatigue, Mike became aware that his right arm was dangling, probably due to a dislocated shoulder, while his left hand was badly injured. As he felt another jab at his kidneys, he realized that the only way to win this fight was to keep Sobatics close enough to prevent his punches from gaining momentum until Mike could reciprocate with lethal precision. The two men rolled around like a couple of bear cubs for several minutes, each unwilling to give up his grip on the other. This was no playful romp, however; each was trying to force the other's head into a corner or a door frame in an attempt to subdue, in Mike's case, or to kill, in Sobatics's.

To break the stalemate, Mike, in desperation, cracked Sobatics's head with his own. Rather than achieving the desired outcome, however, the sight of blood gushing from Mike's forehead seemed to create a greater sense of urgency for Sobatics. He pushed Mike off of him and rolled on top, freeing up his arms for another attack. Mike could feel Sobatics's fists pounding on his head, reigniting the pain his encounter with a lead pipe a couple of months earlier had left him with. *Except this time, no one is coming to help me. Shit shit shit!*

It was now a fight to the death. All bets were off.

Mike poked at Sobatics's head with his bloodied hand to distract him while scanning the room for something—anything—that could be used to land that one debilitating blow. *That's all I've got left in me. Shit!*

Frantically, he looked for something to knock Sobatics out with. A lamp. A nightstand. A handful of jewelry even.

And then he saw it—the weapon he was looking for—sitting to one side on the dressing table: a vintage art deco telephone, its heavy receiver calling out to him. Wielding his makeshift weapon, he lunged for Sobatics. The first blow glanced off Sobatics's head with little to no effect. Without giving

Sobatics time to respond, Mike smashed the receiver down on his head a second time, stunning the man. The third made the sound of a melon hitting the ground. The fourth, fifth, and sixth were, Mike realized, probably gratuitous: Sobatics was down for the count.

Mike collapsed on the floor against another blood-splattered wall to catch his breath, two people lying dead or near-death within spitting distance of him. His head and body throbbed with pain.

And then he chuckled. *Oh fuck. Mom's going to take one look at me and have her mail redirected to my house.*

Mike took another look around and then dragged himself over to the bed to check Katherine's vitals. Relieved to find that she had a pulse and that the bleeding had slowed, he reluctantly crossed over to where her husband lay, the blood still oozing from his head wounds.

Seeing Sobatics's chest rise and fall, Mike knew he was alive. Mike wasn't taking any chances though: The man was a suspected murderer first and a victim only second, so he instinctively patted Sobatics's body down to search for evidence or weapons. *You never know what these fuckers will do.*

Chapter Thirty-Five

"For the love of God, Mike," Amanda's voice rang out loud and clear, "can you show up at work for just a couple of days in a row without getting your head bashed in?"

"Sorry, boss," Mike said with a smile from the gurney, his head held immobile by a neck brace, the view of the ceiling in Emerg all too familiar. "You should see the other guy."

"I did. He's in serious condition. Better hope to hell he lives. Amy did too much work on this one to have our accused die."

"So he did it?"

"Oh, yes. Strands of his hair were all over her body."

"Lovely."

"We should have more murderers wrap their victims in plastic wrap. Stuff is great for preserving evidence."

"How is Katherine?"

"Critical, but alive."

"You're a rock star, Mikey!" Julia Vendramini announced as she yanked open the curtain that shielded Mike from the busy hallway.

"But *you* saved my life."

"Again?" Amanda said.

"If it wasn't for Julia," Mike explained, "Sobatics, the missus, and I would probably still be lying on their bedroom floor."

"The housekeeper would have found you." Julia set her huge black Prada purse down for a moment on the foot of Mike's gurney before pulling it closer to her body. "*Mingia Fach*. You never know what kind of germs you'll pick up in a place like this."

"How did *you* end up involved in this?" Amanda asked.

"Well, I was on my way home from the station and thought I'd stop in at the Diplomatico to pick up some *bruttiboni* for Keith and me to have with our espresso this morning before I went to bed. I couldn't find parking so I turned up one street and then another, and then I ended up on this street and thought I recognized Mikey's truck—"

"Because it's a shitbox?"

"Well, yes. Anyway, I'm thinking 'What's Mikey's truck doing here?' when I see a Tahoe dumped on the hacked-up lawn. I look a little closer and see that the house door has been smashed in, so—"

"You called for backup? Tell me you called for backup."

"Oh, *cara mia*, I've got a gun, pepper spray, and God only knows what else in this purse. I don't need backup." Julia laughed. "But I did call the station to let them know where I was. Anyway, I hear something up the stairs, and there's Mikey."

"So if Sobatics dies, I can always say that it was you who landed the fatal blow?" Mike asked.

"*Non chiedermi alcun segreto, non ti diro bugie*," Julia said with a smile. She pulled a paper bag from the depths of her purse. "Since it doesn't look like I'll be home any time soon, can I interest either of you in a—"

"Excuse me." A young man in scrubs pulled open the curtain. "There's a woman here who says she needs to speak to the patient. I think she's a reporter."

Amanda pivoted on her heel and marching out of the cubicle. "Leave this to me."

"And no food just yet, sir. We've got a few tests we want to run first."

"In that case, do you want one?" Julia said, holding out the bag of biscuits to the nurse.

"Don't mind if I do."

* * *

"Excuse me, Inspector?"

"Aren't we done with that game yet, Janelle?"

"Sorry?"

"Never mind. I'm assuming you want an update on James Sobatics's condition?"

"Sure, but first, what about Detective O'Shea? How is he? Let's get a soundbite or two about O'Shea that we can run for the 8:30. Camera up, Craig? Okay. Janelle Austin here at St. Mike's Hospital where I'm speaking with Detective Amanda Black—"

"Detective *Sergeant* Amanda Black."

Chapter Thirty-Six

7 p.m., Wednesday, October 17, 2018

"For the love of God, Michael!"

"It's not as bad as it looks."

"As what looks? Holy shit, Dad!" Max exclaimed when he saw Mike.

"Straight upstairs with ye, child!" Mary-Margaret commanded, teetering on her crutches but not taking her eyes off her son's face.

"Sorry, Gran," Max mumbled, aware that he had sworn in front of his grandmother.

"No, lad, I think that about sums it up," she conceded, leaning back to take a better look at Mike.

"It's not—" Mike began, frozen in the doorway.

"Max, put a kettle on for us, will ye? Yer da is clearly in need of a cuppa. And how did ye get yerself home, then?" Mary-Margaret looked out the door, trying to see past Mike.

"Taxi."

"Ach! Where's Ronnie"

"His wife—"

"Oh Jesus, Mary, and Joseph!" Mary-Margaret pulled the crutches in with her elbows as she crossed herself.

"No. Not yet, anyway. She's in a hospice and he—"

"Say no more. Sitcheedoon. Max, have ye got the tea, then?" Mary-

Margaret tried to lead Mike towards the nearest chair while Max scurried past them into the kitchen to plug the kettle in.

There was a faint knock on the open door.

"And who would this be then?" She twisted around and saw Carmen, Mike's estranged wife, in the doorway.

"Hello, Mary-Margaret. Surprised to see you here."

"I could say the same."

"Where's—? Shit, Mike, what happened?" Carmen pushed past Mary-Margaret to get a better look at Mike.

"If ye hadn't run off with yer boy-toy, ye would know, wouldn't ye?"

"Mom!" Mike cried, standing up.

"I'm just sayin' what we're all thinkin'. I'll just go and see how Max is gettin' on with that tea. Are ye stoppin' in or just come by to pick up yer remains? Ach, I hear the kettle screamin'. Sort yerselves out."

Carmen glared at the older woman hobbling towards the kitchen.

"I guess I should ask: Are you back or…?"

"I just thought I'd drop by. See how you are. See how—"

"How is life with the Little Shit?"

The two stood no more than a foot apart from one another, and yet worlds separated them.

"Meh. It's okay."

"All that glitters is not gold, Carmen?"

"That was uncalled for."

"Was it?"

"How long has your mother been here? Didn't take her long to move in, did it?" Carmen sniped, stepping back from Mike to look around the nearly empty space that had been her former home.

"She came to help."

"Always does, doesn't she?"

"Does it matter? Now?"

"No. I don't suppose it does. I was hoping that—"

"Look, Carmen, what do you want? I just got home from the hospital. And I'm on my way to bed. Alone." Mike shuffled towards the stairs, then turned and added, "But that was never my issue, was it?"

"If you're going to be—" Carmen called after him.

"If I'm going to be what?" Mike said calmly. "I think you should leave."

The two looked intently at each other, perhaps for the first time in many months.

"I'm sorry, Mike." Carmen's eyes softened and a slight smile crossed her lips as she lowered her head.

"I'm sure it's all for the best."

"Do you honestly believe that?"

"I honestly believed that we were married for life."

"We are. Still are, if that's what you want."

The two looked closely at each other again.

"It's done, Carmen. I think you should leave now."

Carmen looked at Mike before stepping towards the door. He watched her walk out on him for the second time.

As soon as Carmen was gone, Mary-Margaret called out from the kitchen. "Tea, luv? I've got these gorgeous almond biscuits that Julia dropped off this afternoon. Max is just bringin' them out. Did I mention that Julia dropped by? She looked very tired. Still no children. I canna believe that. God must have His blinders on. Such a lovely girl."

Mike turned and walked up the stairs without answering. He made his way to his bed and lay down without pulling down the covers or even taking off his clothes. He was asleep in no time.

"Time heals all, me son. Time heals all," Mary-Margaret said as she gently placed a quilt over him, giving him a kiss on his forehead before quietly hobbling out of the room, closing the door behind her.

"Max!" she called down to her grandson. "How do ye feel about drivin' me home to pick up Sally-next-door's dog? The wee thing needs to be walked tomorrow, but I'll not be in any shape to do it then or thereafter. Spoke to Sally-next-door, thinkin' ye might take the walkin' over for a wee while and we'd just bring the dog here, if yer willin'?"

Chapter Thirty-Seven

8 a.m., Monday, October 22, 2018

Mike looked up from his desk as Amanda walked into the investigative office. "Ron not coming in?"

"No. Dependent sick. Surprised to see *you* here, though."

"You know me: company man through and through. I see you've got Sobatics in the cells."

"Made a miraculous recovery. As soon as we get the bare-bones paperwork done, we'll get him off to court to be arraigned. In the meantime, I'm going to do a quick stand-up out front. How's my hair?"

"A little face time with your buddy Janelle Austin?"

"As if! Story's gone national. Everyone wants a piece of it."

"Great."

"Don't go too far. You're coming with me to court."

"Even better."

* * *

"Do all the roads you travel lead to my office, Detective?" Bridget asked Mike as she walked into the Crown's office, her trendy, overpriced designer purse dangling precariously close to the equally trendy and overpriced coffee in her left hand, litigation bag dragging behind her in her right.

"Hate to break it to you, Madam Crown Attorney, but I'm not here to see you today," Mike said with a grin, juggling a bankers box of files in his arms while using a foot to jam the door open for them both. *Holy shit, is that a slight look of dismay I saw on her face?*

"Thanks for carrying that, Mike. Richard wants— Oh, hello, Bridget," Amanda said from inside the Crown office reception area. She had already briefed the lawyer who would be running today's Show Cause court.

"Amanda," Bridget acknowledged with a nod, returning to her balancing act, surprised at herself for how awkward she felt at this moment.

"Just take that box over to that office, Mike." Amanda pointed to what had been a storage room up to about a week ago. Mike hesitated. "New guy on our case. Richard Wajowitz. Just transferred down from Newmarket courts. Poor bastard. Doesn't know what he's in for down here. He's got it all electronically, but I want him to see the actual photos. As far as we've come, you still can't beat an old-fashioned picture. Nice purse, Bridget. My husband got me one just like it for Christmas last year. Cost him a fortune. Totally worth it. I have several pairs of shoes by the same designer. Smashing. Mike?"

"Yes, dear." Mike dutifully followed Amanda, winking at Bridget as he intentionally brushed up against her, adding, "I'll be in 101, just in case the jury comes back early."

Bridget smiled. "I'll find you."

"Detective O'Shea. Richard Wajowitz." A diminutive eager young man thrust his well-manicured hand out, the cufflinks on his crisp white shirt managing to shine despite the inadequate overhead lighting. "Not at all like my office back in Newmarket, but it's a start. Word on the street is that you're a pretty good copper."

"Thank you." Mike held fast to the bankers box, not taking the extended hand. Tassel shoes, double-breasted suit, paisley tie, and stylishly unkempt beard. Another Little Shit.

"Well, great." The young Crown attorney withdrew his hand, turning his attention to Amanda. "I have to say, Detective Sergeant, I have my reservations about your matter."

"Oh, really?" Amanda said, her voice and the expression on her face barely able to hide her disdain.

"Circumstantial at best." He flipped through the paperwork in front of him. "Ex-lover can place Sobatics in the house. Dump employee can place his kid and his vehicle in possession of the trunk that held the body. Trying to bugger off to Australia doesn't help, but there's no crime in that. The most I'm seeing here is Indignity to a Human Body."

"With all due respect, my friend, I think all you need to do today is handle his bail. This is a circumstantial case, but I believe—and the JP who signed the Information believes—that there is enough evidence to proceed on the charge of murder."

"Far be it from me to argue with a Justice of the Peace, I suppose. Good call on the tie, Detective O'Shea. I would expect, given the media coverage you and this case have already had, that we will see a jammed courtroom."

"Not my first rodeo, Mr. Wajowitz. Is it yours?" Amanda asked with a smile.

"Hardly." The young lawyer looked pointed at Amanda, then at the stack of Crown briefs on his desk before looking back at Amanda. "I'll see you in 101 at ten, then. I won't be needing you, Detective."

Mike adjusted the bankers box as he and Amanda made their way down the worn marble stairs to courtroom 101. "Not making any friend on this one, are we?"

"Arrogant prick. Oh shit!" Amanda looked down at her cell phone. "Never a good morning when I get a call from home. Hello?"

Mike stepped away, giving her what little privacy one could expect outside of the still-locked bail court. Looking around, he saw the usuals: distraught parents with sleep-deprived eyes looking around frantically in an attempt to find something—someone—to ground them; friends who had received yet another early-morning call looking for a bail-out; cops in suits with briefcases, carrying a cup of the cheap coffee from the vending machine down the hall; girls on the verge of becoming women who already had that look of distrust bordering on hatred, carrying babies; a couple of too-thin women with steno pads, one of whom both Mike and Amanda recognized as Janelle Austin, bottom-feeding in the hope of stumbling across something to send back to their news outlets. Just a typical Monday morning in bail court.

"Is it that hard to pee on a goddamned stick?" Amanda said, returning to where Mike was standing. "My fucking kid, the one who has everything going for her, may be pregnant. How does that happen, Mike? How?"

"Well…" Mike began, adjusting the box so that it could rest on his belt buckle.

"I mean, she's training eight, ten, twelve hours a day. She's got a scholarship—a fucking scholarship, Mike!—lined up for the next four years in the States. She doesn't even have a boyfriend! This is *not* how this goes!" Amanda looked at the young women in the corridor with their babies and shook her head.

"Has she peed on the stick?"

"She won't do it. Not with just Tony home. Afraid of what he'll do. Wants to wait for me. Like she shouldn't be more afraid of me."

Mike nodded in agreement.

"Don't get me wrong, Mike. I love children. They're wonderful. My children are wonderful. They really are. But this? She doesn't even have a boyfriend!" Amanda repeated the last phrase, as if that would clearly disqualify her daughter from the pregnancy group.

"Don't need a boyfriend to get pregnant."

"You are *so* lucky to have a son." Amanda glanced anxiously at her phone. "Fuck! Now she's not returning my texts."

"Give the kid a chance. If she's pregnant, she'll be pregnant tonight. Wait till you get home. Have a nice dinner together. A heart-to-heart. It will all work out."

Amanda was about to say something but stopped short. "Is that Janelle Austin over there? Tell me it's not. Oh God, Mike. I want to choke that woman out."

"There's nothing you can do right now," Mike continued calmingly. "You know this. I get that you're surprised. I'd be surprised. But nothing is going to change right now. And besides, how do you think she feels?"

"Scared to death. My poor baby." Amanda looked at Mike. "You know, for a guy who lives with his mother and can barely dress himself... Thank you. By the way, how is your mother?"

"Broke her foot."

"Oh no. Well, tell her I'll be by tomorrow morning around ten to pick her up."

"Why?"

"We're going to Sibby Mac's funeral together. Anyhow, here's our illustrious Crown. Let's get in quickly so we don't have to talk to anyone or sit in the back."

Bail court was always stuffy. And stinky, particularly on a Monday. The room itself was arguably the smallest in the courthouse, but its direct access to the cells continued to make it the logical choice for in-custody appearances. Extensive discussions about expanding the room or rejigging the passageways to facilitate an unencumbered entry into a larger room had taken place over the years, but to no avail. As a result, those who lacked ties to the community, or were recidivists, or were charged with crimes deemed to be overly dangerous to the public safety, or just did not play well with others were paraded before the sitting Justice of the Peace, who would then decide whether they would be released to friends or family or returned to the overcrowded prison cells pending their next court appearance.

Uniformed court officers brought up the prisoners three at a time, in alphabetical order, handcuffed together in a daisy chain. When a name was called, the court officer would remove the shackles from the prisoner's wrists and hand him forward to the waiting guard, who would hand back the offender who had just had his matter spoken to, ensuring that there were always three men chained together. There would be a slight pause in the proceedings as one team took their group of three back to the cell area and another team brought up their trio. Occasionally, the wrong prisoner would be brought forward, much to the consternation of the sitting JP, who would either sigh patiently or admonish the guards for not having their prisoners in order.

Seeing James Sobatics among the rabble made Mike happy. Not as disheveled as most but certainly not his picture-perfect self, the accused murderer waited with every other criminal for his name to be called. As predicted, a family friend was there to post bail and take responsibility for him. Aside from acknowledging before the court that the lead investigator was present, the Crown did not object to releasing Sobatics with the appropriate bail conditions. Arraigned, bailed, and gone in about three minutes.

Mike and Amanda rose, bowed ceremoniously, and then left the court-room, immediately followed by both of the reporters they had noticed hanging around.

"Detective Sergeant Black, what are your thoughts on James Sobatics being released on bail?" a man from one of the national newspapers asked.

"I trust that His Worship took all factors into consideration and the correct decision was made."

"Is it true that the victim picked Sobatics up on a chat line?" Janelle Austin asked.

"No. It's not true." Amanda continued to walk away.

Janelle followed closely behind Amanda, tape recorder in hand. "Would you say that her lifestyle played heavily in the motive for murder?"

"No, I wouldn't." Amanda stepped around the reporter, making her way past the friends and family who could not get into the overcrowded bail court. "That box must be getting heavy. Let's take the elevator, Mike."

"Detective Sergeant, Elizabeth MacDonald, as I'm sure your investigation has revealed, was quite a loose woman who had numerous sexual partners over the years," Janelle continued, following far too close for Amanda's liking.

"Her character is not on trial." Amanda focused on the elevator, looking up hopefully at the descending numbers indicating its imminent arrival.

"But you'd have to say that she—that any woman—who routinely has sex with strangers is putting her life at risk."

"No, I don't have to say that. And I never have. Elizabeth MacDonald's sex life is not on trial here. A man who murdered another human being is on trial. If you want to ask me about that, go ahead. Otherwise, we're done."

"Fair enough, but she was a—"

"We're done. Thank you." Amanda turned her back to Janelle and the other reporters. After a few uncomfortable moments, the elevator doors opened.

"Parasites," Amanda muttered, stepping aside to let a woman pushing a cart full of court briefs exit the elevator before she, Mike, and a well-dressed young man stepped inside. Realizing that Detective Sergeant Black had nothing more for them, the reporters remained in the hallway as the doors closed.

"They're just doing their job. You know that. Maybe you're just a little over-sensitive because—"

"Do not even *think* of going where I think you're thinking of going."

"Seriously, though. She did lead a pretty… uh, adventurous life."

"Christ, I expect so much more of you, Mike. Tell me you're still on your painkillers and your brain isn't working."

"Mike, why don't you fucking ask yourself who women are sleeping with," Amanda went on. "You guys screw everything that moves and no one says anything. Look at Sobatics. No one has ever mentioned his sex life. But let a woman enjoy her body and suddenly she's a slut? I'm not buying it, Mike, and you better not be, either."

"Fair enough."

The elevator doors opened and the young man pushed past the two cops.

"And yeah, my kid may be pregnant, but my kid isn't a slut. Or easy. Or desperate for attention. My kid had sex with a boy. She got caught. He gets to walk away. She doesn't. That's how it goes. Same with Sibby Mac. She had sex with men. She got killed. Sobatics will not walk away. I gotta go to the little girls' room. Meet you out back at the car?"

"Sure."

Mike had just put the bankers box from the Sobatics case into the back of the unmarked police car when his cell phone rang.

"Jury's coming back. Room 205. Do you want to be here, or do you want me to call you later?" Bridget asked.

Mike sent a text to Amanda and dropped the police light on the dash of the car, rushing into Room 205 just in time to hear the verdict…and to watch

Gregory Sanderson turn slightly to smirk at him.

"So what's next for you, Mike?" Bridget inquired absently as she packed up her briefs. "I see you and Amanda have another homicide on the go. The new Crown didn't put up a fight to keep Sobatics in custody?"

"News travels. Want to grab a drink sometime?"

"Sorry, Mike, I don't think so."

"Suit yourself."

Mike walked back to the car where Amanda was sitting in the passenger seat waiting for him. She was on her phone.

"Mike O'Shea?" the well-dressed young man who had been in the elevator with him and Amanda a few minutes before called out just as Mike reached the car.

Mike nodded.

"Damien Fraser. Fraser Document Services." The young man tapped a document on Mike's arm, then handed him a clipboard and pen. "You've been served. Sign here, please."

Separation papers. Carmen's not wasting any time, is she? At least, it'll be over and done with soon. Mike signed the sheet on the young man's clipboard and stuffed the paper into his jacket pocket.

Chapter Thirty-Eight

2:41 p.m., Friday, October 26, 2018

"Do you want to go for a beer?" Ron asked cautiously, looking up from the mounds of paperwork that seemed to perpetually cover his desk.

"Now?"

"Yes. Just the two of us. You know, like partners."

"We *are* partners."

"Yes, but you know, like *real* partners. You don't have to, though. I mean, if you've got something else to do. I was just thinking..." Ron retreated behind his computer monitor.

"No, I'm free," Mike replied, putting off calling his lawyer to get the separation agreement finalized.

"How are things going with you and Bridget?"

"What things?"

"Oh. Sorry, I thought you two were dating."

"Nope. Not that I'm aware of, anyway."

"Well, she sure seems to like you. Might want to consider?"

"I just got served yesterday, Ron. Might want to give it a couple of days." Mike looked over at Ron, took a deep breath, and then realizing that this was a stab at relationship building on his partner's part, rephrased. "I'm sure Bridget is as nice as she seems. I just don't think the timing is right, you know?"

"Looking for something a little more...hmm, fun?"

"No, not looking at all." Mike returned to his monitor, noticing that an email from the unit commander had just come in for him.

Some info that might be useful, the subject line read. Mike clicked on the message. A series of attachments rolled out.

"So, I suppose you've heard that I'm retiring?"

"Uh-huh," Mike grunted, scrolling down the list of attachments: Transphobia in the Workplace, How to Accommodate a Transgender Employee, Help: My Friend Just Told Me They Are Transgender.

I'm not seeing Help: I've Got Too Much Fucking Work to Do on this list, Mike thought. *Now that would be helpful.*

Ron was still talking. "I didn't want it to be common knowledge. Not yet. I wanted to tell you myself, but the boss asked if he could tell you. Sorry about dumping Karl on you."

"How so?" Mike looked up.

"Well, I mean, he's certainly one of the boys, but no investigator, you know."

"Yeah."

"It should make for interesting times for you, though."

"Oh?"

"Well, you've got that ongoing Sanderson investigation; I don't suppose Karl can help you with any of those interviews. And then the Johnstone pre-trial coming up, and I'm sure Amanda will have you doing more on the Sobatics case..." Ron let his voice trail off. "I don't want to retire, you know."

"I know."

"This isn't the way I thought it would be. I mean, I realize that I'm no Police Officer of the Year, but I kind of thought I'd finish my thirty-five, and Marie and I would move to the cottage full time, at least for a few good years..."

"It's okay, Ron. You're gonna be fine. It's just a rough patch. You'll be back for the Johnstone trial, and I'm sure Sobatics is going to go for a judge and jury trial; that should take a couple of months. You'll be around. Want to go grab that beer?"

"Before you boys go off for a beer—and man, do I wish I could go with you," the unit commander said from the doorway, "I just spoke to a fellow at the front desk. Chris Williams. His father was your old boss, Robby Williams."

"Yes. I know. I've already spoken to Chris. What did he want?" Mike asked, slumping back down in his chair.

"He was asking about a box that he dropped off for you. Wanted to make sure you got it. Said it was full of old photographs and things from his father's storage locker that he thought might be better off in our hands than in someone else's. Did you get the box, and is there anything I need to know about this?"

"Got the box, and I'm sure there's nothing you need to know."

Ron raised an eyebrow when he looked at Mike and then quickly looked away.

"You do realize, of course, that if there is anything criminal, you will be reporting—"

"Sure." *Reporting my ass. What went on in the JPTF stays in the JPTF. Especially when most of the players are already dead.*

Landon looked at Ron. "How is your wife?"

"As good as can be expected," Ron mumbled, beginning to shuffle his papers again.

"I imagine you being home with her will make a big difference."

"I suppose."

Amanda entered the room.

"Well, Detective Sergeant Black," the unit commander called out. "Please tell me this is a social visit. That there isn't another homicide in my district?"

"No, sir, there isn't. Just dropping by to see my favourite detectives."

"I doubt that," Mike said.

"You're right. I just need that statement from you for Johnstone sooner rather than later, Mike. His lawyer—guy named Reiner, never had him before, sounds like an idiot—is pushing for an early pre-trial date." She shook her head, then continued. "What a shitshow this Sobatics thing has been. Can you believe that Janelle Austin? Wow. Remind me to never talk to her again. Ever. Lovely funeral, though. And your mother, Mike—what a sweet woman. Cried through the whole thing. Adorable. Anyway, get me those notes by…let's say, Monday morning. I have to fly. Picking up my daughter."

Amanda turned her intensity on the unit commander. "I have a few loose ends to tie up with you when you have a moment, sir."

"I am at your disposal," Landon replied, leading the way out of the investigators' office.

"So, first things first. Beer. On me." Ron returned to his original plan.

Mike nodded with a half-smile and was shutting down his computer when the phone on his desk rang.

"Mike, it's Bridget Calloway."

"We were just talking about you."

"I know this is a lot to ask, but I don't know who else to call. I feel so stupid even calling."

"What's up?"

"I just got a call from home. My dad. He's dead, Mike, and I didn't know who else to call."

"Where are you?"

"At work." Bridget's voice began to tremble.

"I'm on my way."

"I'm sorry to have to call you, Mike, but there's no one…" Bridget was barely able to hold back her sobs.

"Bridget, I'll pick you up in fifteen minutes."

"But it's Friday afternoon. The traffic—"

"I'll be there in fifteen minutes." Mike hung up the phone.

"Everything alright?" Ron asked, looking back from the doorway, coat on, fedora in hand.

"Bridget Calloway's dad just died."

Mike didn't have to say any more. Ron knew, as did every cop, exactly what that meant and what had to be done. Death and coffee: the two constants in policing.

"Want me to come with you?"

"No. I got this one. Thanks. Maybe tomorrow night?"

"I'll be at the hospital most of the day with Marie for her treatment. Maybe afterwards. My place, around four?"

"Sounds great." Mike dug his hand into his coat pocket and pulled out his car keys. *It's going to be a long night.*

The End.

Acknowledgements

Without you, my reader, there is no Mike O'Shea or any of the other characters on these pages. When you read the books in *The Mike O'Shea Crime Series*, you give them life. You also remind me that getting these words down on paper is not done in vain, and that gives me life. On behalf of me and my characters, I'd like to acknowledge you, my reader, and the time you spend with us. Thank you.

About the Author

For almost thirty years, Desmond P. Ryan worked as a cop in the back alleys, poorly-lit laneways, and forgotten neighbourhoods in Toronto, the city where he grew up. Murder, mayhem, and sexual violations intended to demean, shame, and haunt the victims were all in a day's work.

Whether as a beat cop or a plainclothes detective, Desmond dealt with good people who did bad things and bad people who followed their instincts. And now, as a retired detective, he writes crime fiction.

Desmond now resides in Cabbagetown, a neighbourhood in Toronto where he is currently working on *The Mike O'Shea Series* and *Pint of Trouble*, a more traditional mystery series, both published by Level Best Books.

SOCIAL MEDIA HANDLES:
  Twitter: @RealDesmondRyan
  Facebook: RealDesmondRyan
  Insta: desmondpryan
  TicToc: @RealDesmondRyan

AUTHOR WEBSITE:

www.RealDesmondRyan.com

Also by Desmond P. Ryan

10-33 Assist PC (Book 1 of The Mike O'Shea Crime Series)

Death Before Coffee (Book 2 of The Mike O'Shea Crime Series)

Mary-Margaret and The Case of The Lapsed Parishioner (Book 1 of A Pint of Trouble Series)

Printed in the USA
CPSIA information can be obtained
at www.ICGtesting.com
LVHW090328170924
791213LV00001B/92

9 781685 125462